# LIQUID CRYSTAL NIGHTINGALE

An Abaddon Books™ Publication
www.abaddonbooks.com
abaddon@rebellion.co.uk

Published in 2020 by Abaddon Books™,
Rebellion Intellectual Property Limited,
Riverside House, Osney Mead, Oxford,
OX2 0ES, UK.

10 9 8 7 6 5 4 3 2 1

Creative Director and CEO: Jason Kingsley
Chief Technical Officer: Chris Kingsley
Head of Books and Comics Publishing: Ben Smith
Editors: David Thomas Moore,
Michael Rowley and Kate Coe
Marketing and PR: Hanna Waigh
Design: Sam Gretton, Oz Osborne and Gemma Sheldrake
Cover Art: Adam Tredowski

ISBN: 978-1-78108-650-6

Printed in Denmark.

# LIQUID CRYSTAL NIGHTINGALE

eeleen lee

*To my family*

# CHAPTER ONE

TYRO PLEO TANZA made a vow as she rode the T-Car network to the ends of Chatoyance, her home city settlement.

*Leave.*

Although not right at this moment. She sat in the last carriage of the T-Car as it sliced through the air, and if she jumped out now she would end up on—and like—the streets below: a total mess. All T-Cars ran along miles of track suspended above the streets, and she could see the moss green band of a minor canal flowing beneath the window on her right. People assembled on the station platforms built above the tracks; the passing T-Car illuminated their faces and Pleo glimpsed them staring into the middle distance like the passengers in the carriage. The six passengers teetered on the edge of narrow seats or leaned against beige walls scoured so often they acquired a uniform sandblasted finish.

Chatoyants ensconced themselves in cocoons of inattention on the T-Car network. After the death of Cerussa, her twin sister, Pleo duly swapped her cocoon for armour. Unlike these people, her life would not degrade into routine—thanks to her vows she rode with purpose today. They provided her with much-needed spiritual ballast, no different from the prayers wrapped together with amulets and mementos sold to the tourists and devotees at the Temple of Gachala, the emerald sun at the centre of the Archer's Ring system.

The commuters around Pleo covered their eyes at the same moment as if taking part in a choreographed dance. It meant the T-Car was nearing the temple. The looming prism of vivid teal speckled with gold mirror fragments was an architectural marvel, but the sunlight reflecting off the cantilevered roof made the view dangerous despite the thick UV film coating the T-Car's windows. Pleo averted her gaze as the diffused light bleached the carriage interior for a few seconds. Right now there would be a few senior nuns at the entrance to greet devotees and visitors, exhorting them to pray to Gachala the Emerald Sun for better tomorrows.

An emerald sun made as much sense to Pleo as the temple's architectural opulence. Gachala was a simmering green at sunset for only a minute, when its light was scattered through a cleaner atmosphere due to a lull in activity between Shineshifts. Still, she had visited the temple once a week and only stopped going when Cerussa died.

Over the past year she attempted to keep a journal in

Cerussa's honour since her sister had always confided in her diary. The expected outpouring of words failed to manifest after Cerussa's unplanned funeral, but during the early rush hour commutes Pleo found herself scrawling the same words over and over again onto her standard issue moth-wing paper pad:

*Chatoyance means 'cat's eye' in old Terran French. People who live here are called Chatoyants, and those who don't live here assume the city blinks when seen from space. But they're wrong: there is no giant eye that opens and closes. We have city zones which light up, one after the other, in bands of light that travel towards each other at the centre of Chatoyance and meet at the Pupil. When a band lights up the other zones remain dimmed. Chatoyants who work when their professional zone lights up call the eight-hour period a Shineshift. Those living in the unlit Zones are supposed to rest and sleep. I can't sleep since Cerussa died.*

Other passengers never cared for Pleo's notes; their sporadic attention turned to the highlights, news updated in real time and printed on moth-paper strips generated by a pair of specialised carriage columns. One detailed T-Car running times, delays and station statuses, and the other column was for news. These highlights fluttered like prayer flags every time the T-Car hit the switch tracks. Each passenger tore off a highlight and discarded it after reading, where it fragmented into transparent specks before settling on the carriage floor. Sometimes a highlight did not break up and remained on the floor, twitching until the energy contained in its splicing of butterfly neurons, cellulose and gossamer ran its course.

Pleo was old enough to remember panelscreens in stations and on T-Cars before the highlight columns replaced them. Chatoyance Metro had decided it was harder to vandalise columns housed in reinforced glass than screens.

A fuchsia square containing a stylised black moth symbol was embossed onto both columns at eye level. Pleo figured these physical hazard warnings also deterred vandals, especially when they were unsure of the nature of the hazard. She knew exactly what it was because she had to memorise all types of warning signs in Polyteknical. The liquid inside the columns, from which the highlights were manufactured, was a mixture of insect-derived silk proteins and chemical stabilisers, and it also had an affinity for keratin in its unprocessed state. The fuchsia warning sign was also a challenge: puncture or burst a highlights column and find yourself sprayed in a quick-drying liquid that stuck skin and hair together, or sealed eyelids and mouths shut.

A pair of autonomous municipal-drones clicked and whirred as they scrubbed down the walls at every stop. When the T-Car was moving they rested on the ceiling like fluorescent yellow beetles. Pleo ignored them and watched two Constabulary officers, both female and decked out in their municipal indigo uniforms, boarding the neighbouring carriage through its roof-hatch and perform a cursory sweep before moving on to the next carriage. Through the scratched glass she glimpsed them going through the same motions before they moved out of sight.

On this morning Pleo added a new sentence to her story: *Today is the day I took her body to Leroi Minor Canal.*

She finished and tore out the page. The minute golden scales covering the paper's surface ensured it remained stuck onto the bottom rail of the window next to her seat. That she had changed nothing in her story just meant that her life was the same a year later: still a tyro-level gemmologist at Chatoyance Polytechnikal.

When she got off at the circular hub of Polytechnikal Station, leaving the drones to wipe away her note before it fell to the floor and joined the highlights, she regretted the amendment. She was leaving an extra part of herself behind in her eagerness to disclose a thought, which hitherto had been too personal to express in public.

# CHAPTER TWO

THE APERTURE HATCHES contracted in the T-Car. Marsh felt all of them closing around his neck.

Chatoyance was too small for him—especially in the mornings.

This sense of confinement befitted him. Marsh was from Cabuchon, the elder sister city of Chatoyance, and the administrative capital was the vanguard of the Archer's Ring. Over generations the Corund had governed from Cabuchon to realign disorder into order, generating prospects on the many settlements and constructs orbiting Gachala. The documentaries Marsh had seen in school hinted at the giddy promise of those formative times, embodied in the catchphrase: "Same dreams and same destinations."

Those pioneer Waves of settlers may have held to the common dream of seeing the Archer's Ring in their lifetimes, but not all of them ended up on the same settlement. Past successive Waves had relayed people to Cabuchon, the more beautiful elder sister, but more recent arrivals settled for second-best on Chatoyance, the younger Cinderella sibling relegated to the drudgery of manufacturing and industry.

Chatoyance had thrown itself into this role with a single-mindedness Marsh begrudgingly admired. Observing Shineshifts made Chatoyants proud of their ability to smoothly transition between work and rest. The air during Shineshift changes vibrated so much that he stood inside station entrances to absorb the energy. Segmented acoustic barriers lined the T-Car tracks to absorb the noise, but the klaxons blared loud enough to rattle teeth in commuters' jaws. If it drizzled there was so much ozone at ground level he could taste it through his mouthguard filter. This brief thrill came at a price though: it always nauseated him before he made it to a station platform.

Not all Chatoyants were so resigned to their stations in life, and the view of the Tiers from the T-Car windows attested to the success of some of their number. Marsh spotted the structures rising out of the north sector of Chatoyance, all staggered like coral outcroppings set on a sheer reef wall. The Tiers housed the abodes of the city's wealthy and holiday retreats for those stifled by Cabuchon's administrative order. Marsh could make out tiny figures inside the habitats on the lower levels from this distance, but the haze always reduced his view to a dreamlike impression of decaying grandeur.

He shifted his attention back inside the carriage. Marsh

had been riding on T-Cars and working Shineshifts for nine months—still not long enough to shake off the feeling that the passengers were giving him sidelong glances when they were not scanning the highlights. Defiant, he stared back as a Cabuchoner, although one in self-imposed exile. He was still too fresh-faced and bright-eyed to pass as a native Chatoyant. *Give yourself enough time and you won't know the difference.*

Movement attracted his attention despite the rattle and jerks of the T-Car. Marsh recognised the woman who had been scrawling in her moth-paper pad and sticking the pages on the carriage walls. She lifted her face to gaze at the roof hatch, presenting her profile to Marsh. Her refined angular features and proud bearing reminded him of his Chinese great-grandmother, one of many during the Second Wave of mining colonists who had settled in the outer Kuiper Belt and Oort Cloud before the establishment of the Archer's Ring.

Perhaps this woman was an offworld empress in austere disguise, paying an incognito visit to Chatoyance. Diplomatic immunity would permit her a spot of irreverence. But her minimal modifications told him otherwise—Gemmologist: Tyro level. A few students obtained similar modifications back on Cabuchon, outside the minor satellite campus of Polyteknical, but here the students went all the way as they channeled vocation into profession. Marsh had seen those with full modifications travel in T-Car carriages reserved for them, no doubt courtesy of government and Chatoyance Settlement Transport. Over several months Marsh had seen gradual changes in the appearance of other students on the T-Cars and he foresaw hers with depressing inevitability. The nostrils would be stoppered with silicone plugs or entirely sealed off with white cartilage implants, her thick black hair shorn off and her slate-grey eyes glazed over with intraocular lenses. He cringed at the thought and hoped the lenses were removable, but it was unlikely; the more modifications gemmologists and lapidarists possessed, the higher the wages they commanded.

Today she changed tack, leaving a note at the bottom of the window level with her seat. A pink keloid scar wrapped itself around her wrist like a shiny bracelet and a bone-white forcep emerged from under one chrome-plated fingernail. The paper made a raspy protest as she used the forcep to tear it. When she was done, the forcep retracted and she rose from her seat to grasp the carriage pole.

At Polytechnikal Station the T-Car shuddered to a stop under the weathered platform. Klaxons blared as the woman stood up, along with six other passengers, and grabbed straps attached to the top of the carriage pole in front of them. As she stepped onto a rung set into the foot of the pole, Marsh glimpsed the back of her head. Her hair was coiled into a large bun at the nape of her neck, like a lustrous black ammonite. The roof hatch slid open and the pole hoisted her and the other passengers through it, like a firefighter's drill in reverse. Before the next wave of passengers descended into the carriage, Marsh got up and quickly occupied her seat to see what she had written before the drones could scrub it away.

As per his unspoken routine en route to work he always read what she had written after she had alighted at her stop, and over time Marsh found her repetitive notes more enthralling than the news highlights fluttering on the columns. Still wary of Chatoyant conventions, he never approached her on the T-Car to ask what compelled her to write the same words day after day.

Today Marsh discovered she had added an extra sentence:

*...I can't sleep since Cerussa died. Today is the day and I took her body to Leroi Minor Canal.*

During his spell of work on Chatoyance, Marsh had handled a few specimens of cerussa—lustrous white lead. In its crystalline form, cerussite, it displayed a distinctive twinning habit, most commonly expressed as chevrons radiating from a central axis of growth. He guessed that 'Cerussa' was the name of the woman's deceased sister or lover, although he could not work out the association with Leroi Minor Canal, one of Chatoyance's numerous waterways.

The roof hatch of the carriage hissed as it contracted shut and three stations later, the T-Car pulled into the sprawling Water Hyacinth Terminal Interchange, or The 'Cinth as all Chatoyant commuters preferred to call it. The sky darkened to burnished steel, promising heavy rain later, although it was already shot through with wispy clouds generated by airbourne cloud-seeders.

As the pole hoisted Marsh to the opened ceiling hatch he reached out to tear off a fresh highlight, but two came away instead. Liquid—he used to think it was either stored water for emergencies or vehicle coolant—sloshed inside the column as the T-Car swayed with the new weight of embarking passengers. The damp translucent highlights stuck to his fingertips as he quickly read the first one:

*SIGNET STANDS FIRM IN DISPUTE WITH ANIUM OVER CLAIMS ON MARINER ASTEROID BELT*

The other two Sister Ring Settlements were embroiled in their own politicking and negotiations would break down to start up in perpetuity.

He read the second highlight and decided it was of even less consequence:

*ARONT CORPORATION CONFIRMS ITS NEW NORTH-SOUTH CANAL TO OPEN ON SCHEDULE.*

As soon as the pole lifted him to the platform area Marsh dropped the highlights onto the floor and did not speculate about the woman further.

# CHAPTER THREE

THREE YEARS EARLIER the narrow street outside Pleo's home had turned into a scarlet river.

She peered out of her bedroom window and on to vivid red flowing past it. The road was covered with paper nightingales; their creators had sought comfort in repetition by folding each bird out of dyed coffee filters and decorating their little wings with prayers for their loved ones' safe return.

Passersby had dropped freshly-folded nightingales into the paper river and hurried on with their business. Two boys knelt on the other side of the road, gathering up handfuls of the nightingales and tossing them into the air. Their shrieks of delight broke the reverent morning hush. Paper birds drifted down like red snow in the crisp air.

A woman's voice called out to the boys. Her words had been unclear but when they did not acknowledge what she said she came running down the street to drag them away. Her hair was wrapped in an orange scarf. Their mother, Pleo assumed.

Pleo had yanked down the shutter. Today was going to be like yesterday and the weeks before; all of Blue Taro and Boxthorn on edge as they waited for the names. She didn't want to append the clauses 'of the dead' or 'of the living' until she received confirmation either way.

Her father, Idilman Tanza, had been one of the forty miners trapped in the Bhakun Mine on the asteroid Kerte Yurgi. Pleo had no time to think of him or the other thirty-nine—it seemed all of Blue Taro and Boxthorn was milling in and out of her home as it turned into a communal meeting point. Pleo's memory of the day the news broke was disordered. It began with with a flurry of knocks on the front door, accompanied by variations of: "Tell us it's not that asteroid, tell us it's not Kerte Yurgi. It's a mistake!"

People began streaming in, hugging her mother, Guli, holding her hands or crying on her shoulder. They either refused offerings of menthe tea and manti dumplings or drank gallons while emptying the pantry. Pleo's back ached from the weight of the frozen bags of dumplings she hauled out of the freezer. But all of them wanted to know if Guli had any news not reported in the highlights, as if she could access an exclusive source because her husband was the mine manager.

The only people who had not come for information were the two Mining Union leaders. Pleo had never seen them pay a visit before. It seemed inappropriate for them to only turn up when a tragedy dovetailed with a longstanding issue. Both men had come with greetings and reassurances that rang as hollow as an emptied mine.

"We don't know yet if it's an act of war," Guli told the two union men. "So far CIM has still kept quiet." The men had fidgeted with their cups of tea before setting them down on the wooden coffee table. Pleo watched them watching each other, realising both were waiting for the other to broach a sensitive subject.

"If this was perpetrated by the Artisans, the company can't keep quiet. The truth will emerge," the elder man began.

"Artisan involvement is neither confirmed nor denied," said her mother. "I thought the Archer's Ring, Signet, and Anium defeated them years ago. We all believed it."

"Well, in the worst-case scenario—and I pray with you that it won't happen—the union would like to bring your attention to the war exclusion clause in the miners' insurance policy."

He looked pale and soft in the middle, and Pleo wondered when he had last set foot in a mine. She had caught his name as Erden.

"I'm well aware of it. So what?" her mother snapped.

"Now would be an opportunity to seek to overturn it. With your involvement, as Idilman Tanza's wife..." Erden hesitated.

*Hesitation is your mistake*, thought Pleo. She wanted to shove manti dumplings filled with ground glass down the men's throats.

"We all have shares and stakes with CIM, but you two have nerve! You won't even wait for the inquiry," fumed

Guli, sweeping up the cups of half-finished tea.

She threw the union men out of the house. Afterwards Pleo asked her mother to get more sleep.

"I'm too tired to sleep," was the reply.

Pleo was not convinced. Her mother was tired of being trapped in stasis by the ongoing radio silence from Chatoyance Industrial and Mining, unable to move or live until all of Blue Taro and Boxthorn received confirmation: dead or alive.

When the visits had stopped during the wee hours Guli took to grinding salt in the living room until sunrise. According to miners' custom, if Idilman Tanza's name was not among the dead the salt was to be scattered outside the front door of the Tanza container home to ward off further bad luck. If he was confirmed dead, Guli was to fill a table lamp with the ground salt and light it for forty-four nights.

"Ours is a small community," Pleo heard her remind Cerussa on the morning the paper nightingales covered the street.

"It's microscopic," replied Cerussa, pacing in front of the salt grinder to relieve the tedium of waiting.

"Don't you mean 'claustrophobic'?" Pleo suggested as she stepped out of the bedroom they shared. She glimpsed the hollow-cheeked faces of her mother and twin sister as she walked past. The porthole window in the narrow hallway offered a better view of the paper river.

"Gachala's teeth and nails!" Cerussa shot back. "Stop projecting because you're taller than me—"

"Stop it, both of you! Will arguing speed up the news

and bring back your father?" Guli thumped the grinding stone on the floor as her tone shifted from mother to harried mining supervisor.

Chastened, Cerussa shut up and Pleo did the same. Their mother's brand of discipline was to issue directives and statements like the boss she used to be, envisioning every worst contingency in order to prepare herself for them. However, a miner's death never felt entirely final. Their names were included in various reports and therefore enshrined in administrative banality.

Miners might die but were not normally born in a mine; Pleo and Cerussa were the exceptions in Blue Taro and Boxthorn, arriving during one of their mother's 36-hour shifts. She'd stayed at her post in the on-site control room as labour pains had her doubled over.

Pleo pushed open the porthole window. A solvent tang of ink and dye, long dried on paper, drifted in. The river's impromptu beauty contrasted with the rows of container homes in the Blue Taro and Boxthorn New Areas. The smallest container homes were single boxes; interconnected stacks held larger families. The neighbourhoods were built around five threadbare parks, in clusters of seven homes facing each other over central courtyards. With instant guilt Pleo thought there ought to be more disasters if it took a crisis to jolt the residents into offsetting the ugliness.

In a touch of mockery, the windows of the stacked homes were framed by staggered steel balconies that looked like mining shaft cages; Pleo was convinced it was deliberate. She and the other kids hated looking up at them so much they hurled rags soaked in paint to break up the balconies' outlines. But no one ever bothered to throw paint or rags at the dingy windows of the Tanza home. Despite what had happened on Kerte Yurgi, this six-sided tin was still her home, a refuge of brewing tea, Cerussa's pressed flower and leaf art, and manti dumplings made by the concessionaire. The gaps in the panes were plugged with strips of greased cloth and hammered sheet metal to keep out rain and drafts, but Guli had installed a new panelscreen in the cluttered kitchen, next to an extra freeze-drier unit. Pleo and her family had stopped living on surplus provisions from the mining commissaries since Idilman Tanza's promotion to mine operations manager five years ago.

Pleo and Cerussa were not allowed to use the good set of lounge furniture. It was carved from genuine Catru forest teak and therefore set aside for guests. The polished burgundy grain attested to a very comfortable existence once her father retired. His presence in the home was signified by cast-off heavy-duty boots stacked by the front door and teetering shelves of assorted rock carvings. According to him, it was stultifyingly boring between mining shifts.

"No one's there for the scenery," he liked to joke on his occasional visits home. "Also, we're bored because we aren't machines. The job still requires the human touch. A robot can locate a hydrocarbon pocket but wouldn't have the experience to know how deep to drill into it."

Space had long ceased to hold wonders for him and his miners. It was a cosmic junkyard filled with ore and hydrocarbon-rich rocks, but when you saw one asteroid you saw them all. The only real difference was which ones yielded rich yet finite pickings for Chatoyance Industrial and Mining.

BY THE TIME a CIM company transport had rolled its way through Taro and Boxthorn, its ridged wheels were slicked with sodden paper nightingales. From the porthole window Pleo watched the boxy green vehicle stop outside her home and drop off two people like an urgent delivery: a tall woman, wearing a white uniform and the sky-blue veil of a psychiatric counsellor, accompanied Idilman Tanza to the front door.

Slump-shouldered, he stumbled through the door, and her mother caught him just before he tripped. Pleo's heart stopped at the sight of the visor covering his face.

"Your father is still processing his experience," the tall woman said through her veil, hanging back on the porch.

"What's wrong with his face?" asked Cerussa, and Pleo noted the strangled quality in her voice. She restrained her sister from following their parents to the master bedroom: Ma had taken it upon herself to guide Idilman over the threshold and hence back into normal life. She would refuse help from her daughters.

"Nothing," the woman said. "But his eyes are sensitive to light after being inside the mine for so long. Leave him be."

Her mother returned to the porch and asked the counselor inside to offer her some menthe tea. The woman shook her head and tightened her veil over her grey hair and face, not bothering to hide her disdain of the neighbourhood. Her immaculate tailoring made the street around her look rundown.

"What happened to my father?" demanded Pleo, her mind racing in all directions. "And the other miners? Where are they now? Are they getting the same treatment too?"

"I'm not at liberty to answer any questions for security reasons."

Pleo had stared after the counselor as she returned inside the CIM transport and lowered its gullwing doors. Was there movement behind those tinted windows, making the vehicle rock slightly? There had to be more Kerte Yurgi miners in the transport besides her father. It was a large vehicle and it was sure to make its rounds. The rest of the survivors were waiting inside and the counselor was safeguarding her patients' confidentiality and privacy.

But the CIM transport moved off the street and onto the main road connecting the gates of Taro and Boxthorn to the Lonely Heron Bridge. The company had only brought back her father.

Before the transport slipped out of view Pleo ran after it in disbelief, as if its departure was a mistake. Breathless, she stopped in the middle of the street, treading on sodden paper nightingales while evading the stares of people standing on their porches.

# CHAPTER FOUR

GUNFIRE ECHOED DOWN the wide main corridor of the Polyteknical. To Pleo it always sounded like a target practice session gone awry, but the two ever-present Spinel Guards, resplendent in cardinal red armour, never left their posts outside the Multipurpose Hall. The Spinels were aware there was no danger; the sounds just signified the commencement of another intense training session.

Yet their ready stances—slightly swaying, long legs planted shoulder-distance apart—suggested these Spinels were well aware of another risk. In spite of the noises, no guns or ballistics were involved, just the manifold sounds of heels striking the floor, enhanced by the acoustics of the hall. A pair of reinforced heels worn by Saurebaras Arodasi: Polyteknical's resident and sole fla-tessen instructor. She feared nothing—you could afford to be fearless if you lived at her speed of life. To peer through the doors revealed nothing, until you saw a blur darting towards the metal fretwork screen behind the doors as Saurebaras delivered a single blow, forcing the heavy screen into your face. She did not tolerate interlopers and unauthorised bystanders. The Spinel guards protected them from Saurebaras, not the other way round.

Most of the time, students gave the fla-tessen hall a wide berth, deliberately separating strenuous physical activity from the unwavering focus required of theory and lab work. However, Pleo's intake had the first of their twice-a-week fla-tessen sessions this morning. Pleo trudged up the staircase, spiralling around a support column of malachite, leading to the fla-tessen hall and an open corridor overlooking one of the Gardens of Contemplation. She stopped halfway to touch her palm to the polished surface, a frozen storm of green and white swirls and concentric rings, and when she reached the top of the stairs she always traced the tips of her forceps over a cluster of crudely-patched holes, just below shoulder height on the column. Five perforations, now filled in with imitation malachite. The contrasting textures of the genuine and synthetic was engrossing to analyse.

One of the Spinel guards raised a gloved hand at Pleo, warning her away from the doors. The guards appeared human as far as she could tell, but they definitely possessed some physical ameliorations; they stood watch for days on end.

Pleo ignored the pre-sessional chatter and studied the murals outside the hall. The lustrous paintwork incorporated the oblique angles of the surrounding wall into the images. Recent touch-ups had imparted the whirling figures of dancers with an urgent vibrancy; if Pleo stared long enough, they would leap off the wall. The linear flow of images and accompanying placards gave Pleo a concise summary of fla-tessen's origins. As a martial art, fla-tessen originated from "...cross-artistic exchanges of oral and abstract heritage during the settlement of Cabuchon and the Archer's Ring." This was the principle, but as for the reality, Pleo had her doubts. A footnote to one of the placards mentioned fla-tessen was developed by travelling dance troupes and based on various forms from Earth.

Saurebaras was notably absent from the mural sections depicting the more recent history of fla-tessen, but the reason was an open secret and clearly no footnote. She had spearheaded fla-tessen's revival, with more emphasis on developing it as a hybrid fighting style. She was rumoured to have consolidated her position by murdering seven other instructors and principal dancers during a demonstration gone awry three years ago. Constabulary had taken Saurebaras into custody and Chatoyance government subsequently sanctioned her. After a period of intensive subliminal reconditioning, she had been permitted to live out the remainder of her natural life in pedagogy. As the noise inside the hall abated, Pleo hoped Saurebaras's reconditioning was still completely effective. She felt the cultural ministries of Chatoyance and Cabuchon could not afford to eliminate Saurebaras yet. To do so was to eradicate the art of fla-tessen, since she was its last living creator and proponent.

Pleo also felt that in an ideal world, the Polyteknical curriculum would be immune to the interferences and idiosyncracies of policy makers and their Tiew Dweller associates.

One of these associates was commemorated on the section of mural opposite the doors, a lone woman draped in stylised violet fla-tessen shawls which flowed down like a river to the painting's foreground. The late Ignazia Madrugal, who invented the responsive fabric used to make the shawls. Now she held her hand out to the viewer as an invitation, as if to ask: "How will the future generations of the Archer's Ring connect to their heritage without ensuring the existence of its artistic traditions?"

Pleo didn't think the absence of fla-tessen would make much difference as she observed her classmate Gia Aront, a dozen beginners and five high-intermediaries and adepts arrive for class. Making fla-tessen compulsory for Polyteknical students was another kind of lofty distraction.

They waited near the doors, stretching out their bodies, flexing their arms and massaging their knees in preparation for class. Pleo spotted Gia watching the warm-up but not joining in. She was determined to not blend in like a normal student, and her presence resulted in a charged atmosphere of indulgence.

Gia approached Pleo, holding out an opened lacquered case containing sticks of eyebrow paste and grip powder. Pleo shook her head as politely as possible. She didn't need the paste, because she had no implants to protect. And she always brought her own powder.

Just as Pleo expected, Gia snapped the case shut and tsked.

"Nosebleed's sister." Exaggerated indignation made Gia's voice loud yet brittle. "Admiring those murals won't improve your fla-tessen skills."

Keeping quiet never stopped the taunting, but today was different—Gia had gone straight for the jugular and did not stop there.

"Using your family's name won't improve your scores and test results." Pleo also knew Gia's many sore points and zeroed in on the most sensitive one. "No matter how many canals your father has built."

A shocked hush fell over Gia's friends. This was too blatant, even for Pleo.

"Mining scum! How dare you—?"

"And what are you doing sharing the same oxygen with mining scum like me, Gia Aront?" Pleo interrupted. "Did another overpriced finishing school in Signet Capital kick you out?"

"None of your business!"

"It's all over the gutter highlights," replied Pleo. "Next to a story about mismanagement at one of your father's water treatment plants."

Gasps from Gia's gang broke the prolonged hush. Now the other students drew away from both women, expecting a fight. Pleo was not worried; she could have floored Gia. She was pleased to notice that Gia was half a head shorter than her and petite like her mother, Matriarch Aront, whom the gossip highlights dubbed 'The Gorgon.' Both mother and daughter had the same bright yellow eyes.

"Shut up, you *ant!*" Gia snapped. The word hung in the air between her and Pleo.

Instead of anger, an odd relief came over Pleo. She had been waiting for Gia to call her that in front of everyone.

"You picked that up from your parents? Do Tier-Dwellers still refer to us as 'ants' during their parties?"

Pleo almost laughed. But the word was not only meant to sting, but as a threat. Gia could crush Pleo like an ant—and Pleo's life mattered less than a mite living on the ant. Pleo's neighbourhood was based around a central spine of repurposed administrative blocks at an Aront water treatment plant. Hence the functional ugliness of the neighbourhood, and also Gia's attitude towards her: as if Pleo and the families of the Forty were squatting on her father's land.

And was it not earlier this term that some toadying Polyteknical instructor got worked over by a dozen Dogtooths, the personal guards of the Aronts? The incident allegedly happening in an underpass because he remarked to Gia that she was the mirror image of her mother.

Gia held her fla-tessen fan in front of her face. With a flick of her wrist the weapon unfurled with a soft rasp, revealing its leaf of intricate black lace covering ribs of gold-lacquered wood. Pleo instinctively backed away from its arresting beauty, brushing up against the mural behind her, next to Ignazia Madrugal's outstretched hand. Fla-tessen fans appeared to be made with lace and wood, but the "lace" was actually layers of living membrane grown over a mesh of threads finer than silk. Modified stinging cells, harvested from offworld coral farms.

"You're only a tentative candidate for Adept. Threaten

me and you'll be off the longlist before Shineshift," Pleo warned.

"Threaten you? With a training fan?" Gia smirked and stepped closer to Pleo. "There's no blade, and the venom will only give you bad rash. Once they award me with a real fan, I won't hear another word out of you, right?"

Pleo extended her index and middle finger forceps and used them to parry aside Gia's fan. The tips of her forceps tingled as they came into contact with the mild venom, and she drew back her arm.

"*One* little tragedy and thirty-nine families are entitled to special treatment forever," continued Gia.

"Forty miners!" Pleo shot back.

"Apologies, I forgot one survived. Luckily the salvage teams found your father in time. So let's imagine if all Chatoyants were handed a free pass due to some tragic occupational event. This time it's forty, then comes another incident—300, and after that, 3000 more?" Gia gestured to the rest of the students. "Soon enough, Polyteknical classrooms, and even the Tiers themselves, would be overwhelmed with the children of other miners, war veterans and long-haul pilots—"

A sudden bang interrupted Gia's grandstanding. The doors of the hall flew wide open, framing the figure of Saurebaras, and Pleo marveled at her strength. Saurebaras flicked her arm up in a gesture of exasperation and hurled something small at Gia and Pleo.

Both women covered their faces as the thing flew past their faces and hit the mural, smack between the eyes of Ignazia Madrugal. It was shaped like a sea star, matte black and bristling with silver mother-of-pearl spikes. Aside from training footage, Pleo had never seen a flatessen caltrop in use before.

Saurebaras took long strides as she approached the mural, not so much walking but flowing towards it with purpose like mercury at room temperature. Gia and Pleo stood to attention, but Saurebaras dismissed them to get changed with the rest. Gia darted off but Pleo stopped halfway to the changing rooms to watch Saurebaras.

She drew closer to Ignazia Madrugal, reaching out to touch the face of the painted image. Saurebaras was more interested in sizing up the damage she had just inflicted on the mural than admiring the artwork. *Not enough*, Pleo thought, judging from Saurebaras's piqued expression. She had been aiming for the eyes.

# CHAPTER FIVE

BLUE TARO AND Boxthorn had seethed like a wound turned septic, belying the deserted streets. Before the confirmation of Kerte Yurgi casualties, the neighbours could not keep out of the Tanza household; after receiving certified news from CIM there was only one survivor, they refused to acknowledge its existence.

As soon as Idilman Tanza had returned home, Pleo set about shutting all the windows of the container home. She closed the porthole window last, shutting out what was left of the river of paper nightingales. Her mother had shunted her father into the cramped master bedroom where he remained, standing and staring at his surroundings. The bedroom remained closed to Pleo and Cerussa for a fortnight, although the light from the bedside table lamp seeped through the gap at the foot of the door.

At the end of the two weeks, Guli had hurled the table

lamp and the ground salt on to the porch. She ordered Pleo and Cerussa to leave it where it landed. Pleo would discover the shattered lamp fragments and the rock salt kicked over during the night, the word "akma" scratched on the door in reverse, to emphasise the word's negative meaning: *unfit*. She covered the vandalism with paint before the rest of the neighbourhood left its mark on the door as well.

Home had transformed into a vacuum—nothing went in and nothing went out: sound, light or emotion. Pleo's initial relief at her father's return vanished. Her mother understood Idilman Tanza was not the same man: less than a ghost. An imprint of ashes in his likeness, left behind after his personality and lifeforce had burned away.

Remedies were available if he had come back as a ghost, as various annual festivals and household decorations testified: exorcism, appeasement or long-term tolerance. But he was a physical presence, unavoidable; he slept during the day and spent his rare moments of lucidity poring over the schematics of the Kerte Yurgi asteroid mine, or he worked himself to exhaustion by making unnecessary repairs to household gadgets and plumbing.

The *Incident*, Cerussa and Pleo immediately started calling what happened, with their mother's reluctant approval. A neutral shorthand, for exclusive use within their family. But nothing was neutral about what had happened to the other thirty-nine miners under her father's supervision.

One night, Pleo heard more movement in the kitchen

than the usual house geckos. She was surprised to hear her mother and father in the kitchen at the same time. She had long given up trying to sense when either parent was awake.

Guli asked Idilman, "Did you see the others die?"

When Pleo heard that, she dropped her practice reticule and loupe to clatter on the study table, and Cerussa stopped tracing patterns from victory cedar leaves onto paper. The sisters exchanged a glance and winced at their mother's directness. Any trace of mine supervisor or partner in her voice was shunted aside; this was confrontational. The voice belonged to someone who was close to giving up, even though only she was allowed to speak freely of what happened.

Cerussa pressed a finger to her lips. Both sisters crept into the narrow passage outside their bedroom and stood to the side of the kitchen entrance.

Idilman remained silent, and Pleo turned to go back to her desk. If he was not going to answer the question, her mother would leave him to watch the new electric lamp fuse and sputter out in the kitchen. He'd found a new terror of salt and salted water. The mere sight and smell were enough to make him run outside. Pleo had kept the remaining salt lamp in her bedroom.

But after a beat he replied, sounding like he was speaking from behind a screen.

"In the beginning, others passed news of fatalities to me. They stopped me from going to every dying person's side. We had to spare each other the pain. What could I have done differently?"

"Nothing," insisted Guli. "You can't afford regrets."

"I told our captors to take me instead, spare my crew."

Pleo and Cerussa waited for him to elaborate, because they did not dare broach the subject of the Artisans. When he did not, their mother spoke again.

"Whatever you could've done, there's always another choice."

"I keep telling myself that. It doesn't help. Maybe I can join my crew soon. Still better than sitting at home and dying thirty-nine times a day."

A thump as Guli leaned forward and slapped both hands on the kitchen table. She replied, "You have nothing I've not seen before in other miners. Recovery is within your reach."

Pleo saw her father pointing at the front door and beyond it, to the clustered neighbourhoods of Boxthorn and Blue Taro. "They will never let me forget. I was supposed to die with the rest. Their minds were made up as soon as CIM brought me back. But I can't blame them. Now they curse me, saying I died too, but brought something else back with me."

"Superstition," muttered Guli in exasperation.

Stories were rife, and Pleo had heard them while growing up. She didn't understand all of them, but absorbed them like the filtered recycled air that had entered her lungs when she drew her first breath. Superstition was to be expected when hydrocarbon miners liked to joke, "Shift ends when you're dead." Similar to bats in dark caves, miners had developed sensitivity in the dark. Due to the strain of their work, a few were more susceptible than others, when one fear was replaced by another larger one. Everything was possible in darkness.

Reports of hearing voices over the intercom and seeing ghosts of deceased colleagues were common. Stories of seeing colleagues in two mine locations at once. An apparition that could beckon you away from a section of tunnel that was going to collapse, or lure you inside it.

"The old beliefs are unavoidable. The more high-tech we become, the more stubborn it gets. Do you know how much time is wasted on opening ceremonies when new shafts are begun?"

Idilman didn't wait for Guli's reply; she already knew from her experiences. He went to the sink and splashed water on his face. "But you know, and I know, you can't do away with the ceremonies. It's a trade-off; if we don't burn paper nightingales for protection, or allow miners to pray to Gachala or whatever divinities they believe created them, we save at least three hours on the first shift, but morale is affected. Most of the time it's simply not worth it."

Pleo saw the eyes of her mother burrowing into her father's back as she came to a realisation.

"You didn't let your crew perform the ceremony?"

There, she had to say because he was unable to bring himself to say it to her.

"Not that time."

"Why? You sacrificed your crew's morale?"

"I did it for you, for Pleo and Cerussa."

Her father returned to his seat, drying his face with sleeve. Or was he wiping away tears? He spoke, and managed to keep his voice from trembling. "It was my tour before my next performance review for promotion to project control manager. I had to bring in the crew's work ahead of schedule. My record needed to be faultless. But it's as if I invited the Artisans with that aspiration."

Two metal kitchen chairs yawned and squeaked as they were pushed under the table. Pleo and Cerusa hurried back to their studies. Both parents' voices floated past their room.

"Well, don't jump off the Lonely Heron Bridge, that's what they want you to do. There's even a betting pool going on." Guli's voice suddenly rang with indignation. Pleo heard Cerussa gasp and punched her in the shoulder to keep quiet. "As if the others don't know the risks we all live with. An asteroid mine is always one mishap, one human error away from becoming a tomb."

"You should've never resigned." Pleo heard the admiration in her father's voice.

"Don't change the subject."

There was a small victory in her parents trying to resume their old banter, no matter how stilted.

In Pleo's mind there was a canyon blasted out of the landscape by the Incident, leaving her mother, sister and herself clinging on to the edge. It would not take much to push them below to join her father.

Yet her mother remained hopeful. Perhaps his old self was still within him, or at least a version his family could still recognise; perhaps it could eventually be reached.

*It's not only our father who suffers, dear Mother,* Pleo thought. When Idilman Tanza had returned home, their community pronounced judgement. The canyon extended and came between the Tanzas and the other thirty-nine families. They acknowledged this difference by branding Pleo and Cerussa the children of a coward who had abandoned his fellow miners.

Children of a *survivor*, the daughter of Idilman Tanza, Pleo liked to correct the gawkers and journalists who gathered on the street corner outside her home. She did not deny who she was.

A MONTH AFTER the Incident and the confirmed news of the Forty had broke, CIM, Polyteknical, and the Investigation Committee were very kind, or made a good show of it. They found various ways to soften the blow. They deployed exosuited construction workers to resurface the roads going in and out of Blue Taro and Boxthorn and make basic repairs to roofs and walls. All the residents' utility bills were subsidised for the rest of the year. A visiting apparatchik from the Corund, Cabuchon's lower chamber of representatives, presided over the groundbreaking ceremony of a new community hall. In his speech he emphasised that the neighbourhood upkeep and the new hall was the least the people of the Archer's Ring could do for the Forty until a proper monument was built in the city space.

Pleo had sat in the back row of New Community Hall, facing the wall of glass and wooden panels next to her seat. The impression the decor was trying to achieve was not worth the fumes given off by the chemicals used to polish the wood. Were those same substances applied to the faces of the guest speakers? They all looked the same to her—waxy complexions smoothed over by endless cosmetic procedures, or by being fossilised inside. She witnessed them struggling to keep their masks of concern from slipping off. She bunched her hands into fists on the arms of her seat. *How naive and provincial we must look to them, a bunch of low-class uneducated mine rats.*

The questions the other children of the thirty-nine had for the speakers were met with the same rehearsed answers and commiserating faces:

"When will the bodies be returned to us?"

*After processing, next of kin will be invited to make formal identification. We ask for your patience in the meantime.*

The rows of people below Pleo glanced up at her and Cerussa. Pleo had sunk into her seat.

"Are we in trouble with CIM?"

*No.*

"Will the Artisans attack Chatoyance? Or the Archer's Ring?"

*According to the Corund our system's defences are strong enough that it'll never come to that.*

The answer did not reassure Pleo.

In the wake of the Incident, CIM were going to decommission all the hydrocarbon mines in the Spilled Ink Lacunae. Pleo had read the planned procedures outlined in an auto-generated memorandum delivered to her home by company servitor, still addressed to her father:

1. *Isolate all hydrocarbon-bearing asteroids.*
2. *Prevent leaks of hydrocarbon into surrounding space.*
3. *Remove all traces of mining structures so that asteroids can be rehabilitated.*

A shrewd move, thought Pleo, to rehabilitate CIM's image. Restore the Spilled Ink Lacunae to its original emptiness before CIM had earmarked its asteroids for profit and sent people into the void. Make a fresh start. *Isolate, prevent leaks, remove, rehabilitate.* Terms that also applied to the families of the Forty.

CIM had almost convinced her there was no punitive motivation on their part. The company needed to keep the survivors' children distracted with resurfaced roads, fixed roofs, and free utilities until the initial panic of the Artisan attack on Kerte Yurgi had calmed down. The end of the memo offered to assist any direct family members of the Forty to retrain or relocate on other settlements in the Archer's Ring or Anium.

She took the memo to her mother in the living room. She read it once and quickly gave it back to Pleo.

"You don't believe CIM will give us assistance?"

"I used to work for them. First piece of advice given to me by my predecessor was, 'Check every mine three times. If CIM says it's safe, check four times.'"

"That's another miner's joke," said Pleo.

"They told me help was coming when I went into labour with you and your sister."

"The medics did come, right?"

Her mother stood before the shelves of rock carvings, toying with a piece of soapstone shaped into the likeness of an ant.

"Yes, after I was on the floor for two hours. I was so scared and angry. But it didn't matter when I saw you and your sister. Your father loves to say how he thought the most miraculous sight was a field of asteroids, glittering with iron pyrite and olivine, drifting past a red gas giant. Until he saw his newborn twin daughters."

Pleo bit her lip and folded the memo. She never had an appropriate response to the story.

"I've seen CIM assistance: their type of help actually hinders. I don't trust them *not* to put us on some backwater moon or deploy your father and I on a five-year tour to a mine and then close it in two years." Her mother placed the ant sculpture back on its shelf. "CIM will conveniently forget about us after Kerte Yurgi."

With or without relocation and retraining, Pleo would have been more than happy to conveniently forget about CIM, *and* Chatoyance.

Polyteknical was not so ready to forget about the Forty, which made Pleo suspicious of its sudden concern. Education was subsidised, especially in the areas of earth sciences, geology and gemmology, as a recruitment incentive. Apprenticeships and on-the-job training with CIM had already been available for years.

"We came to listen and we believe you can be of assistance to us," said the three Polyteknical speakers when they took the stage in the new community hall.

Something in their voices had told Pleo they were

downplaying the importance of their visit.

"How so?" someone in the front row asked in a voice that lacked deference. One of the Shojib brothers, sounding surlier than usual.

"What would you say is the main difficulty facing all of you after Kerte Yurgi?"

"Compensation," Pleo heard from the front.

"Finding work," piped up the middle rows without hesitation. The rest murmured in agreement.

Three nods from onstage; the speakers were pleased with the reply. Without changing tack, they pressed upon their audience that these new lapidary implants, to be used from training level to advanced, somehow increased your employability, and made the wearers viable.

Join the vast Chatoyance industrial machine as a component—as equipment. Your place is guaranteed.

*We aren't pieces of equipment,* Pleo wanted to scream, but she bit down on her knuckles. She feared ripping her vocal cords if she did.

Asteroid miners did not regard all implants as taboo. If any necessary implants enhanced performance and health, they were permitted, although not encouraged. Yet Polyteknical took a dim view of this attitude. They insisted that making yourself more viable equated to better pay.

The speakers had half an hour. Near the end of it, they reiterated how they were here to gauge as many responses as possible and of course—*of course*—all concerns about the implants and the TI would be addressed.

"Polyteknical and CIM owns the licenses and the implants are patented. At the end of your training, if you opt out of it or at any time during your working years, they will be removed."

"You think they mean it? About the removal?" Kim Petani, who had lost both parents in the Incident, muttered in the seat next to Pleo.

Polyteknical's sudden interest, and the speakers' enthusiasm and attention to detail, only gave lie to their concern. Pleo raised her hand.

"Why do you say these experimental hand and ocular implants are indispensable?"

Her question sent waves of unease rippling through the hall. Someone at the back laughed, although nothing about her question was funny. She looked around to gauge response; all eyes were on her. She sensed an undercurrent of conflict, but it was insubstantial.

For now.

The three speakers on stage—two male Polyteknical instructors and one medical functionary in her blue veil of profession—exchanged knowing glances. Immediately Pleo saw what they were thinking: *the daughters of the sole survivor.* They were expecting trouble. Their masks finally slipped, only to be replaced with another, just as fake and grotesque. Pleo imagined endless layers sloughing off and forming moist piles of translucent skin next to the podium. No point in hitting one of these representatives in the face, there was nothing to hurt.

"'Indispensable'? No, we never said that."

"That's what we're hearing," replied Pleo. "Or else why are you so insistent on them?"

On the 'we' she felt the disapproving glances boring

into her back. *Speak for yourself, Tanza.*

*Oh, I will speak,* she thought. *Especially when no one else is speaking up.*

"New technologies—as they surpass the advances of the past—create new roles for people."

When they can't answer a question they fall back on their pitch. She had been hearing and reading it for days.

"Specious bullshit!" she yelled, shocking everyone in the hall, but mostly herself. Out of the corner of her eye the flapping red robe of a Spinel was making its way towards her, along the centre aisle between the rows of seats.

The speakers raised their hands, and the collective gesture said to the Spinel, *let this one speak.* Pleo saw the guard stop halfway up the aisle, poised for further action.

"Care to elaborate?" asked the taller instructor, a man with a pinched face and shorn head. He pointed at her. "You're Pleo Tanza, yes?"

"Correct."

"Idilman Tanza's daughter? Is that your sister, Cerussa?"

"Right."

"We hope your father's recovery is going well?"

Pleo ignored the question. "All we've seen so far are vague promises and technical details which only masquerade as benefits."

"That suggestion offends us and insults our intelligence," the tall instructor said all too readily. "Don't take what we've presented to all of you out of proportion—"

"Proportion to what, exactly?" Pleo shot back. "To your fucked-up ideas of proportion?"

"And what alternatives do you propose? For all of you? None of you are in any sort of position to object or bargain," he said and shook his head, as if Pleo embodied all sorts of stupid in questioning him.

The audience was watching her for signs: incredulity, disbelief or outrage. She gave them none, and took her time in sitting down as if she had just asked the most important question.

"Why be afraid of change?" the other visiting functionary asked. "When the discomfort—we won't guarantee the process is completely pain free—will be temporary." She waved at the ceiling. "Lights down and screen up, please."

The internal schematics of the implants appeared onscreen, line by line and grid by grid as though traced out by a meticulous invisible hand. When completed, they were gradually laid over anatomical diagrams of the human hand and eye. One by one, labels appeared at their corresponding parts: *metacarpal scaffolding; distal, radial, and proximal phalange sheaths, digital flexor tendons...*

*Groundbreaking implants indeed,* she thought, *and at what cost?* Too tired to argue back, Pleo stared at the screen and sided with the Polyteknical speakers and CIM for a moment. *Why be afraid, indeed?* she asked herself in an instance of exasperation. *Why* not *be afraid?*

The house lights returned and so did the specious bullshit, which became more elaborate. "But consider the attendant benefits: you skip at least three years of physiological adjustment and training. We can now afford to be very optimistic. The process has been shortened to a handful of operations.

"Please understand you have no enemies in CIM or Chatoyance. You've all suffered an unimaginable trauma and you have our sincerest sympathies. But now is the time to look objectively at available and realistic courses for your future. So, please come forwards and submit your names to the TI registry."

Pleo was not impervious to the heads drawn together in the rows of seats in front of and behind her. The mumbling increased in volume. Out of respect for her father's standing, no one had openly contradicted her but they were herded together by common tragedy. With dismay, Pleo recognised the conflict, now no longer insubstantial: the others were still so anguished that any talk of putting the future in order was welcomed.

Let all of Taro and Boxthorn judge her then, since she was the only one seeing their futures with horror. The job security Polyteknical was offering to the children of the Forty was nothing more than a prison sentence. The shackles were fitted on the inside.

The other male instructor finally spoke, and his voice was bureaucracy set to music. "None of you are viable as potential employees; not valuable enough to retain or retrain. But it's not like you can work anywhere else in the mining industry. What happened on Kerte Yurgi will cast a very far-reaching shadow, across to Steris and Anium and down through the years. Such is the effect of tragedy. No one will want the association with Kerte Yurgi—or to employ someone with this association—no matter how tenuous."

"Mierda del toro," Pleo swore, confident that the Polyteknical speakers and the functionary did not understand Terran Spanish. She had seen enough for today. With a whistle, she slapped both arms of her seat and rose from it. Cerussa and Kim Petani followed her into the aisle as Pleo brushed up against the Spinel and squeezed past. Kim tried to follow her friend, but the guard refused to make way and shoved Kim aside.

People cried out and stood up, finally showing some defiance. Pleo turned around and sprinted back up the aisle. With great presence of mind, Cerussa took Kim by her shoulders and pulled her out of Pleo's way.

Pleo charged at the Spinel and the guard unofficially added another item to the CIM memorandum:

4. *Removal of stubborn deposits formed during heat exchanges.*

The Spinel flicked her arm up, grabbed Pleo by the shoulder and tossed her to the floor. She slid down the aisle for half a metre before the Spinel stepped forward to pick her up again.

The entry doors of the hall shook in their frame as a new group of uniformed personnel poured through them.

"No one move!"

A shaft of bright light hit Pleo in the face (*Gachala's teeth, was it Shineshift already?*) and four figures clad in indigo uniforms stepped out of it. A commotion without chaos followed. The officers did their jobs and Pleo did not resist, although the people inside the hall raised their voices in protest and tried to form a human barricade. Encouraging, but it would have little consequence. Besides, she didn't want them standing up for her only because she was Idilman Tanza's daughter.

\* \* \*

IT HAD BEEN a long ride to the main station inside the detainment Shirpen transport. The four Constabulary officers had not told Pleo the type of vehicle they were travelling in, but she had heard them talking amongst themselves. She was sure the station was not that far from Blue Taro and Boxthorn; its drab twin blocks, bridged by a glass-walled corridor on its roof, were visible from the T-Car as it approached Aqueduct Station.

The officers were taking a long drive to shake her down and suck the fight out of her. Pleo sat up as straight as she could on the bumpy seat. Well, she'd show them no sign that their tactic was working. Occasionally the officers glanced at Pleo through the partition and she stared back at them with a perplexed expression. As if this was all one big misunderstanding.

Her ruse had no apparent effect on the four officers. They remained unimpressed with her as the Shirpen pulled up outside the station's entrance. She got out of the transport and looked up at the twin blocks. What a splendid and ridiculous adornment that bridge was, she thought. Up close and under Gachala's light it glittered like a golden crown and clashed with the buildings' grey and black walls.

"Get inside."

The officer holding her arm pushed Pleo through the entrance while the other three left their colleague to handle the latest detainee. *Probably because she's a rookie*, Pleo thought as they walked together across slick corrugated metal tiles, staring at her arresting officer's immaculately pressed uniform, with its shiny buttons and new baton nestled in its belt holster. She had a sharply pretty face, and a purple birthmark at the nape of her neck, half-concealed by the collar of her uniform. She was maybe a year older than Pleo.

The end of Shineshift had brought a rogues' gallery into the station reception area. Pleo stared past them: gang members, biohackers, drug dealers, even a pair of women arguing that they were not picking tourist pockets in the 'Cinth. In contrast, officers were huddled around terminals trying to enter details or access records and forms, inured to the movement and chatter of the human zoo. For once Pleo was grateful for Blue Taro and Boxthorn's isolation from the rest of Chatoyance.

"Trooper Iryna Devinez, what have you dredged up from the canals?" asked a thin metallic voice, distorted as though treated with software filters. It came from a white polycarbonate screen behind the booking desk.

"Not from any canal, Desk Sergeant," Devinez replied and pushed Pleo up against the desk. "Not my beat at all."

"We'll attend to her in a second."

"Canal Police were suddenly called in to pick her up from the New Areas for public disturbance. Why?"

"Dispatch sends their apologies. Kindly understand Constabulary are understaffed," said Desk Sergeant, although Pleo had the feeling no actual apologies had been made. The sound of movement came from behind the screen before a pair of androids of indeterminate gender stepped out from behind it. Two voices had been speaking together—this explained the distortion. Both androids had reflective faces devoid of features, and they moved in tandem.

"But oversupplied in the vehicle department. I had to swap riding in a Canal Newt for a detainment Shirpen," said Devinez. Pleo was not sure why the exchange would cause her such distaste. Departmental pride, maybe.

"You still got a chance to dry your feet," rejoined Desk Sergeant. Their sense of humour must have been preprogrammed.

Trooper Devinez placed a hand between Pleo's shoulders and pressed her forwards over the desk.

"Look into Desk Sergeant's face and smile," advised Trooper Devinez. "Or don't smile, up to you."

Pleo found herself looking into one of Desk Sergeant's mirrored faces and back at her reflection, curved and elongated like in the back of a spoon. She gazed past it and into a dinghy squad room behind reinforced glass partitions.

A blue light flickered across her reflection followed by the hum emanating from behind Desk Sergeant's mirror-mask face. Pleo's face had been scanned and uploaded into the system.

Trooper Devinez walked Pleo through a series of heavyset doors and shoved her into a tiny cell at the end of a corridor, sans a visit to the interrogation room. Then she sauntered off down the corridor with the satisfaction of a rookie task well done.

The corrugated door of a cell to Pleo's left yawned

open, and a man stepped out. As the door swung shut he straightened his coat and sighed heavily. Pleo sized him up: he'd be elegantly attractive if he weren't so tired after what must have been a tough interrogation session.

She had not spoken, but he clocked her looking at him just the same. Unnerved, Pleo felt he had instantaneously filed away all details about her into his memory. Then she saw the enhanced-hearing implants lining his outer ears.

"Investigator Dumortier," said Devinez from down the corridor.

"Trooper Devinez. Why're you here?"

No joking between these two, only a courteous professionalism. Investigator and officer types must be above the preprogrammed canned humour of Desk Sergeant.

"Dispatch sent me. Desk Sergeant says we're short of officers."

"Dispatch processes requests, but they don't make the decisions." Dumortier looked at the ceiling, as if it contained the source of his suspicion.

Trooper Devinez shrugged. Pleo watched both leave before hunkering down for the night, simmering in her thoughts and picking at the frayed threads in the worn mattress pad.

An hour later an officer slid open the cell door to lead a man and a woman inside. Pleo had sat up, although she was only half-awake, expecting her parents.

"How can we help your situation, Pleo Tanza?"

This couple were not her parents. They would never be so abstract with their questions. And they never addressed her by her full name. The fog of sleepiness suddenly cleared and she saw the tall male Polyteknical instructor and the functionary standing next to the mattress pad.

"Excuse me?" Pleo stood up, brushing specks of grime and loose threads off herself.

"How can we help?" repeated the man.

*Apart from the immediately obvious?* But Pleo bit back this comeback. *Don't answer yet, let them fill in the silence.*

"Here's what's missing in Chatoyance," murmured the instructor in faint disgust. "A hero."

"A rebel," corrected the woman.

He shrugged to say both meant the same to him. "But maybe you're thinking this heroic or rebellious routine will help you bargain for something from Polyteknical."

Displays of excess emotion would disadvantage Pleo before this couple. She nodded, but willed herself to speak as if referring to someone else's ideas. "Leave us alone with our lives. In peace. Remove us from Blue Taro and Boxthorn if you must, but leave us."

"Can't do that. It"—the man waved his hand as though to describe the machinations of something vast and invisible—"has been mobilised."

"Leave us."

"No, sorry. Forty of you is a good number."

"A good number for what, exactly?" Pleo felt the air inside the cell get chilly all of a sudden.

The woman's reply did not reveal anything. "No number is definitive, but forty ensures the results will be varied enough and observable over time."

Pleo waved her hand around too, reminding the couple she was still detained by Constabulary. "Anything can happen overnight in a cell like this."

The woman raised her eyebrows at her companion in a *what-did-I-tell-you* expression.

"If you die tonight, by your hand or otherwise," she said, "the new training initiative will proceed, regardless. Along with your sister. You'll be of more help to her and yourself outside this cell. Or stay here and let this 'anything' you speak of happen to you."

"Maybe I just will."

"Fine words, but you won't," challenged the woman. "You're smarter than that. Don't let it go to waste. Conform with the initiative first. Reform yourself later, if you must."

"Once you're in the initiative, we promise to leave you alone." The man drummed his fingertips on the cell door, impatient but satisfied with a better-than-expected result.

Pleo felt she had listened quite enough. She called out, "Guard!"

The couple were led out and the door slid shut again.


"WANT TO TELL us about it?"

"About what?" asked Pleo.

"The point you were trying to make back in the community hall?" asked her mother.

Constabulary had not bothered to interrogate her, so after the couple's visit Pleo had been left overnight to stew in her own perspiration and stale recycled air inside the cell. Now, she faced her parents back home with her tongue suddenly stuck to the roof of her mouth. She wished she was back in the cell.

Cerussa stood behind her parents, in the kitchen entranceway, and made a slicing motion in front of her throat for Pleo's sake. The gesture meant: *It's a trap, it's one of Mother's rhetorical questions. She's looking to what you did to hang her feelings on. Let it slide, don't answer it, don't even—*

"That the Spinel had no right to shove Kim Petani around. No Spinels have the right to shove any of us around."

Cerussa sighed, covered her eyes with her hand and slumped against the kitchen wall. But her father showed a more favourable response.

"I can agree with that sentiment," said Idilman Tanza with a shrug. He peeked through the lowered blinds of the kitchen window in case busybody neighbours were lurking outside.

Guli glared at her husband. "You're not helping me here."

"I'm just stating my opinion. Apparently I'm not the only one holding that view."

He stepped away from the window and took a seat opposite Pleo but not quite next to Guli. It was a neutral position and one that would give him space if anyone lunged at each other.

"We didn't pay your bail," he told Pleo.

"Was it the Petanis?"

"No. And neither was it anyone in Blue Taro and Boxthorn. No one took up a collection."

Pleo sat down on a worn stool, held her face in her hands, and viewed the scuffed kitchen floor through grimy fingers. Out of everything that had happened over the past day and night, this unexpected—albeit positive—revelation completely drained her energy. She had been too exhausted to consider bail when Cerussa and Kim Petani arrived to collect her from the station.

"Praise and thanks to Gachala." For once Pleo meant it.

"Someone, somewhere—maybe up in the Tiers or behind the scenes at CIM—likes you enough to pay your bail. They like you more than you like yourself." Pleo's father picked up on her unspoken question. "If we knew who this mysterious benefactor was, we wouldn't be talking about it now. Neither can we accept such generosity."

Pleo thought of the couple but kept her mouth shut. Her mother pressed forward again. "So, what were you trying to do in the community hall?"

"Something, anything. The rest clearly weren't," Pleo said in a tight voice.

"Acting a hero?"

"*Guli*, please."

Pleo looked at her father, who retreated to the kitchen window again. The question had inadvertently touched a raw nerve in him.

"That I'd heard enough from them." Pleo decided to be honest with her parents. "And their apparent goodwill. That when it comes to their so-called *voluntary* training initiative, they mean to impose it on us. I have no illusions about it. In my cell they told me, 'Forty is a good number.'"

"Good for what?" asked Cerussa, still in the doorway.

Guli did not quite believe it. "Experimentation. But they wouldn't dare, it's unethical."

"Their intentions were made clear and so I made mine clear."

"We can talk to Polyteknical," Pleo heard her mother say, but she sounded unconvinced by her own suggestion.

"Ma, you and Papa have no influence with them. Maybe both of you can still talk to CIM as ex-employees of CIM if you want to, but not Polyteknical. I don't trust them."

"Or we make their lives difficult, when we need to. That's how we handled CIM over the years. If we hadn't insisted, do you think we'd be still living here?" Guli asked.

"It's not CIM this time," replied her father. "If such a mandate reaches us all the way down here, then imagine from how high it comes."

"Our children should not be coerced into this experimental training..."

"Do they know whether these implants will work or not?" Cerussa interrupted from the entranceway.

Pleo replied, "Remember, they said they were 'optimistic'? Do you believe them?"

Silence ensued in the kitchen. Pleo took it to mean her parents and sister did not believe the optimism either.

"There may be threats if you refuse," began her father. "Some of our current benefits could be yanked away from us, from Blue Taro and Boxthorn."

"They'll cut off the water? And send Spinels to drag Cerussa and me away?"

"More indirect," suggested her mother. "And less indiscreet."

"Khrysobe Spaceport," said Pleo. "It's the only way left."

Cerussa reminded Pleo, "They already know we exist. Especially after what happened, they know your face."

Her sister was right. The children of the other thirty-nine were waiting to dive into a vat of necessity Polyteknical had created and emerge saturated with the same colour. And Pleo did not believe she'd be so lucky to get her bail paid for a second time.

# CHAPTER SIX

*WAS IT POSSIBLE to outrun heat and noise?*

*Not a chance*, Marsh answered himself. The air inside the main concourse of the 'Cinth was warm and heavy. He checked the calendar on the station infoscreen again, which told him it was not the Festival of Gachala yet. A station announcement explained the packed crowd: maintenance work on three southbound lines.

Marsh changed lines inside the 'Cinth to the Subaltern's Parade. On the T-Car network map, the Subaltern's Parade was a scarlet zigzag boring under Planisphere Mansions Park and terminating in the Retail Sector 6 hyper-elevated station; his destination every morning.

*You can't outrun the smell.*

Not that he was able to run inside the 'Cinth. A distinct metallic tang cut through the announcements of departure times and the melange of sweat, lubricant oil from the tracks and ozone. Shoved into a haphazard queue by the remaining passengers from his T-Car ride, Marsh approached the phalanx of sentry turnstiles.

He filed past two servitors hard at work, their telescopic arms spraying white foam over three bodies sprawled on the floor behind the sentry turnstiles. Three commuters had been shot dead by the turnstiles, most likely for trying to run through them. The foam generated a rising mound of streaky red and pink flurry as the bodies dissolved.

"Dissolving's faster than bagging the bodies up," a woman remarked from behind Marsh. "Lucky for those who die straight away."

"I've seen some move," a man replied. "Heard them screaming too. The turnstiles' programmers like a bit of variety: bullets, acid sprays, even darts."

Marsh gripped his string of fare tokens, willing the queue to move faster. Sensors mounted on the turnstiles registered his presence and emitted a sonic frequency that broke one token. The fragments fell into an overflowing tray.

Lightheaded from the commotion and witnessing the gory work of the servitors, Marsh found some space to sit at the grubby base of the nearest column, one of twelve sculpted to resemble giant flower stems. They supported the massive turquoise-tiled roof of the hypostyle main hall of the Water Hyacinth Terminal. He made out the drainage channels flowing across the ceiling in dendritic patterns and felt like a fish looking up at a cluster of water lily pads. Lighting panels had flaked away (or been torn off?) halfway up the columns or clung together in tatters.

The servitors finished cleaning up and left. For a minute, three human-shaped spaces on the floor of the 'Cinth were shiny and pristine. Passengers poured out of the next T-Car, obscuring them. Marsh stood and plunged back into the throng.

HE WAS TWO hours late for work when the 'Cinth released him.

The early afternoon haze sank below the Chatoyance skyline and the next Shineshift was going to begin in three hours as Marsh began his delayed lunch of glass noodles, only eating for the sake of subsistence. He stood behind the display counter and stabbed a pair of chopsticks into a palm fibre tray of slippery translucent strands garnished with pomegranate seeds the size of his thumbnail. The juice dyed the noodles a vivid fuschia. He knew he should have bought something more substantial from a station vending machine this morning, but all the ones in the 'Cinth had been switched off to discourage the crowds from loitering.

Giving up on the food, he snapped the chopsticks in half and left the remaining seeds in the tray. Marsh could have left the shop and walked to the Cormorants Leaping Foot Bridge and then along Aront Major Canal to Polyteknical, but the food was worse in the educational and industrial zones. Most of it was consumed intravenously, adapted to their denizens' various body modifications, or compacted to translucent wafers and frangible bars overloaded with supplements, with nutritional emphasis on eye health and nerve function.

During his first day on the job, Marsh had paid the price for being a food tourist during his lunch hour. After scarfing down a packet of vivid orange wafers and vomiting them up an hour later he had stumbled over to the nearest medical booth around the corner. The booth had drawn a pinprick blood sample and announced the result an agonising minute later—a mild vitamin A overdose. Capsules of powdered ginger root and diuretics slid out of the dispenser slot and on to a tray in front of Marsh. He swallowed them one at a time to counteract nausea and help flush out the excess nutrient, and he had remained inside the booth until his stomach had stopped heaving. Marsh's throat now tightened at the memory. *Experimenting with food ought to warrant Cabuchon military intervention.*

He didn't like to leave the jewellery shop during lunch for another good reason—the view outside the main window was of the piazza in Retail Zone 12. Its fountain was adorned by a huge sculpture—three stallions hewn from weathered boulders of Shepherd Moon olivine and pietersite. Each horse was balanced on one leg and playing out a perpetual gallop in space and time as water spurted around them. When viewed directly from the front, all horses appeared to merge into a single charging form. The fountain lacked the ambition and grandeur of the marble behemoths in Cabuchon public parks, but the vibrant interplay of art and glinting water jets reminded him of home.

Marsh resumed his place behind the shop counter and orientated himself towards the shop entrance. The shimmering crowning-shield over the arched doorway reinforced the self-tinting glass, reducing daytime and Shineshift glare. The crowning-shield had myriad uses for protection and containment, but its secondhand generator was unstable when not properly maintained. In an impromptu test of its integrity, Marsh retrieved a fragment of Desert Rose, crystallised gypsum, from the potch waste tray under the counter and hurled it at the door. The crystal bounced off the barrier and landed on the platform in the window.

"Pick that up now!" snapped the woman standing on the platform behind a display leopard.

"Sorry, ma'am."

"Call me *madame!*"

He had almost forgotten about Jean-Ling Setona posing on the platform, for she did it so well. His employer was able to stay motionless for hours, even week-long stretches. Sometimes not all of her body was on display in the window: her upper body could be placed on a dais with her arms reaching skywards and festooned with bracelets and rings.

Today, Setona was in a floor length black dress, and she had brought out the display leopard. Passers-by stopped to admire the big unmoving cat with amber-hued fur, the latest jewels set into every spot on its face and platinum claws. In person, Setona was a little underwhelming, like most former celebrities. She was still beautiful, like a piece of restored artwork, and her limbs were customisable, all printed skin and muscle coating laser-sintered titanium bones. Currently her exposed arms were covered in hexagonal sequins and gold embroidery. This was a nod to the matador-chic that had been in vogue on Chatoyance last year, according to Setona. Marsh took her word for it—she had years of experience in navigating the caprices of fashions in the Archer's Ring.

But Setona's funerary choice of clothing and guardian animal meant only one thing—the Doyen was paying her a visit today.

Marsh suddenly craved a flake of gypsum; nervous tension always triggered his pica. He went back into the storeroom for another cluster of Desert Rose sitting on the highest shelf. Snapping off a translucent flake, he placed it under his tongue and sucked hard. The jagged edges dug into the surrounding soft tissue and the gypsum's powdery saltiness provided temporary distraction.

AFTER SHINESHIFT'S END a tall shadow blotted out the streetlights twinkling through the doorway. From behind the display, Marsh switched off the crowning-shield over the shop entrance and braced his knees against the counter. He had glimpsed a group of Doyens before, loosely congregated on the expansive viewing deck of a sleek pleasure barge passing under a T-Car track, but it was always unnerving to see one up close. They were retired gemmologists and lapidarists but retained their implants and modifications after retirement, mostly out of professional pride.

This Doyen had arrived without his usual towering Spinel bodyguards. Marsh took one look at him and decided to stare at the jewels displayed in the counter. The Doyen was like scaffolding in a human form with skin stretched over it, covered by a maroon overcoat in a grotesque acquiescence to fashion. His spindly physique seemed to be held together by sheer curiosity; he made straight for Marsh, who was brushing non-existent dust off the counter.

"Are these new hydrogel beads?" asked the Doyen, tapping the countertop.

Puzzled, Marsh looked down through the glass, scanning the rows of cut gemstones shining back at him.

"I refer to the red beads in the tray."

Some Tier Dwellers had never eaten street food in their lives, Marsh thought, reaching to sweep his lunch tray off the counter. Setona would scold him again for not tidying up. It was too late, though, as the Doyen had already reached out one spindly hand and picked up a pomegranate seed. He extended the forcep of his index finger and pierced the seed. The juice squirted onto the counter in a fine spray and mottled the Doyen's sleeve. Frantic, Marsh searched behind the counter for a cleaning cloth while the Doyen blinked slowly in contempt and flicked the seed onto the countertop, showing minute grid lines under the papery skin of his eyelids.

"Deities were believed to dwell within a particle of gemstone. A handful could fill a room with the colours of a supernova. Now these *novelties* overwhelm the market."

Marsh crumpled up the cleaning cloth and dropped it behind the counter.

"I regret to observe that Chatoyant retail standards are slipping—much like everything else in this city." The Doyen directed his voice at the window platform, but kept his gaze on Marsh.

"Only because what passes for fashion is slipping," replied Setona.

The Doyen swivelled around; the quick staccato movement implied delighted surprise.

"She acknowledges me!" exclaimed the Doyen as he moved towards her, but Setona had already stepped off the platform and was walking towards the display counter. "After weeks of passing your shop and talking to you as you posed in the display window, you finally grant me an audience."

"You shouldn't have tried to interrupt me when I was working," Setona muttered, but the admonishment sounded as tired as she did. She popped the burst pomegranate seed into her mouth and arched a knowing, groomed eyebrow at Marsh.

"Why don't you hire automata to populate your window displays?" asked the Doyen.

Setona tilted her head back as though astounded by his question. "The essence of being modrani is defined by presence. Standing still and suddenly flowing into the next pose at the *perfect* moment cannot be done by automata."

"I wish for the old days of automata servants," sighed the Doyen. "Instead of these servitors. It's like being surrounded by giant creaking insects."

"Common servitors, in use on the Tiers?" Setona paused. "Are standards slipping up there?"

The Doyen waved his hand in dismissal. "Of course not. Except for the one I own, the other Tiers bore me... well, to tears." When his wordplay failed to get the desired response from Setona, the Doyen hastily added, "A visit from you would make the Tiers less dull."

Setona shook her head and called to Marsh, "Wake up the display leopard."

"Yes, madame." Setona had received many visits from admirers and former lovers, but she was tolerating the Doyen for longer than usual.

He went to the window and jumped onto the platform. It swayed under his weight as he reached under one of the leopard's ears to press a tiny copper square embedded in the skin. Like a human modrani, the display leopard could pose for hours without movement or sound. It yawned like it was waking up from a long nap, arched its back and growled at the Doyen. Marsh held on to its bejewelled collar to lead the big cat inside and into storage, but it had other ideas. Giving up, Marsh left the display leopard to lick itself in front of the counter.

Setona stepped out of the shop entrance and surveyed the piazza, as if hoping for something to happen and give her a good reason to close up for the day. She kept her back to the Doyen as a brief motorised bubbling, like a rundown vending machine, emanated from him. The Doyen was clearing his throat.

"Make it easier on yourself and leave Chatoyance," said the Doyen. "Nothing has happened yet, but the city is still beyond the Demarcation."

"I'll go when this place has had enough of me, or I

of it. But who's to say Cabuchon is still safer?" Setona dragged the question, sounding both curious and dismissive.

"Provided the incompetent seat-warmers of the current ruling Corund can guarantee the entire Archer's Ring security." The Doyen stabbed the air before him with his forceps. Marsh noticed they were transparent, like fish scales, instead of the bone-white ones belonging to Polyteknical students.

The Doyen mistook Marsh's interest in his forceps for real attention. "All three systems should've abjured any form of expansion and concentrated on housekeeping. The Corund enjoys finding fault in the other ring settlements. Steris and Anium have already reinforced their defences."

"Aren't these the same Corund members who also said nothing can breach the Demarcation?"

"It's not a single wall or barrier in space. Even the thousands of military satellites become useless when Archer's Ring traitors have already let the enemy in."

"The ring settlements of Signet and Anium already seek their independence. Perhaps the enemies have always been on the inside," said Marsh.

"Trust me, one will notice." Setona made an exaggerated sigh. "The canals can flood half of Chatoyance, yet when Chatoyants consult the highlights all they remember is the name of *that* family who built the canals."

The Doyen stepped aside to allow Marsh to lead the display leopard into storage.

"Are you from the Third Wave?" asked the Doyen.

"Marsh is Second Wave. From Europa," chimed in Setona from the door.

"'Marsh'?" said the Doyen, struggling with name. It had never officially existed: it was a combination of 'Mars' and 'Schist', his surname. Most families had landing names which been assigned them arbitrarily upon arrival in order to speed up processing through Cabuchon. The more recent arrivals had raised objections to the procedure, and the landing names and their usage faded over the years.

After three months in Chatoyant, Marsh had learned to avoid letting on that he was from Cabuchon. At best, it provoked insults or heated discussion; at worst, a challenge to a street brawl, as if he was a representative of the Corund Senate itself. No matter, Setona liked having him around since his presence kept thing interesting. Chatoyants loved stories: the more iridescent and embellished the better. Every major and minor detail crushed together like faience until the original tale was lost in repetitive or digressive layers.

Marsh also knew he looked too young to be descended from the Second Wave. Emboldened by catching the Doyen off guard, he continued:

"My family on my mother's side were lunar settlements administrative back in Home System. They oversaw the running of urbanised orbital rings, crater cities, and tunnel towns located around the shepherd moons of Saturn and Jupiter. Her father expected my mother to follow him into the family business, but instead she fled the tedium to join sea jade prospectors on Europa. She made enough to buy three places for herself, my father and her mother on the Second Wave."

"You should tell more stories like that. My customers always love a slice of personal history." Setona clapped and glared at the Doyen as she added, "And those customers also include the ones who actually buy something."

The Doyen put Marsh back on the spot. "Let this Cabuchoner employee tell you about the Forty Pearl Miners."

"I read the highlights at the time," replied Setona.

"They were found covered with mother-of-pearl." Marsh shuddered at the detail.

The Doyen nodded. "Correct, except that 'covered' is not quite accurate. They would have died faster if they'd been covered. The Artisans are not mindless thugs if they can display such meticulous sadism when they strike a mining outpost."

"Why did Chatoyance Industrial establish a mining outpost so near the edge of the Spilled Ink Lacunae?" Setona asked with annoyance.

The Doyen paused as though he was going to elaborate but jerked his shoulders in an approximation of a shrug. Or a shudder. The gesture was theatrical, although Marsh glimpsed a hint of terror slipping through, of what the Artisans would do to the citizens of the Archer's Ring.

Marsh did not want to know more and turned on the blackout mode for the crowning-shields over the windows. During Shineshift the whole street was lit up in a blinding display.

"My door is always open to you, Setona," said the

Doyen, turning around in the doorway. "You don't need to be here—you were above all of this. You still have time to rise again."

Before he left, he swept out his arm to indicate the shop and beyond it, the piazza of Retail Sector 12. The shadow cast by the crowning-shield bisected his face diagonally, highlighting one less-augmented eye and a patch of forehead as if these were all that remained of the person he used to be.

Setona whistled for the display leopard. It bounded away from the counter and ran over to her. She caressed its head and neck while removing the numerous gems set in its spots.

The Doyen's offer rejected, he departed.

"I need to rest," she said to Marsh.

The leopard settled back onto the platform, sphinx-like, with its amber eyes staring out at the empty piazza. Setona sat on the leopard's back and would remain there until Shineshift was over. For a moment, Marsh was able to put her into context. A new sky had showcased new stars: the usual procession of entrepreneurs, actors, actresses, singers, interactive virtual celebrities and augmented sports personalities. Modranis soon moved from the sidelines of the procession and on to center stage; men and women who modified their bodies to varying extents on the fast track to fame. Diverse and Protean in form and appearance, they sparked controversy when they first appeared in various adverts and films. When it came to modranis the public could not look away. She had taken part in visions of glory and beauty, darting in and out of every social sphere like an overreaching migratory bird. Long before she came to Chatoyance, Setona had fallen to earth and never realised her dreams were in pieces until years after impact.

As soon as he was sure she was occupied, Marsh slipped back into the storeroom, and a minute later he stepped outside the shop for fresh air. He had slipped two more flakes of Desert Rose under his tongue. Madame had sworn that if she caught him, she would deduct it from his pay; so far, Marsh suspected she'd not made good on her threat because as an ex-modrani she understood his craving. But he did not want to push his luck too far; Desert Rose flakes were abundant, Madame's goodwill was unlikely so.

Excerpts from

# A REPORT ON THE
# FORTY PEARL MINERS INCIDENT

Compiled with the express cooperation of the
Chatoyance Industrial Investigation Committee,
at the request of the Inner Chamber.

The final report has been published to inform
the military Chain of Command and the Corund
of the findings of the inquiry, together with
recommendations on further courses of action.

## FOR INTERNAL CIRCULATION ONLY

## Important Note

This report is not to be distributed to any members of the public or any ordinary upper and lower House members of the Corunds of Cabuchon, Signet and Anium.

(The document and its attachments and pages are shot through with a touch-sensitive retriever watermark which tracks document readership and unauthorised distribution.)

Reseal and return this document in its original sheaf to the Spinel or Tagmat personnel who couriered it to you.

We understand that required reading at such short notice is particularly vexing. However, we most respectfully ask you to have patience and resist the impulse to judge until you have fully absorbed the contents herein.

Unauthorised distribution, dissemination, reproduction and sale of this document and any of its contents is an offence carrying the harshest of penalties.

# INTRODUCTION

This report selects from accounts of the circumstances of the incident at Bhakun Mine on the asteroid Kerte Yurgi in 3444, in which Artisan military forces kidnapped and tortured to death thirty-nine mine workers and left one survivor seriously compromised. It is based on the involvement of those in the search and rescue attempt and in the full investigation that followed.

## Summary of the Incident

On the morning of 15 September 3444, Archer's Ring Standard Calendar (ARSC), shift work was about to be completed as usual at Bhakun Mine, a medium-scale hydrocarbon mine on the asteroid #2599 VP58, informally known as Kerte Yurgi, in the region of gas clouds informally dubbed The Spilled Ink Lacunae.

At 5.45 am, approximately Chatoyance time, Idilman Tanza, the site manager, declared end of shift and over the next half hour or so, the other forty-five workers clocked off. Around 7.00 am as per procedure, the first ten out of the forty-five miners ascended two kilometres closer to the surface where the accommodation nodes were located.

At around 11.00am explosive charges of unknown origin were set off. The blast released a large body of wastewater stored within caches which were adapted from old hydrocarbon seams. Water flooded the working stalls, where shale was being extracted, and where the mine manager and the foreman, Idilman Tanza, was at his usual work post. Two other workers, Erxat Tasrin and Halida Baten, were also nearby.

So great was the volume and speed of the inrushing water that five miners were immediately overwhelmed and died. Idilman Tanza was injured but managed to escape through the old workings and emerged on the surface about an hour later. Section Supervisor Jannah Petani, who was farther away from the work post, just managed to escape to the asteroid surface in order to activate the distress beacons. Since her injuries were too severe, she authorised her husband, Crew Chief Rus Petani, to raise the alarms.

According to Idilman Tanza's statement, the three escaped miners were immediately captured and brought back below.

Search and rescue operations conducted over the next four days proved unsuccessful. Over the following week, an initial investigation was started as part of a major joint investigation led by Offshore Mining Police (OMP). The investigation was supported by other key members from Chatoyance Industrial and Mining Rescue and Recovery (CIMR2) and available personnel from the nearest Tuzher, Little Twigs and Han Yeng asteroid mines.

Plans for extracting the mining crew were rendered unfeasible as soon as Artisan presence in The Spilled Ink Lacunae was confirmed. Missile bombardment of Kerte Yurgi was ruled out due to high hydrocarbon content, thus creating a high risk of setting off a major explosion.

Invaluable support was also provided by specialist contractors, equipment suppliers, and other personnel with long experience of working small hydrocarbon and mineral shale mines in C-type asteroids. Their combined efforts and dedication kept Kerte Yurgi partially accessible for the duration of a very difficult investigation carried out in challenging circumstances.

Chatoyance Industrial Mining has continued to assist OMP beyond the the scope of the site investigation phase, including helping plan and carry out interviews with key figures and other organisations.

# BACKGROUND INFORMATION

## Bhakun Mine

Bhakun Mine was a medium-scale hydrocarbon mine set high on the southern slope of the crater Nanshe, on the southern hemisphere of Kerte Yurgi, a type C asteroid. With about 100 trillion cubic feet of gas and hydrocarbon-rich shale deposits detected within, it turned out to be highly profitable. In the decade leading up to the merger of Chatoyance Industrial and Corund Mining it accounted for a fifth of the revenue from mining. It was one of very few such mines remaining in the #2599 asteroid fields.

The mine had been owned and operated since 3436 by Chatoyance Industrial Mining Ltd, who in 3439 had a licence granted by The Interstellar Fracking Authority to mine shale from the No.2 Rhodu Seam. Planning permission granted by Lacunae Regional limited the extraction of hydrocarbons to the area defined on The Kerte Yurgi Territory Authority licence.

The mine had been working under a parade of owners and subsidiaries under Chatoyance Industrial and Mining for many years. Operation was not continuous, and there were sometimes months of inactivity. In the two years before the incident, shale production was highly intermittent, ownership was changed three times, and there were five different mine managers. The manager at the time of the incident, Idilman Tanza, was appointed in April 3444.

In the six months before the incident, Bhakun Mine

had been producing crude hydrocarbon shale on a daily double-shift basis. Between thirty to forty-five miners were employed in this period, including a supervisor and a mine manager. The method used to extract the hydrocarbon was a traditional 'bit-drill and expand' technique, where holes are drilled into the rock face via remote tools, explosives are inserted into these holes and are expanded to break down the rock layers over the hydrocarbon seams.

Contact was lost with the mining outpost on September 27th 3444. Thirty-three days of comms silence followed, and remote sensing was able to detect faint heat signatures within the mine but not movement.

# SURVIVOR INTERROGATION TRANSCRIPT

*What follows are key excerpts from session transcripts conducted by E[name redacted] of Mineral and Pipelines Department in Chatoyance Industrial and Mining Corporation, of the sole survivor Idilman Tanza in the investigation into the incident at Bhakun Mine.*

## Background Note

Idilman Tanza's background and training were in construction. His colleagues described Idilman Tanza as "loyal, taciturn, and the first to get his hands dirty." In asteroid miners' parlance he was the reliable choice, which, as he explained, meant that he combined a degree of formal camaraderie with a healthy respect for anything dangerous. It was not enough to hire personnel who could work on an asteroid, hires had to work and survive despite being stationed on a rock in space.

Hence it made sense to his employers that Idilman transitioned from managing transshipments of cargo frigates to mining because he hurled himself into any role.

[Interrogator's name redacted]

E: We're ready to begin when you—

Idilman T: My father was Curzo Tanza. You know of him?

E: I can find out, surely the company keeps personnel records.

Idilman T: He swore by the belief that hard work entails

dignity. However, he also insisted the work should not destroy our bodies.

E: We can discuss any possible compensation after the inquest.

Idilman T: My version of events stands. Did you see the bodies?

E: We still need to go over it. Why did your captors release you—and only you?

Idilman T: [raising voice] What's your implication? I escaped.

E: [Pause] All this is going on record.

Idilman T: You still don't believe me?

E: Your account is rather... fantastical.

Idilman T: I'm here before all of you, am I not?

E: Take your time.


[Session begins one hour later]


E: Let's begin again—from before the time of the flooding: was the shift going well?

Idilman T: Yes: no equipment breakdowns, personnel disputes. No problems. We were preparing to sign off duty and return to accommodations.

E: Is it standard practice for mine personnel to be housed in the subterranean tunnels?

Idilman T: Kerte Yurgi has a thick layer of regolith and no shelters are built on its surface due to risk of landslides and bombardment from meteors.

E: Point taken. Continue.

Idilman T: As Deputy Section Supervisor, Rus Petani

took over from his spouse, Jannah, and tried to activate the distress beacons. But that's when we discovered the Artisans had disabled the communications probes around Kerte Yurgi.

E: We found all of the probes covered in [pause] diamonds.

Idilman T: A taste of what they would do to us.

E: So, upon discovering that eventuality you ordered distress signals to be broadcast on all available frequencies?

Idilman T: We were desperate. Some started shouting and banging on the tunnel walls before I told them not to waste their energy.

E: What did you do after that?

Idilman T: I let them. There wasn't much energy left in us to waste. The Artisans did not flood the tunnels around the accommodations to kill us.

E: It was to drive you and your miners to any available surface exits?

Idilman T: They did it to trap us.

E: And they performed on all of you, in your own words, the pearl experiment?

Idilman T: Not at first. For several days they left us alone. They made food drops although most of it was inedible. [A pause.] They broke us down. A miner's best defence is psychological. The ones who last in the job are those who respect the weight of the rocks around them and the void of space beyond the rocks. I kept telling my miners that if we survive this we will live forever.

E: Were there any suicide attempts?

Idilman T: If we weren't immobilised I would have given the self-destruct order—with or without us inside Kerte Yurgi.

E: They left all of you to die? That is difficult to believe after all the trouble.

Idilman T: They do not feel enmity towards us. They were performing the duty of protecting their territory; this absolves them, in their view.

E: You presume to speak for your captors?

Idilman T: Have you ever seen an Artisan in real life?

E: From archival footage. But that is irrelevant right now.

Idilman T: [whispers] They're crystalline deities [*unintelligible*]

E: [to auto-transcriber] End this session now. Do it!

Idilman T: [louder] they're reshaping the universe into their vision.


[End of recording]

# RECOMMENDED COURSES
## OF ACTION BY THE COMMISSION

1. Relieve Idilman Tanza of duty.

2. Idilman Tanza is to be released back to his family as soon as he is deemed fit enough. Security concerns are moderate level for the time being. The stigma of being the sole survivor of a tragedy that affects a close-knit mining community will limit his profile and movement. To detain Idilman Tanza indefinitely, force his disappearance or keep him under a pretext of quarantine for longer than necessary is to invite suspicion from his relatives, community and the general public.

3. To buy and ultimately guarantee the silence and cooperation of the children of the other thirty-nine, and thus serve the purposes of the Inner Chamber for the time being.

4. Pertaining to (3), we suggest restarting one of Polyteknikal's Training Initiatives involving experimental implants. Test subjects are now, so to speak, serendipitously available.

5. Surveillance satellite production and maintenance to be stepped up in preparation for future hostile incursions and recurrences on scientific and trading outposts under the jurisdiction of the Archer's Ring.

6. Pertaining to (5), redeploy the outer section of the Corona on the edges of the system to reinforce the Demarcation.

7. Bring Chatoyance under martial protection of the Demarcation if, and when, necessary.

**END OF REPORT**

# CHAPTER SEVEN

*Conform.*

Tyros were allowed to retain their hair until they chose their vocation and went on the track to professional.

Pleo held onto her hair. It connected her to an innocent time before her hand and elbow implants, an era which ended on the day of the surgery. Despite the compulsory talks and counselling sessions by the Polyteknical medical functionaries, Pleo had been dreading the assembly line surgery. Her nightmares involved lying on a freezing bed or pallet before it slid through a shutter door and stopped to rest under the polished ceramic face of a surgical android, its unblinking compound eye covered in an oversized surgical loupe.

*Reform.*

On the scheduled morning two human technicians had ushered her into the low-ceilinged theatre. All they required of her was to lie down on a padded operating table, stick her arms and shoulders through the white surgical drapes hanging down on both sides of her, and wait until the procedure was over.

She heard the robot surgery assistant say, "Put the patient under."

A notification chime sounded as the surgeon pulled up Pleo's chart.

"Don't put this patient completely under!" He raised his voice although there was no reason to. A pause followed before he glanced at her hair in disbelief: "She's *still* a tyro. Basic implant set required. Administer local."

The anaesthetic did not take as well as the surgeon had thought. Pleo felt her fingernails getting prised off. As she lay shivering on the table she heard them dropped one by one in a metal tray. During the initial tortuous minutes, the surgical instruments descended behind the drapes and intensified their metallic humming as they made a series of fine incisions along her fingers and arms. Her skin was parted all the way up from her fingertips right up to her shoulder blades. She could not help but visualise them laying bare her bones, muscles, and ligaments, until her nerve endings were all exposed to the cold air inside the theatre and impassive gaze of the surgeons. The surgical instruments reappeared, streaked with her blood and she fought back a scream. From Pleo's position the backlit ceiling panels formed a barrier of muted greys and harsh whites, as if she was trapped beneath an avalanche.

There followed a pause, yet no respite for Pleo. After the interlude a pair of reciprocating saws buzzed to life and went to work on her arm and shoulder bones. She felt them making incisions at intervals along the length of her radius and humerus, glimpsed bone dust blurring the air above the drapes.

The humming resumed but louder this time; a different set of instruments, which inserted the forceps and elbow spurs. She felt her hands and arms lifted in turn and then suddenly dropped and left to dangle over the sides of the table. This exercise was repeated three times, maybe as a kind of test. When her blood splashed the edges of the drapes, Pleo focused on the ceiling and gritted her teeth, telling herself that if she died on the table her soul would drift through the ceiling and away to the stars.

Pleo survived the operation, although after being admitted to the shared ward, she wished she hadn't. Waking up was like struggling out from a waste disposal chute, stench included. She stayed for eight days, her upper body immobilised in a traction frame which raised her arms over her head to prevent blood from pooling in her fingertips. She remembered yelling at passing hospital servitors for extra sedatives, not for the pain but to take her mind off the blank stares and groans of the other tyros in their frames. On the fifth day, the traction frame was adjusted, and she was able to move her arms again. On the sixth day, a passing servitor knocked the corner of a tray against her left hand and ruptured a large suture across the wrist. Despite her constant and extremely verbal requests for attention, the wound lay open for another day.

After her discharge, Pleo rested at home. She didn't remember how she got there. She had woken up in her tiny cot back in her bedroom, facing the narrow study desk shared with her sister. She had hoped either Cerussa or their parents had brought her back. According to Cerussa, it had been a Polyteknical transport.

The elbow spurs had been the easiest to get used to because they functioned as extensions of the ulna, the bone stretching from the little finger to the elbow. Pleo felt them as smooth titanium bumps when they were sheathed and not in use. She appreciated how they increased stability on various surfaces, so that the hands would not shake and drop when analysing valuable specimens or when balancing stones on dop sticks.

Aside from her new chromed fingernails and the keloid scars stretching over her wrist, her hands looked like her hands. Under the skin the forceps were housed in sheaths which had been integrated into the bones of her fingers, but she felt the sharp edges of the sheaths when she bent and flexed her fingers.

Pleo recalled the practice drills from the demonstrations and videos: make a fist and slowly open it, digit by digit, starting from index to little finger, to extend all forceps. Bend fingers in reverse order to retract forceps. Keep fingers away from face and other vulnerable areas.

Scratching her scalp and the tops of her thighs was now rendered more pleasurable and tactile. The forceps intensified the nerve endings in the index and middle fingertips, although rubbing her eyes and cracking her knuckles was now inadvisable. After too many near misses, Pleo moved away from mere drills and tried experimenting with her forceps in unconventional ways, such as running them along rough walls or submerging her hands in various liquids and releasing the forceps. Daily inspections by instructors prevented too much abuse among tyros.

The derogatory term for the forceps was "Nosepicks." Extreme stress, high infection rates and the difficulty of adaptation meant that suicide rates for tyros were still high. Once implanted, there was no reversing the process. If you paid a back-alley surgeon to extract your forceps you risked turning your fingers inside out and paralysing your arms. Cut the forceps off and they grew back crooked, often emerging sideways out of the fingers or curling back into the bone.

But not every student was able to tolerate their implants. The preferred method of suicide among tyros was indeed nose picking carried out to its grisliest extent: ramming two fingers up the nostrils and extending the forceps past membrane and into brain matter. Pleo now knew all about it—Cerussa had been a Nosebleed.

PLEO'S SHOES WERE covered with filth after treading in a shallow drain. She swore, hurled her used fare tokens into the drain and hurried out of the station. She ran onto one of the numerous walkways suspended over the rundown networked density of Chatoyance below them. The walkways intersected and wound their way around the accommodation node so much so that the structure resembled a loose knot of tattered black ribbons. Cerussa's former dormitory was suspended underneath the main node, resembling a giant leafcutter ants' nest but displaying much less activity. Pleo walked past a few rooms that had been sealed off, ostensibly for maintenance, although someone had daubed the ancient numeral *II* in red onto the doors. The students had adopted it as the symbol for Nosebleed, representing the blood gushing out of the nostrils.

Draped in a beige lab coat, Kim Petani was already outside her room. She was named for Kimberlite pipes. Pleo recalled the term from her remedial theory classes, the vast subterranean deposits that produced the highest-grade diamonds back on old Earth. Kim was studying the opposite door with interest when Pleo walked up behind her and peered over her shoulder. There was a different symbol on this door, a crude daub of an *I* at eye level. The red paint was still wet.

Pleo thought the graffiti artist was sloppy or rushed. Kim turned to face Pleo with a scowl, obviously not in a mood to share opinions on the artist's execution.

Kim had shaved off her brunette bob on making Mid-Level Gemmologist two weeks ago. Pleo tried not to look at the glistening black cannula inserted under the skin of her face, snaking out of the corners of Kim's eyes and flowing down into her nostrils. The tubes were needed to moisten Kim's eyes and drain off excess fluid in preparation for her intraocular lenses. White stents had been inserted into Kim's browbones to enlarge her eye sockets for future implants.

"Cerussa died at home, if you must know."

Kim glanced again at the mark on the door, as if Pleo

had confirmed something she had long suspected.

"Did your parents grant her final dignity?"

"I gave it to her myself."

A touch of admiration softened Kim's expression. "But if your parents wouldn't do it, then it's not like you had a choice."

"I didn't."

Kim nodded, not so much in sympathy as to change the subject. "You going to tell me what happened to you during your resits?"

"Nothing happened."

Exasperation flushed in Kim's cheeks, making the cannulas stand out more against her skin. "Exactly—you failed your qualifying exams and did the same with the resits."

*Conform.* This time the directive came from Kim.

"You're correct in observing I do so every time." Pleo shrugged. "And so what? Does my failure affect you or the others?"

"If you're malingering, then yes."

"Who says I am?"

Kim began reciting names as if the list was printed out and hung on the door before her: "Tasren, Bhaten, Asan, the Shojib brothers..."

"Idle talk."

"Then why can't you pass?"

"A good question." Pleo bared her teeth to challenge Kim, but she ended up looking pained. "It belongs with: 'Why can't I sleep well?' or for the two us now: 'Why can't we talk like before?'"

The question hit home. Kim sucked in a wet breath through her cannulae before changing the subject. "Do you still have dry eyes?"

'Before' never included chit-chat relating to modifications. Pleo fell back on a stock reply. "Not since I started the taurine supplements."

Kim tapped the side of her nose to stimulate tear flow and coughed, the kind that precedes a grand speech. She did not disappoint.

"Discomfort is nothing when you realise the significance of your role. Even the tiniest part has its function and integrity. Each unique from its neighbour and yet, all variations are accounted for."

Pleo had noticed a similar fervour with Cerussa before she had her implants. It was especially pointless to talk to students who revel in quoting wholesale from the Lapidarist Manual (Third Edition). The implants subsumed the people they used to be, sparing only the necessary for locomotion and interaction.

"Everyone who passes Tyro level is awarded their implants. It is a mandatory precondition of our future work. You're the only one out of the rest of us, the children of the Thirty-Nine, without intraoculares or extraoculares. The child of the sole survivor is still against the idea of the TI."

*Reform!* Kim now beseeched.

The sanctimony brought out Pleo's evasiveness, and yet she could not resist baiting Kim. "When I fail it's not deliberate. I just don't achieve the prescribed standards set by Polyteknical and—"

Kim was not convinced, judging from the way she pursed her chapped lips. "You think your mother, your sister and you are the only ones who've suffered?"

"I never said anything like that!"

"At least your father survived and your parents are still together. You can mourn him with pure dignity when his Designated Time comes."

Resentment flooded back into Kim's face. It was the truth, and Pleo could not say anything against it. Kim had lost both parents and, like the other thirty-nine families, was unable to claim the bodies of her loved ones.

Or unwilling to, Pleo thought, given their grotesque condition upon discovery.

Kim and Pleo looked away from each other, both unwilling to talk about the Pearl Miners so early in the day. Pleo made a show of examining her thumb forcep, allowing the tension between them to swell, wondering if Kim would back down first. Kim finally gurgled and emitted a wet prolonged cough. With the cannulas clogging her friend's airways, Pleo realised that Kim had just attempted a nervous laugh.

Suddenly she took hold of Pleo's arm, and her breath caught in her throat because Kim's grasp was cold and hard. The sleeve of Kim's lab coat had slipped back, revealing a hand wrapped in thin variegated copper bands that extended over her wrist and reached up to the elbow. The bands had been tightened until the entire forearm was the same thickness as Kim's wrist. The slot for the elbow spur was outlined with a ring of white collagen.

Pleo had never seen these banded copper gauntlets

before. She expected little comfort from the implants but there was nothing reassuring about these. Each successive batch of implants increasingly reinforced what the medical functionaries promised during the preparatory sessions: "The hands will be able to reach any point, in such a way that the student can manipulate, draw on and move objects towards or away from their body. The main function of the arm and elbow positioning spurs are to stabilise the hand for functional activities…"

"Put in more effort for your resits." Kim turned around and pointed at the *I* painted on the door. "Otherwise you're no better than one of them."

"You're saying I'm a potential Nosebleed?" countered Pleo.

"No offence meant to Cerussa."

"None taken."

Kim circled the red *I* with one of her forceps and sighed in uncomprehending exasperation at Pleo's defensiveness.

"But when you see half of the sign, it means an 'Attempted Nosebleed.' This person failed at failing. Like you."

As Kim left the dorm she pushed her way past Pleo, who recognised the dry click of an elbow spur unsheathing and made no effort to evade Kim or defend herself from the jab of righteous fury. Maybe she deserved to take the brunt of Kim's rage.

The pain temporarily filled the void within her.

# CHAPTER EIGHT

PLEO TRACKED THE twinkling paths of four Corona weather satellites above the horizon as she waited for the crunch of worn wheels trundling onto the bridge. The Salt Sellers would start crossing at dawn with their carts struggling under the weight of the white crystalline blocks. Her mother always bought three, although Pleo deemed that an excessive amount for mere food preparation and household use. The remaining salt filled the lamps outside the entrance. After Cerussa died, she bought an entire cart's worth to crush up and sprinkle throughout the home.

With Cerussa gone, all comfort and illusion had disappeared as well. Her twin sister had left Pleo locked in a war of attrition with her parents: the home buzzed with a tension she couldn't bear. Pleo felt like the child in the story of the quartz lamp shadows—deceived by the charade of adults who should know better.

At the unexpected memory of giving Cerussa over to the Charon at Leroi Minor Canal, Pleo threw up over the railing. Colourless bile hit the water and merged with the effluents on the surface. Her vomit was her contribution to Chatoyance, making her part of the ecosystem. She couldn't leave yet.

She settled down on a worn bench on the Leroi Major end of the Throat Singing Waveform Viaduct. The structure's curved ribs formed an alcove which sheltered her as she watched the end of Shineshift play out, momentarily transforming the sky into a black canopy. All mining families knew that Constabulary rarely patrolled the viaduct, because it couldn't spare the manpower. She leaned her head against one of its undulating steel ribs, listening to the aqueduct's famed vocalisations, vibrations generated by the sporadic footfall on its deck and transmitted by the canal. When she was young, the bridge was closed to the public because part of the deck had given way, rotted away by years of pedestrians and stray dogs urinating on it. The children took the risk of playing under the bridge whereas their families gathered to listen to its uluations in the evenings. Occasionally, layers of rotting wood fell off and disturbed their reverie.

The viaduct conveyed water to the households of the Blue Taro and Boxthorn New Areas. Their dim lights appeared like Pleo's faded dream of her neighbourhood. How odd that such a sprawling place could feel so claustrophobic, but also welcoming.

A grave evoked the same feeling if it was deep enough.

Pleo took stock. She needed more time to find her way off Chatoyance. To be precise, 70 days, or two more Chatoyant months, as the city settlement took two thirty-five day orbits of Gachala. With the aid of nutritional supplements issued to all gemmological students of Polyteknical and some tweaks to her diet she grew her hair back to waist length within sixty days. She needed 84,000 uta and since Cerussa died, Pleo had sold her hair five times at 14,000 uta each, cutting it off at a middleman's stall in the Back Bazaars. He accepted only long hair—natural, dyed or treated—due to the continuous high demand for naturalistic hair extensions with a lived-in look among wealthy Archer's Ring denizens.

In the meantime, tension exhausted the Tanza household and came to a head via outside intervention.

Since Cerussa had been a Nosebleed, she was not to be cremated and her ashes were not to be infused into the glass of an oil lamp for her family to keep lit on the altar next to the entrance. Polyteknical took Cerussa away, and Polyteknical returned her; she had given them no choice.

Pleo had stopped figuring in her sister's day-to-day existence. Pleo and her parents were soon replaced by details of Cerussa's implants and adapting to them, another barrier between them as fraught as the Demarcation. Cerussa's procedure had betrayed her sister, replacing their adolescent dreams to get off Chatoyance. The nights spent walking over the Lonely Heron to Leroi Minor Canal, a preview to a better life with both sisters sketching out their plans and filling them in with aspirations in every colours and shade, were secretly disregarded. Cerussa had scrawled a line of old song lyrics many times within all available margin space: *Nightingale sings while lovers kiss in corners of lonely stations.*

Her handwriting started out meandering, but near the end it ironically regained its clarity. But Cerussa had never been a music lover. Pleo went over the line countless times but nothing clicked; the incongruity of the lyrics with Cerussa's day-to-day-day existence nagged at Pleo. Out of frustration, she had taken the journal to Leroi Minor Canal and dangled the notebook over the barrier, her sudden tears merging the lapping water and sky into a blur.

A page slipped out and landed on a resurfacing Canal Police Newt. The amphibious vehicle shone its yellow floodlights up at Pleo, forcing her back. She shielded her eyes as it went under and sped off, churning up foam and scum as it cut a swathe through a dense floating mat of stonewort and water spinach.

Pleo knew what was written on that loose page: a story told to reassure children of miners absent during year-long work cycles. About parents who went out to the asteroid mines, leaving their children at home. The eldest sibling comforted the younger ones by pointing to two shadows cast by a pair of quartz lamps and said, "Do not fear. See our mother and father watching over us now?"

A medical functionary and a pair of Spinels had arrived at the Tanza home with officious inevitability on the morning after Cerussa's death. The Spinels' red robes and the streamlined cyan topcoat worn by the functionary imparted the three with a righteous zeal, like emissaries on a religious crusade. Sweeping through the home, the Spinels had collected Cerussa's body as if they were repossessing the Catru teak furniture set. They swaddled her in a skein as translucent as the wrapping on manti dumplings and carried her into a waiting transport. With a proprietary gesture, the functionary handed her parents a folder containing documents to sign and imprint before the Spinels left.

"Joint acknowledgement of your daughter's deprocessing is required," said the functionary, impatient to discharge her duty.

As Idilman Tanza and Guli hesitated to place their palms on the documents, Pleo ran outside to the transport.

"Pleo!" Guli called after her.

Pleo had reached the door of the CIM transport, the forceps of her thumb, index and ring fingers already unsheathed and locked together in the glass-cutter configuration. No crowning-shield on the vehicle to stop her.

*Glass is a solidified liquid and, no matter how reinforced or composite, always has a shatter point.* Before she had a chance to put this fact to good use, a pair of red gloved hands hoisted her until she was kicking the air a metre off the ground. She lashed out with her elbow spurs. The Spinel holding her turned around to make Pleo face the medical functionary, who had been standing a little too close. Pleo's arm swung out in a wide arc and raked the functionary's cheek with the elbow spur.

The functionary jerked to a halt in front of Pleo as glistening blood trickled down her jaw and stained the cyan top coat. Pleo heard her mother gasp in the doorway as Idilman Tanza held Guli back.

Touching a hand to her cheek, the functionary studied the blood on her fingertips.

"Tyro Pleo Tanza?" she asked, emphasising each word.

Pleo knew she was not anonymous, especially not after her outburst in the community hall. Now she was going to be a marked person for assaulting and injuring a medical functionary.

By way of reply, Pleo slumped in the Spinel's grasp, horrified by what she had just done and by what it was going to mean for her.

"I had expected this sort of response."

Something about the functionary's look and manner of speaking was very familiar. *Conform and then reform,* she had told Pleo in the Constabluary cell.

"There were special talks," Pleo suddenly recalled. "When you all promised that recipients' minds and bodies will accommodate the prototype implants with no trouble..."

She knew, as the words spilled out, how feeble and disjointed she sounded.

"We mentioned the necessary preventive measures. But we cannot account for every recipient." The official adjusted her sleeves while she spoke. Now she was not one of the slick panjandrums who had shilled the implants and augmentations to Blue Taro and Boxthorn all those months ago. "Your sister's body is to be returned," she added with what passed for kindness, to Pleo and by extension, to her parents. The functionary's thin mouth twitched in what may have been a fleeting smile. She seemed to be preoccupied by a private dilemma beyond Pleo's knowledge or comprehension.

"I've never seen this reaction when we collect Nosebleeds. But be warned: such spirit will get you ahead in some way, and then it will get you killed."

The functionary nodded at the Spinel, who unceremoniously dropped Pleo to the ground. With a thud and billowing of dust she landed on her hands and knees. After what felt like decades in this position Guli came out and took Pleo by the shoulder, ushering her back inside.

She remembered her mother placing her into a chair at the kitchen table and leaving her alone, while Pleo noticed the functionary's blood was still coating her exposed elbow spur. A drop fattened at the tip before it fell onto the worn tabletop to make a shiny circular stain. *The blood is too slow in the clotting*, Pleo observed with a shudder. *By Gachala's shining brow, these Polyteknical staff really aren't human.*

"Your mother was right," said her father from his usual position by the window. "I should've died rather than live to see all of this."

Pleo smeared the blood into the tabletop. This really was not her father talking to her now. He'd never say things like that before the Incident. Death on the job and all the variables that might lead to it occurred to the unlucky or the incompetent. He had prided himself on being neither. Burnout happened to machinery and equipment, but when it happened to people it was negligence, and therefore a personal failure.

But her father had sounded just as cold and inhuman as the medical functionary when she heard him say, "Since you found Cerussa in your room, you can dispose of her when the Spinels return."

"Stop, stop! Can't you stop being a pair of mine managers?" yelled Pleo, her vision blurring with tears of frustration. "You and Ma always sound the same. Your default settings are set to 'delegate'!"

Idilman Tanza leaned on the other side of the table for support, but made up for this sign of weakness by raising his voice even as it trembled, betraying a pre-emptive grief for the duty he was going to foist on Pleo. But his message was clear: Become a Nosebleed like your sister and the person (most likely Guli) who discovers your body will have the same burden. We won't cremate you, we will leave you outside or under the bridge for the dogs.

Now, he kept his eyes averted as if he was concealing his absence of self from her.

Three Spinels and the functionary had returned Cerussa to the Tanza home the next day, still wrapped in the skein. When Pleo lifted her sister from the stretcher, Cerussa weighed less than the shadows cast by quartz lamps in the fable. Her eyes had been removed and the sockets were sealed over with black resin. Her forearms were slit open from the elbows to the fingers and stitched up again. They had reclaimed the eyes, forceps and elbow spurs: even her nails had been peeled off with sickly meticulous precision. Desperate for any advice, Pleo stood in the Spinels' way and asked them what to do with Cerussa's dry husk of a body.

"Go find the Charons at Leroi Minor Canal," the medical functionary finally muttered as she pushed past Pleo, fixing her with vivid gold eyes, perhaps out of pity or disdain. With that directive, she left Pleo to carry Cerussa inside.

"Don't carry that—her—inside," Idilman Tanza said.

Pleo remained in the doorway. "I can't leave her outside. Cerussa must have *some* dignity."

"But not inside," he repeated.

"I'll take her to Leroi Canal myself."

"You will not take her."

"She's still my sister! It's what she wanted. She needs the ending she wanted."

Pleo showed them the crumpled suicide note: ...*bring me to the Leroi.*

She noticed the other residents of Boxthorn and Blue Taro peering out of the dingy windows of their container homes, alerted by the raised voices and departing Spinels. Men and women clustered on the path outside, their necks craning forward towards any raised voices from the Tanza household that might be fodder for gossip. Their unwavering gazes lent an intense carved quality to their faces. Some people pointed at the front door, shook their heads and covered their mouths while talking to each other.

If her father had heard them, he made no show of it. He remained at the door. She had carried Cerussa to the back of the container home and stopped under her bedroom window. Pleo slid it open and climbed inside first, before hauling Cerussa through. Pleo lay her down on her cot and rummaged through the closet they once shared, for jewellery and clothes. Her father banged on the bedroom door, but Pleo ignored him. Cerussa deserved to be given dignity.

Pleo tore off the translucent skein and it came away from Cerussa too easily, already dry from long exposure. Out of the jewellery Pleo found a pair of beads that approximated the rich hazel of Cerussa's eyes and pressed into the resin-filled sockets and fixed them in place with nail sealant. Nothing needed to be done for the nose, which was curiously untouched. She wrapped one of Cerussa's white scarves around her face. After dressing Cerussa in a loose black shift Pleo lifted her from the bed, carried her through the home and out of the front door. She walked through Taro and Boxthorn, staring ahead and ignoring the people watching from their container homes.

She had not stopped at the Lonely Heron, disappointing those who thought she would jump off the bridge with her sister's body. Pleo went up the terraced stairs at Aqueduct T-Car station. Constabulary presence be damned: the rules of carriage prohibited pets, loitering, drinking, live ammo, littering and smoking, but they never mentioned carrying a corpse on public transport.

The passengers on the platform and inside the carriage hardly noticed anything unusual with Pleo's burden. Late evening Shineshift crowds were dreaming of dinner or their beds. Cerussa's body must have looked like an oversized doll. As the T-Car hit a switch, Pleo mentally went over the ritual for summoning a Charon. Like most folk wisdom and beliefs, she never thought to question its origins. You accepted it as necessary if you could not accept it as true:

*Running water liberates all the spirits of the dead. Place the body in water and say your prayers for the deceased. Any requests of the departing spirit should be made at this time. If the request is to be granted, wait for a sign of acknowledgement from the deceased. This may occur in the form of passing clouds, random snatches of conversation or song lyrics heard on broadcasts. When the Charon appears, give your offering or token. If or when, after repeating your request five times and nothing happens, and no Charon appears, do not stay to plead your case or press the issue. Leave the deceased for the Charons. Don't look back especially if one collects the body. Never look back.*

The procedure was detailed and elaborate, to make it emotionally easier for the bereaved. Pleo had decided to reserve judgment of that until she was finished with her duty. In the station underpass, Pleo heard the water lapping the banks of Leroi Minor Canal. It smelled different from the Throat Singing Waveform Viaduct, its earthy coppery odour both challenging and yet welcoming.

Leroi Minor Canal was one of the dozen waterways on Chatoyance. Once, the minor canals were an efficient method of transport and even the odd pleasure cruise on Tier Dweller barges. Pleo gleaned a growing sense of gradual neglect from the disused surroundings as she walked, and saw fewer people strolling and frolicking along the canal banks. Since the Downturn, the Leroi was always a dumping ground for the unwanted deceased, although the Nosebleeds were a much later addition.

From where she was standing, all Pleo heard was the creaking of support struts, traffic noises and water gurgling out of a row of metal culverts. She stayed for a while in the humid dimness scented with soil and rust. The culverts had presented her with a tempting alternative. They could keep a secret until it rotted away. But Cerussa was so light and desiccated she would rehydrate when submerged in water. Pleo shuddered at the thought.

She emerged from the underpass in the empty docking station of Leroi Minor and passed a row of older sentry turnstile models. One swivelled its head to scan her, but the lights in its eyes were flickering out. Conditioned with Chatoyant respect for sentry machinery, Pleo held up her chain of fare tokens for it to scan but the tokens remained unaffected. Even the formidable sentry turnstiles felt the effects of neglect.

Holding on to Cerussa, she followed the *Exit* signs hanging crooked on the walls. Fatigue caused Pleo to lose her hold on her sister's body as she stepped onto the canal bank. The ground was rough yet slippery after a spell of rain, and Cerussa's inanimate legs dragged in the dirt. Pleo tripped and fell face-down, letting go of her sister. Gasping, she got up on her knees only to see the dirt smearing the white scarf around Cerussa's face. Pleo cried and slapped the ground in frustration, past caring what sort of attention she attracted.

Water dripped onto her hair. She closed her eyes and welcomed it; if it was raining again, she hoped to fall sick and die. More wetness fell onto her shoulder, but it did not feel or smell like Chatoyant rain; it was freezing cold and reeked of algae.

Pleo opened her eyes and saw an expanse of wet black cloth. She backed away from it on her hands and knees. A figure stood before her, cloaked in black, its face hidden inside a hood. It had slung a roll of sodden cloth, also black, over its shoulder. The figure bent down to drape Cerussa's body with the cloth and picked up its new burden.

"Don't touch my sister!" Pleo got up and ran. Perhaps she was running too fast, or the hooded figure slowed down just enough to let her catch up. She had no weapons on her except for one of Cerussa's old metal hairpins.

The figure stopped moving. It held out a hand that was more a wet cloth-covered stump.

"You're a Charon," Pleo blurted, trying to recall the correct order of the ritual. But it all seemed so unnecessary when she could give her offering directly. She put the hairpin on the hand but its owner remained immobile. Pleo added four fare tokens to the hairpin. "That's all I have on me."

The Charon dipped its head and continued down the steps on the canal bank. *Don't look back,* Pleo remembered. The last part of the ritual.

But she did. The Charon had entered the waters of Leroi Minor Canal and slid under with Cerussa's body. Maybe it was using some sort of submersible tech under its black cloak, but she did not dwell on it.

Out of fare tokens for the night, Pleo had followed the Minor Canal Network back home safely. Her encounter with the Charon had bestowed her with her own cloak of invisibility.

# CHAPTER NINE

SAUREBARAS INSTRUCTED A senior Adept to lead the warm-up session in the hall. While the students arranged themselves into rows, she nudged open one of the double doors and threaded her body through the gap.

The senior Adepts were more than capable of leading the first half of the class. She would not be missed for too long. The corridor was empty, so she set off running, passing the two Spinels posted outside. She aimed to execute a flying somersault over the balustrade at the end of the corridor and to finish with a soft landing, pirouetting like a sycamore seed, in the Garden of Contemplation below.

She reached the end of the corridor, and was about to touch the balustrade when the reconditioning took effect. It was always the same flow of sensations: a split second of heightened perception and nausea, followed by a whip of liquid metal bursting out of her chest and lashing itself around her neck. Finally, blurred vision and her legs seizing up under her.

Saurebaras stumbled backwards as if the balustrade had scorched her. Released from a lab tutorial, a throng of students rushed past and she let them sweep her against the wall. If she tried moving too soon, the metal whip took on a python's strength and tightened its grip.

A student called out for assistance. One of the Spinels stepped away from her post and barrelled through the human tide. She picked up Saurebaras by the waist and carried her away like a rolled-up carpet. The Spinel was about to head in the direction of the infirmary when Saurebaras summoned enough strength to point to a nearby bench.

The infirmary was a place of repair, not recuperation, not for a prisoner like her. Under her head she felt the metal surface, worn down by years of students sitting and waiting on it. She craned her neck to avoid the glare of ceiling lights and saw the Spinel resume her position next to her comrade. Both guards whispered to each other and cocked their heads in Saurebaras's direction.

She wished the guards would drop the pretence of their presence being necessary. Better still, leave her wherever she was every time she defied the reconditioning. The guards never spoke to her, but she was well versed in their body language and gestures by now. A periodic shifting of weight from one leg to the other and glances exchanged with each other. These movements seemed to say: we hate to see you hurl yourself against the bars of this invisible prison. Don't resist. Be grateful they gave you a second chance. Why keep torturing yourself?

To this last question, her answer was: they buried me, and my art. The guards thought she was resisting when she was actually testing the confines of her cage. She'd grown to tolerate the reconditioning over time and learned, via agonising trial and error, to work within its confines, and recognised how it inadvertently guided her in its own twisted way.

The noise and foot traffic in the corridor made her yearn for the private gardens on the Madrugal tier. They were more sprawling than Polyteknical's and less cluttered with geodes and intersecting paths.

She had discovered how much the Madrugals adored birds in those gardens. This had been on the morning after her promotion to instructor's assistant, three years before the development of oversized fla-tessen halls, rattling pistes, and the washed-out incessant observation of the screens. A pair of cranes cleaned and shook their black-tipped flight feathers while perching on the roof of an octagonal gazebo. The thick carpet of dew on the surrounding grass was not generated by humidifiers, and peacocks hooted around Saurebaras as she strolled along a stone path lined with crushed seashells.

Like a modrani parading on a catwalk the male peacock strutted towards her, its iridescent blue tail feathers trailing behind it. Saurebaras recognised the bird's challenge and opened her new fan, matte black with transparent membranes, one of two prototypes recently developed by Ignazia. These fans were not classed as training or Adept types, since those terms had not been established when fla-tessen accoutrements were still in development. The peacock raised and shook its tail in a dominant gesture, making the gold and teal background feathers shimmer while the indigo eyespots remained still. Once Saurebaras's vision had filled up with the illusion of a raging gold and teal vortex, the peacock reared its head and spat oily black bile at her.

Saurebaras blocked each incoming bile droplet with the opened fan so quickly that the liquid dissipated into fine spray. Unnerved by its opponent's alacrity, the peacock dropped its tail feathers and retreated behind the gazebo, its sustained cries startling the cranes from their unceasing watch.

Applause exploded from behind Saurebaras as she caught her breath. Two meaty palms belonging to Patriach Madrugal slapped together in common time.

"You have the instincts and stage presence of a tiger." He beamed.

"You're most kind, but thank you."

He held out his hand. Saurebaras hesitated before she took it, reminding herself that enduring his company was also part of the performance. The skin of his palm felt thin and dry, but warm.

*This is nothing but theatre. Afterwards you'll retire to the pavilion for some real indigo peony tea and as many squares of spun sugar gauze to place on your tongue as you wish.*

"Do you choose from a set of pre-planned routines when you move against an opponent, or is it all instinctual?"

"Neither."

How could she begin to explain such intricate processes

to this jaded Tier Dweller? Every body—even Madrugal's with its overindulged waist—moving through the kinesphere wrests artistry from it, consciously or subconsciously. She saw through her dance partners and opponents like water in a basin.

"Saurebaras possesses enough humility for all three of us," Madrugal called out to Ignazia, his wife and Saurebaras's teacher.

"The accents at the end of her movements are still too vague." In imitation of the peacock, Ignazia jerked her head from side to side to demonstrate what Saurebaras had failed to achieve. "More definition and less whimsy, please. Especially with your flourishes."

Madrugal did not defer to her assessment. "Her rhythmic precision is beyond visceral." He addressed Saurebaras again. "Whenever you land or jump from the middle of the beat, my stomach ties itself in knots and my heart bursts with joy."

A chorus of birdsong started up, overpowering Madrugal's voice as he continued to praise Saurebaras's speed and grace to an unconvinced Ignazia. Saurebaras picked up a fallen peacock feather, smiling even though she had heard all it before.

She had seen through him long before the testing stage, and was expecting Ignazia Madrugal to cease their private conversation—which she soon did.

"Put the test fan down on the bench," ordered Ignazia. "Make sure it doesn't drip venom onto any more of my new lawn."

Saurebaras placed the fan on a nearby bench carved out

of a single pallasite meteorite made of iron and nickel. The black peacock venom was still dripping from its opened membranes as Ignazia picked it up. Saurebaras observed the venom pooling around the bottle-green olivine crystals set into the bench.

"Fan membranes display a slightly improved absorbency over previous test batch," said Saurebaras.

"I suggest you proceed with this batch," said Ignazia.

"How much more uta will we have to bleed on another batch?" Madrugal frowned.

"At least ten more rounds of accessories testing are required before I'm satisfied. Then we give our military contractors their much-anticipated demonstration before the year's end."

Ignazia nodded at Saurebaras to indicate her involvement.

"You will allow her to perform the demonstration?" asked Madrugal.

"She's more than capable by now. It'll be a 'touch-and-retreat' style of display. If the contractors remain unconvinced by the end, she could always kill a Tagmat guard to make a point." Ignazia noted her husband's furrowed brow and quickly said, "I'm joking."

Her perfectionist tone changed when she noticed Saurebaras describing a figure of eight in the air with the peacock feather. "Do you have anything else to add, *Arodasi*?"

Without hesitation Saurebaras held out the feather. "Put more of these eyes on my fans."

Ignazia looked askance at her husband. "We have

already finalised the aesthetics over the previous year."

"'Intention fashions the weapon. And—'" began Saurebaras, ready to launch into an oft-repeated speech about the value of distraction.

"I know!" snapped Ignazia. "I coined that so you don't need to quote it at me."

Saurebaras ran a finger along the feather's shaft, waiting for Ignazia's mood to subside. "I know it's a last-minute detail, but it'd enhance the demonstration. I'd perform better."

Madrugal nodded in tentative agreement.

"We're creating a new physical language with every moment. There's still so much potential."

"I'll consider your request," said Ignazia as she picked up the test fan. Before she and Madrugal left the garden she told Saurebaras, "Remember: we found you dancing for uta along the bank of the Leroi—I can easily put you back there."

Against Saurebaras's expectations, six fans were custom made and delivered to Saurebaras within a fortnight. They arrived suspended in a sealed gift box filled with brine solution. The fans were mesmerizingly beautiful when she opened them for inspection; the vivid turquoise eyespots stared at her from the membranes. But their inconsistent placement irked Saurebaras at first; some eyes were too near the ribs, others right in the centre. Ignazia still had final say over the end product.

Saurebaras was down to her last fan when she realised Ignazia's one-upmanship had done her an indirect favour: the fans' unique patterns forced her to adapt to them.

When faced with the unexpected, it helped to shut out distractions. She used the peacock feather eyes on the fans as a focus for her daily meditation—*Be stillness incarnate. When the world is whipping itself into a frenzied blur around you become and remain the eye.*

Years later, this mantra served Saurebaras well when a stale perfume, a blend of oakmoss and benzoin spiked with citrus, heralded Matriarch Aront's arrival with her private security detail. Saurebaras was prepared to be courteous, but planned to cut short the visit by feigning a mild injury.

The perfume seeped through the reinforced door of Saurebaras's private living quarters. *Does the Gorgon subject all of her friends and associates to this odour? Don't these Tier Dwellers send proxies to attend to matters in their place?*

Saurebaras forgot about her planned charade when she saw how nondescript and absurd the Matriarch appeared out of context, where she was not hamming it up at some official function or swanning around the other Tiers. One hulking Dogtooth guard waited outside while the other entered first, sweeping the place. Strings of multicoloured beads dangling from the low ceiling brushed the top of the guard's head. Satisfied there were no threats, he gestured for the Matriarch to come inside.

She walked with a stiff gait, trying not to let the overhanging coloured beads affect the tilt of her head. Her jaw twitched and clicked sporadically, as if it was prepared to dislocate itself at any moment and swallow trays of delicacies or people's reputations whole. Apart from Gia's attendance, the Aronts had no stake in Polyteknical or interest in fla-tessen, and as far as Saurebaras was aware, there no reason for the Matriarch to make an unannounced visit. Of course, she still wanted to inject drama into this tiny space by barging through the narrow doorway.

Fixed in the beam of her disconcerting yellow gaze, Saurebaras hesitated under the decorative beads, repelled and yet amused by the thought that Matriarch Aront was going to plant a big wet kiss her cheek.

And yet she imposed no such familiarity upon Saurebaras during that initial meeting: holding out a hand for her to kiss a ring set with a glittering black diamond as large as a quail's egg. Saurebaras slowly dropped into a deep curtsy and the Matriarch tsked with impatience, flexing her finger and making the flesh bulge around the thick gold band. The choice of jewellery struck Saurebaras as odd; it lacked the characteristic Tier Dweller ostentation. Was Matriarch Aront in mourning, and for whom?

"I've never dropped in to visit you before."

*That voice can scour years of rust off the oldest canal bridge in seconds.* She pressed her hands to her temples.

"A delightful surprise, Matriarch!" Saurebaras effused, removing her hands from her temples, and clapped like a child presented with a choice of gifts. At the same time she wondered when had Matriarch Aront become so concerned about Gia's progress, or the genuine lack of it, that it justified a personal visit?

Matriarch Aront remained Sphinx-like. Without turning, she gestured to the guard to leave Saurebaras's quarters.

"Is this about Gia's involvement in the unveiling ceremony to the new monument Aront Corp is building?" asked Saurebaras, trying to buy time. "I told your daughter only Adepts dance in public shows, and one only attains Adept level on merit."

"I applaud your integrity," replied Matriarch Aront, "but I'm here regarding your involvement in another matter."

"Such as?"

"Did you know the choosing of a successor is the most delicate issue for family businesses?"

*And does Matriarch Aront always begin with an irrelevant question?*

"The issue is better discussed with your husband," said Saurebaras.

But her question proved far from irrelevant, when Matriarch Aront mentioned a familiar name. "Oh, believe me, I've tried, so many times, to discuss Gia's future with him. He's much too sentimental." Her dusky yellow eyes were moist with fervent purpose. Machinations had been set into motion long before her presence in this room, all worked out with a pathological precision. "It's all scheduled."

As she spoke, Matriarch Aront lifted three fingers as though bestowing a benediction on Saurebaras, who was both chilled and infuriated by the gesture.

*This is bad theatre, but you're miles above it.* Act nonplussed. *Show this woman that you're unflappable and that you've been through much worse. Tier Dwellers are so used to buying people with a snap of their fingers. And burying them once they've outlived their usefulness.*

But the relentless precision of the decisions broke her resolve.

"Monster!" Saurebaras had finally spat, despite herself, the word freezing the air in her quarters. "You and your husband, both sick, corrupt monsters!"

"But *ahh,* ones who think ahead," replied Matriarch Aront, without expression. "You're past any sort of refusal now. Be a part of this as I now ask, or face the consequences."

The ground was prepared, no matter how much Saurebaras resisted. Rankling at this intimidation in her private space, Saurebaras visualised a swift blow between the shoulder blades, enough to make warm spinal fluid and blood shoot out of the Matriarch's bulbous nose. Anything to halt these plans, make this awful machinery judder to a halt forever.

But as always, her reconditioning reflex took over and locked her joints in place. The steel whip emerged from her chest and lashed her arms to her sides.

"It helps to remember you don't have a choice, madame. Nothing more can happen to you," Matriarch Aront said lazily, as she brought her face close to Saurebaras's, intensifying the reek of perfume. "Chatoyance has already done its worst to you."

She poked Saurebaras in the chest, making her flinch. The Matriarch raised a tattooed eyebrow, no doubt impressed at the reconditioning she must have heard rumours about.

At this slight Saurebaras retaliated like the peacock in Madrugals' garden. She spat at the Matriarch's golden eyes but missed, flecking her forehead and hairpiece.

A Dogtooth stepped forward to deal with Saurebaras, but Matriarch Aront waved him back. She saw Matriarch Aront pull back her arm before feeling a different sort of pain—a slap across her face, making her forget about the steel whip around her body for a moment.

"They've buried you, but used your own body as a coffin."

And three of her personal guards relayed Matriarch Aront out of the room, no doubt to bathe in foully perfumed waters again. As she left, she pinned a posy of stiff white flowers on the door jamb, flowers that were made of dogs' claws; an Aront calling card.

After the visit, Saurebaras realised she had been wrong about the Aronts: they had suborned her. It was crucial that Saurebaras had to transform from the eye of the storm into shimmering chaos around them to thwart their plans.

"I can become so inspired that I could explode with what is inside of me," Saurebaras had told Ignazia during the fla-tessen trials. Now these words took on a new, unexpected meaning.

The sense of her ghastly purpose consumed Saurebaras until she could no longer keep her fragile surface tension under control. She had no choice but to be swallowed up into the maelstrom kept at bay by the reconditioning. Face down and confront every secret and demon that, for most people, would be quietly lurking in their subconscious, but for her were building funeral pyres and waging battles.

When she did ultimately resurface, she did so with the radiant serenity of a goddess, as if she was reborn with no trace of the agonies that had threatened to overcome her.

If Ignazia hadn't been so dismissive of thoughtforms she would still be alive, long enough to be flabbergasted by Saurebaras's mastery. The body, via the mind, had its own set of memories, and Saurebaras drew on hers when she dove into the inner pit. Her thoughtform never needed summoning—it was always with her, tugging on the chains of the reconditioning. The shawl stretched and twisted around itself until it became as hard and gnarled as a flail. A little crude, but she dispensed with grace and artistry at this moment. Deadly force required less energy but more precision.

Never a problem for Saurebaras.

Back on the bench Saurebaras waited for time and her body to snap back into rhythm. Three years of baseline frustration and discomfort had blossomed over the past weeks into imminent dread and guilt over what the Aronts were forcing her to do.

In her plans, the Matriarch had chosen another victim.

It was not Gia.

# CHAPTER TEN

Pleo tried to slip into the climate-controlled atmosphere of the main lecture lab. Too late—the glares of her classmates were already burning holes into her back. They murmured to each other in desultory tones and she tasted rust as her tongue soldered itself to the roof of her mouth.

She went to sip some water from a wash basin at the rear of the lecture lab, picking her way past students huddled over the benches. The facility was modest by Polyteknical standards, although it was four times the floor area of Pleo's home; ten benches were laid out in arena style. Cables dangled like vines from the ceiling and like insect limbs at rest, retractable lamps folded into recesses set into the benches' surfaces.

"When a material reaches the limit of its strength, it deforms or fractures..."

The focus of the seminar was on the tensile strength of

mineral substances. Current semester work was harder: although she did well in the theory courses and passed the oral examinations, lab work and practicals still eluded her. She excelled at pinpoint handling and manual analysis of mineral specimens.

Pleo sat down and drummed the benchtop with her fingers, risking a glare from the lecturer. When would Kim Petani reach her personal limit, as Cerussa did? Soon after she elbowed Pleo outside the dorm rooms? Would Kim die of complications after her final procedure? A cascade of hemorrhaging from her infected eyebrow ridges, swollen with pus and components that refused to take? A scene that Pleo never actually witnessed but was suggested by the blurred-out images of other Nosebleeds on the obit-highlights in the dormitories.

Pleo performed a discreet prayer gesture for Cerussa and the other Nosebleeds.

The seminar ended soon after, much to Pleo's relief. She scrambled out of the basement of interconnected labs and rushed across the street to the main Polyteknical building, taking the shortest way through the main courtyard and the Garden of Contemplation.

Passing through this oasis of calm brought Pleo's plan into sharper focus. Now she had 70,000 uta and had to wait until her hair grew back to the right length, another fortnight. 84,000 uta was more than enough to cover passage to Steris, on the outer perimeter of the Archer's Ring, just beyond Chatoyance's jurisdiction.

She stopped thinking about money when she entered the fla-tessen changing rooms opposite the hall. She grasped the notch under her collar and tore off her disposable lab smock, then threw on a fla-tessen shift. It marked its wearer as low-intermediate level, a shade of washed-out taupe so bleak and nondescript that Polyteknical students nicknamed them "hard currency block shifts" after the corroded cladding found in the Vice District. She slipped on a stiff padded white bib which protected the chest and abdomen, and gathered her fla-tessen shawl under one arm.

Pleo navigated her way around racks of assorted training uniforms, extremely glad that she had saved enough uta to buy her own shawl and shift. Every time Pleo passed through here she grimaced at this textile chronicle of previous students surrounding her. How many had worn these? Some shifts were musty and stiff from long storage. There were starched white ones for beginners in order to make blood from injuries more visible from a distance, the dull taupe for intermediates now worn by Pleo, and matte black trimmed with gold brocade for Higher-Intermediates. Vests and light jackets were available for men, but they preferred to pair the padded vest with altered knee-length shifts for more freedom of movement. In general, fla-tessen instructors wore what they liked.

Pleo broke free from the eerie mustiness of the forest of racks and reached the prep station, where she rinsed her hands in a trough of milky anaesthetic solution until they were sufficiently numbed. After shaking her hands dry she went to select a training fan from its nine other companions displayed on a wall-mounted rack.

An insistent dripping got louder as she approached. When not in use, training fans had to be kept hydrated in a special nutrient-rich solution—the rack was fitted with pipes for the purpose—or else the membranes would shrink and warp the fan. Pleo discovered the source of the drip when she trod in a large puddle of the stuff below the rack and nearly slipped.

The leaking rack had deprived eight fans of their nutrients, leaving their membranes shrivelled and unusable. She prised the remaining good fan out of its holder and folded it shut, wiping the sticky briny liquid off the guard. The red tassel looped through the head of the fan pulsated in her grip, trying to send minute tendrils into the numbed skin of her palm via processes she never wished to understand. Pleo had to go through this until she reached Higher-Intermediate level. For now she was stuck with common-use fans which had to adapt to the user every session; beginners and intermediaries were not allowed to own personal fans.

She placed the fan on the rim of the trough and took out her case of grip powder.

As she was dusting her palms, she sensed a presence behind her.

"Who's there?" she called out.

Only the creaking racks answered.

She had not heard anyone else enter the changing room. But just in case, she suggested with a sudden exaggerated politeness, "I'm afraid they've taken all the training fans for today. Maybe use your own castanets or practise feints with a shawl."

The unchecked dripping set her on edge. The puddle was extending, expanding, until it looked like a human figure. Pleo stared at it, trying to dismiss it as her overactive imagination.

She had a brief, panicked notion that what had followed her father back from Kerte Yurgi had attached itself to her. Possibly it needed a new victim or host body; her father was already nothing but ash.

More nutrient solution dripped from the rack and changed the shape of the puddle, interrupting Pleo's train of thought. The figure's head was suddenly elongated, its arms raised over its head in warning. She picked up the fan again and allowed it to send out tendrils into the skin of her left palm. It stung, but she welcomed the discomfort; it helped to cancel out her tension.

When Pleo was finally ready, she opened the door leading to the hall and was startled to find Saurebaras already waiting for her outside, impatiently tapping her fan against her thigh. She peered inside the changing room to check for stragglers, her gaze lingering on the human-shaped puddle of solution.

"It was already leaking when I went in," said Pleo, feeling nervous.

Saurebaras narrowed her eyes at Pleo but, to her relief, motioned for her to join the other students waiting for class to start.

The second fla-tessen class of the week was a mixed-ability session which involved more drills and sparring, and less emphasis on footwork. Flames danced inside a double-handled ornate bronze *ting* set into a high niche at the far end of the hall. During her first lesson Pleo had stood near the doors with the other students while Saurebaras told them the vessel was sacred and associated with the process of transformation:

"Every week the barrier between ability and ego burn away in this hall. What will be left is your essence, which in time will steer you to your moment of grace."

The objective of today's session was made obvious by Saurebaras barking across the hall every five minutes:

"Strike the wasps' nest like a sparrow!"

Students were to focus on developing speed and economy of movement. Saurebaras always conducted a strict session, but Pleo suspected fear rather than discipline kept the students in check. Adepts reveled in telling Novices of how a fla-tessen demonstration for Cabuchon defence contractors had gone awry, leaving fragments of the audience members' bones and skin inlaid in Saurebaras's personal fan and caltrops.

Now all the Adepts occupied the far side of the multi-purpose hall, busy practicing a routine. Pleo watched with admiration as they threw off their red and black shawls in perfect sync, spinning to catch them before they fell to the floor. The wall behind the Adepts was overlaid with a projection of a construction site: four towering shapes draped with orange fabric. The image flickered and vanished when the Adepts reached the end of their routine.

"And repeat once more!" Saurebaras instructed the Adepts before reminding them, "The flicker stands in for the moment of unveiling."

When the image reappeared Pleo glimpsed the Aront corporate logo swirling on the orange fabric: branching lines enclosed in a diamond.

Someone thumped Pleo on her back—it was Gia Aront, who asked, "Aren't you supposed to be involved in that?"

"'That'?"

"The Monument to the Forty," Gia said with mock patience, eyes backlit by the reappearing projection.

So the apparatchik from the Corund had told the truth. The promise of a memorial fulfilled as described but without consulting the families of the Forty.

The Adepts resumed their routine but Pleo was not watching them anymore. She slapped her palm with her fan, broadcasting her anger.

"I thought Saurebaras would have asked you," continued Gia. "Given your father's survivor status."

"I'm involved whether I'm dancing onstage or not!" rejoined Pleo. "You only wish you'd made Adept in time for the ceremony."

Saurebaras coughed once in their direction, making Pleo and Gia Aront step away from each other.

Pleo's training fan kept closing of its own volition in mid-strike or parry. The tendrils pricked her palm and the fingers of her left hand itched every time she shook the fan to force it shut. Saurebaras came up behind her, wrapped a bony hand around Pleo's wrist and suddenly released it.

"You aren't sparring yet, so hold your training fan like a fallen nestling with a broken wing. See it as such in your mind."

Pleo could not decide whether she was more fed up with the endless stream of avian metaphors from Saurebaras or struggling with a stubborn fan. She closed her eyes and recalled cradling Cerussa's bloodied face in her hands a year ago. What had surprised Pleo the most was the weight of Cerussa's body. She was heavier dead then than when Pleo had discovered her slumped over at her desk in their shared bedroom after studying overlong.

Pleo shifted her position in the gym as, in her mind's eye, she moved her sister from side to side to check for signs of life. To no avail: Cerussa's soul had escaped before her head hit the desk. A page of moth-wing paper, torn from Cerussa's journal, was stuck to the desk and bore the note:

*I finally heard the nightingale. Bring me to the Leroi if you can—your Ceri.*

With a soft moist click the fan unfurled its translucent membranes and remained open.

When Pleo heard her parents hammering on the locked bedroom door and calling her name, Pleo quickly closed Cerussa's unseeing eyes. Like a giant ornate fish gill, the fan immediately closed up again. The membranes were whip-strong when folded together, and the handles concealed a retractable blade—blunted, for a training fan.

An Adept struck a standing chrome bell, and the low note reverberated around the hall to indicate the start of another sparring session. Students hung close to the wall opposite the giant screens, performing warm-up exercises and wrapping their fla-tessen shawls around their necks or waists. Saurebaras handed out castanets to a few adepts-in-waiting and clicks echoed around the hall in rhythmic *ta-ra-ta-ra* patterns. Pleo hated fan-induced rashes or when a stray castanet took off a layer of skin, but not so much as the sparring sessions themselves. The looming screens on the wall at the back of the hall recorded each bout and broadcast rear-projected footage of each sparring pair frame by frame. Saurebaras loved to dissect technique and make an example out of bad form.

Pleo felt a hard tap on her shoulder and turned around. Gia had dropped to curtsey, holding the folds of her skirt out towards Pleo. Invitations to spar could not be refused in class. Pleo returned the gesture and saw Gia's yellow eyes flashing in glee, probably checking Pleo's face for signs of nervousness. This was how some fighters intimidated each other before a bout, revelling in building up the spectacle. When Pleo curtseyed again, nonplussed, Gia swore in exasperation. Another Near-Adept noticed the exchange, sucked in her breath and ran to tell Saurebaras. Normally students of a higher level refereed bouts between those of the same or lower level. Judging from his reaction, Pleo knew no one wanted to be responsible for refereeing this match.

The bout was to be quick—both women would compete to five touches within a three-minute time limit. Pleo was sure she wouldn't last five seconds, after which she could go rest in the far corner of the hall or run back into the changing room, stuff her fan, shawl and shift down the nearest disposal chute and quit fla-tessen for good.

Six Adepts gathered around Gia and her, but the other students maintained a respectful distance. Wasn't it only last term when Gia had, with great skill and accuracy, hurled her castanets at a boy across the hall because she thought he was laughing at her performance? The Aront family had paid for the boy's emergency medical treatment and reattached nose to hush up the incident.

"Near-Adept Gia Aront and Low-Intermediary Pleo Tanza—on the piste now," Saurebaras called out as the outline of a piste—a rectangle outlined in red—materialised on the floor in front of her. The responsive liddicoate fabric of Pleo's fla-tessen shawl drew itself closer to her skin and wicked away her sweat.

The area inside the piste was lead white, a callback to the early method of refereeing fights by observing blood-splatter patterns on sandstone flooring. At the end of the piste a black oval was marked out: each fighter took their place inside their oval, which moved with them. When viewed from above, the piste appeared like a dynamic, ever-shifting Venn diagram, ovals separating and intersecting from second to second.

Pleo and Gia curtsied four times—once to their spectators, once to the *ting*, once to Saurebaras and once to each other. Gia tapped her heel on the floor once to signal her readiness and Pleo followed suite. Their combined gestures activated the ovals, which clicked and scuttled into action as both fighters moved.

"Three minutes!" Saurebaras announced and clapped her hands twice.

The training fan remained under Pleo's control as she

tried to focus on Gia, now spinning around like a dervish. Pleo stayed close to the edges of the piste, moving from corner to corner, but yelped as tiny spikes on the perimeter of the oval pricked her ankle when she stepped into the penalty area. Once your opponent took to the centre of the piste, you had to keep moving. Gia suddenly stopped turning and lunged at Pleo with her castanet, slicing across and just missing her nose. In a flurry of evasive panic, Pleo dropped her fan outside the piste.

"Halt," cried Saurebaras, making both women freeze in their current positions. "No attacks to the face—this is your first warning!"

"She was careless—" replied Gia.

"Did I give you permission to speak?" Saurebaras cut Gia off. She told Pleo, "Retrieve your fan."

Pleo bent down and picked up her fan. It sent out its tendrils into her palm again and remained open, much to her relief because she had neither the time nor mental fortitude to visualise Cerussa's death again. Charging in, Gia feinted an elbow strike and kneed Pleo in the shoulder, sending her back onto the white floor. Gia's control impressed Pleo despite the throbbing pain; the blow had been hard but not hard enough to dislocate the shoulder and warrant Gia's disqualification.

From her position on the floor, Pleo threw her fan at Gia. It rose and grazed Gia's face before spinning back to return to Pleo's outstretched hand.

"Halt! Pleo Tanza, this is your first warning for face attacks." Saurebaras stamped.

But Pleo heard gasps mixed with a smattering of light

applause for the move. Gia stopped dead as her oval continued rotating around her, and slowly touched her fingertip to her face. A wide jagged slash stretched from the corner of Gia's upper lip to her temple and a trickle of blood extended the line of the wound down her chin and neck. The blade of Pleo's fan had unsheathed in mid-flight and cut Gia in the face. Gia extended her index finger forcep and traced it over the cut, and at the back of the hall, the screens replayed the footage as if to compound Gia's humiliation.

*Training fan blades are supposed to be blunt.* Something had gone very wrong and Pleo knew she had to withdraw right now. She tossed her fan outside the piste before raising both hands in surrender.

"You cheating bitch and coward! Don't try and make it easier on yourself!" Gia swore and pressed the corner of her shawl over her injury.

But there was no point in continuing, and Pleo, already fatigued, didn't know how long she would last against an enraged, wounded Gia. Saurebaras nodded at Pleo, satisfied with her gesture, and tried to wave Gia over.

"Gia, you require first aid and your sparring partner has surrendered—do acknowledge her."

Gia ignored Saurebaras and remained on the piste, glaring at Pleo. She made four staccato claps, which signalled a request for a rematch.

*No,* Pleo mouthed the word at Gia, picking up her training fan with its bloodied blade and handing it to Saurebaras.

"Acknowledge that there'll be no rematch," Saurebaras

insisted to Gia, "or never step foot into a fla-tessen class again."

Gia curtsied once and stormed off the piste. Pleo turned on her heel in wearied misery and heard murmured snatches of conversation from around the hall:

"Who is the low-intermediary with the streaks of mica in her hair?"

"There are no streaks in her hair."

"Look again. Her hair colour changes when she moves—it's so distracting."

"Her fighting style is unusual and yet ingenious—no wonder Gia lost the bout."

Pleo sought refuge at the back of the hall and took off her shawl. She dropped it on the floor and the shawl folded itself up. Outside the piste, she didn't need the liddicoate garment's protection: it would have been useless against Gia and the resources of House Aront at her disposal. She would make Pleo pay for that fluke hit—a minor humiliation for any Adept—but Gia had a reputation as a candidate to uphold, although her prospects for advancement would be less favourable after her latest conduct.

The surrounding air stirred as something flew past the back of Pleo's head. She heard a tearing and her head instantly felt lighter. Pleo put her hand to the back of her neck and felt cool air stirring on her scalp as her coiled bun of hair tumbled to the floor. She heard Gia cackling in triumph as she caught the castanet. Maybe the severed bun was an adequate redress for the cut on her face.

"Pocket," Pleo commanded her skirt.

A small pleat of cloth bunched up near her right hip. She picked up frayed mass of hair and stuffed it into the fold, which closed up by itself. The asking price of her hair at 16000 uta would be reduced to 8000 unless the place near her home could rebond her hair at a discount, but she didn't know of anywhere that could repair her pride. Her supplements would be reduced as part of the disciplinary action for injuring Gia, and possibly delay her hair's regrowth by several months.

Her father once told her the best way to handle bullies who worked in the same mine shaft: "The key is to make them stop. Ignore them and they become more daring, and with tight schedules and fifty miners under me, the problem spreads. Sometimes, allow yourself a necessary show of force."

Pleo's plan to get off Chatoyance was now delayed. She retrieved her shawl, curtsied to Gia and returned the four staccato claps.

*Rematch accepted.*

Taken aback, Gia did not acknowledge at first and stood gawping at Pleo. Pleo clapped again until Gia curtseyed to her. A tall male Adept noticed their gestures, and hurried to the back of the hall to whisper in Saurebaras's ear.

"Call for recess now? Don't be ridiculous," Saurebaras exclaimed, having noticed the pair.

To Pleo's surprise Saurebaras did not command them to stand down. Instead, she did a quick pirouette in apparent delight and crossed the hall with her characteristic flowing strides. She stopped by Gia.

"Gia, if you insist on this madness I must demote you to Low-Intermediate."

"This mining scum fucked up my face, madame!"

"Watch your language in my hall. Speak like the Tier Dweller you are," tutted Saurebaras, holding Gia's chin between thumb and forefinger as she examined the wound.

Pleo saw a forcep emerge from under Saurebaras's thumbnail, and she used its tip to probe the cut. Pleo never considered the possibility that Saurebaras had also been through Polyteknical. Unless her implants differed from the official versions and were obtained via other means...

Patting Gia on the cheek, Saurebaras said, "Tell your parents it won't scar, with the proper course of treatment. You'll be beautiful again."

She then turned to Pleo. "And what do I tell your family, since you insist on this rematch? What if you acquire a slash on your face too? Or worse?"

Pleo thought of her home in the aftermath of the Incident and Cerussa's suicide. She replied, "Nothing, madame. If they notice they won't care what happens."

Saurebaras nodded and gestured to the tall Adept to prepare another training piste and retrieve another training fan from the prep area.

Both Gia and Pleo took up their positions in the new piste.

"I'll remind you both of the rematch rules: all areas of body, except the face, are now permitted. The bout stops with the first touch. One minute."

The Adept emerged from inside the changing room and handed Pleo another fan and half a stick of grip powder. This time she checked the blade and found it to be blunt. Satisfied, she crushed the stick and rubbed the powder into her left palm.

Saurebaras called for both women to begin. Pleo darted forwards. The fighters' ovals intersected on the piste with a furious clicking sound. Gia threw a castanet at Pleo but she held her shawl in front of her face to block the attack. Since Pleo had not issued a command to her shawl it did not fortify itself against an incoming projectile. She saw the silver weave of liddicoate fibres in detailed close-up before the castanet slashed across her mouth. Pleo lost her hold on her shawl and licked her lips—no splash of blood, but the skin was broken.

Gia cursed as the castanet returned to her grasp. She dropped her other castanet and brandished her fan.

*Open up!* Pleo pleaded with her fan as she grasped both sides and tried to force it. She gave up as the fan unsheathed the blade in the handle instead. Lunging back, Gia went into an anti-clockwise spin and prepared to launch her opened fan with a flick of her wrist. In utter desperation, Pleo hurled her closed fan at Gia, hoping to deflect hers in mid air.

Overconfident, Gia did an exaggerated swerve, and her shawl billowed out in front of her, obscuring her from Pleo's view for a second. Before the shawl settled, Gia fell backwards and hit the floor with a thump Pleo felt rather than felt.

"Halt!" called Saurebaras, holding up a hand. The entire

hall fell silent. At first Pleo saw Gia lying on the piste, inside her now deactivated oval. As she took a step towards Gia, Pleo felt her own oval nip at her ankles. She looked down and found that it had shrunk itself around her feet.

"Maintain your last position," commanded Saurebaras, and her voice was subdued. All eyes were on the looming screens. Pleo watched the replay footage with a strange fascination: onscreen, Gia completed her spin and threw her opened fan, but Pleo's closed fan had intercepted it in mid-flight with uncanny timing, its blade snagging on a membrane. The combined momentum of both fans had directed them back to Gia. Now the tang of Pleo's fan jutted out of Gia's eye socket, while the opened fan covered the other eye, its spokes opening and closing on their own.

Pleo heard her voice call out to Gia, but she didn't move. What moved instead were the fans, both pulsating as the leaves reverted to their marine-sponge feeding traits, drawing Gia's blood into their membranes.

Still believing in a ruse, Pleo broke out of her oval and rushed over to her.

"Stay in your piste!" Saurebaras commanded again.

Pleo stopped at the sight of fresh blood pooling in Gia's piste.

*Cerussa, I've avenged you. Sooner than expected.*

A red lagoon formed around Gia's head and neck, reminding Pleo of the false-colour images captured of lakes on alien moons. Saurebaras clapped six times to dismiss the other students. Pleo saw them disperse and leave the hall in a grateful hurry.

She wiped her forehead with her shawl, but the liddicoate fibres could not remove the cold sweat of fear. *Vengeance? Not like this.*

"No one touch her. Let the floor perform its function," said Suarebaras.

The floor under Gia suddenly opened up to swallow her body and the blood cascaded into the hole, leaving wide trails when the floor reformed around itself.

"Surrender your shawl, skirt and other practice accoutrements. Your injuries will be treated, but they must go on record. Your version of events is required—as is mine." Saurebaras spoke with less admonishment than if she had been correcting Pleo's posture.

Another hole opened up in the floor area next to Pleo: when she peered inside she saw a long dark chute with smooth sides, yawning into darkness. Her future from this moment on. She took off her shawl and skirt and dropped them in, along with her never-used practice castanets: a waste of 280 uta. The accessories clattered as they bounced off the sides of the chute before landing with a muffled thump in a catchment tray. As the hole closed up, Pleo winced: she remembered her hair was still in the skirt's pocket.

The Spinels entered the hall only when the last of the students had cleared out.

"Wait," Saurebaras called out to them. "She needs the infirmary."

*No I don't*, Pleo wanted to say, but she appreciated how Saurebaras was stalling for time. She paced the floor in front of Pleo, who automatically stood up straight and pulled back her shoulders.

"Excellent posture. It seems you only progress under immense pressure," observed Saurebaras.

"Don't mock, madame."

"Far from it; I must give you your assessment before you're taken away by the Spinels."

Pleo waited.

"Until something has broken or fallen into pieces, I don't know how it functions. I try to discover individual style in my students by breaking them down. Refinement and polishing don't happen without friction. Now I realise, a little too late, you will never possess grace or fluidity. But you can become quite, *quite* formidable."

"How so?"

"This." Saurebaras pressed a fingertip to Pleo's forehead.

Not understanding Saurebaras—and and not wanting to—Pleo backed away.

"You display skill with thoughtforms. Tell me: was it always in you? Is this ability always possessed by asteroid miners?"

Pleo recoiled from the questions and turned to run towards the doors. But Saurebaras reached out, pulling back on Pleo's shoulder with ease. Pleo tried to shake her off and raised her hand to strike at any part of Saurebaras with her forceps. Like a cobra, Saurebaras's hand caught hold of Pleo's wrist.

Saurebaras said, "Despite what happened today, what everyone saw, and what the screens recorded, you didn't kill Gia."

"It's still an accident."

"I was supposed to arrange the accident. That's why I left out both of you for the opening ceremony." Saurebaras released Pleo's hand. "It seems an accident can be arranged too well; I was not expecting you to try and save Gia."

Pleo rubbed her wrist, still smarting from Saurebaras's grip. "I was on the other side of the piste."

"*You* were, but not that other self of yours. I saw a flash of it. It tried to shove Gia out of the way."

"Enough!" Pleo yelled. "No one will believe that!"

"I already do."

"Akma." The word once used to describe her father slipped out of Pleo. "Madame, your reconditioning is wearing off."

Saurebaras ignored Pleo. "Listen when I tell you: thoughtform, unknown guest, or hidden self, call it what you like. But until activated, it simply resides in a secret space. In most people it sleeps and never awakens."

"Superstition!" Pleo spat.

"Don't dismiss it: it's inherent in the nature of both professions."

"I already know what will happen to me."

"Do you? Please tell me," snapped Saurebaras, bringing her narrow face close to Pleo's.

"Detention, arrest, expulsion and blacklisting. I can still harvest bat guano in a cave on a Pavey shepherd moon, if I survive my prison term."

Saurebaras shook her head. "It's worse than that: Polyteknical will bring you to the Infirmary and tell you that you'll be kept under observation for three days until agents from a certain Chatoyance government department send for you. But no infirmary has such little floor space. You'll be locked in what your interrogators call The Little Room of Forgetting until your limbs and muscles atrophy. Before your body is finally broken, the interrogation begins. Since you caused the death of the scion of the Aront family, I doubt they will observe proper procedure. Pray for a quick death."

Judging from Saurebaras's distant gaze, Pleo realised she was speaking from experience. "Is that what happened to you, madame? When you killed the other instructors?"

"Contrary to that glorious if inaccurate mural tarnishing the walls outside"—Saurebaras pointed at the double doors with such vehemence Pleo expected fire to shoot out of her fingertips—"fla-tessen was not created because some pathetic hired dancers couldn't protect themselves. It was born in the shadows of cargo holds and ship passages during the Waves. It's a fighting art, but some of my *former* colleagues didn't agree to let it remain an art. The first one that was killed was an accident, like your case. The rest were in self-defence. But these noble Chatoyant families, Aront and Madrugal and the rest, disapprove of sudden displays of brilliance. They still cling to the belief that inherent qualities, subject to attrition, pressure and the passage of time, yield the best results and people."

Seeing no choice, Pleo raised the forceps of her index and ring finger and declared, "Then I choose to be a Nosebleed—this is the quickest way."

"Your twin sister is an unfortunate statistic. Do not join her." Saurebaras slapped Pleo's hand away from her face. "If you survive this, give me the chance to tell your parents that they named you well."

"Pleochroism is observed in most rocks and minerals. My name is more common than dirt."

"But *how* you display it: dull from one perspective but unleashing a hidden brilliance from another. What a most useful quality to possess. Trust me, it will serve you well." The instructor placed her hand on Pleo's shoulder, making her flinch. Changing the subject, Saurebaras asked her, "What is the first precept of fla-tessen?"

"'Intention designs the weapon'," recited Pleo.

"What designs a better weapon?"

"A better... intention?" Pleo guessed, unsure of where Saurebaras was going with this line of questioning.

"No, a worse intention," said Saurebaras. She slid her hand up the back of Pleo's neck and pricked the skin over the caratoid artery. Pleo tried to fight back, but her face and arms went numb. Saurebaras's forceps were not remnants of her time as a student or an instructor, but venomous spines. Before Pleo hit the floor, the instructor reached out and caught her by the waist. Head lolling back, Pleo saw the ceiling of the hall jerk into view, a carapace of interlocking golden light-sensitive panels. The inactive screens meant that there were to be no witnesses.

"Be still!" soothed Saurebaras as Pleo thrashed in her hold. "I gave you a controlled dose. It hurts, but the pain won't last."

A high-pitched whistling rang through her skull and

pain exploded in the palms of her clenched fists. Pleo had lost control of her forceps, which retracted and extended under the muscle spasms. Saurebaras wrapped Pleo in a large fla-tessen shawl and hoisted her over the shoulders, like a rug she'd bought at market. The panelled hall ceiling transitioned to the low grubby one of the corridor outside.

"You and I are the results of the very worst intentions," Saurebaras whispered to Pleo. "I hope to salvage what is left of you before House Aront finds you. Pray for death if Gia's parents get hold of you."

Clinging on to consciousness, Pleo focused on familiar names: "Gia?"

"Gia's entire existence was a lie engineered by her mother." For the first time Pleo heard sympathy in Saurebaras's voice. "That poor child. Her struggles are now over, but yours are only beginning."

"Cerussa!"

"I hope she can hear you now," Saurebaras whispered.

"They'll all pay for her death," Pleo muttered before her mind slipped into darkness.

INSIDE THE INFIRMARY, Saurebaras lifted the girl off the examination cot and carried her past the rows of empty beds. The place had been designed to take in thirty patients a day back in the early days of Chatoyance's industrial boom, when Polyteknical student numbers had been much higher. Now, medical bots tackled the infirmary's few patients.

One detached itself from an armoire and tried to sound the alarm. Saurebaras kicked it where its waist would be if it was human, forcing the bot back into the armoire. The impact scattered glass tubes and plastic all over the polished floor.

The old access serviceway was her best bet for avoiding the Spinels stationed in the corridor outside. She knew the place better than most staff and hoped the serviceway connecting the infirmary to the side alley had not been sealed off. Most of the teaching staff and students had left before the end of the Shineshift, but Saurebaras did not want to risk discovery.

She passed through the serviceway with Pleo, emerging from grimy darkness onto an empty passageway, and stood in the shadow of the suspended walkway to avoid any Constabulary officers on evening patrol.

There were none. Saurebaras glanced up at the sky and saw the possible cause: Shineshift glitch. Gachala was throwing a tantrum with a display of solar flares, affecting vital mechanisms on nearby settlements. She drew encouragement from the flashing lights and slipped into an underpass and along a succession of disused tunnels to the nearest Retail Sector. It was the best place to leave an unconscious person: dead bodies turned up all the time in the fountains.

# CHAPTER ELEVEN

THE SHINESHIFT ENDED fifteen minutes late. Marsh stood in the main concourse of the 'Cinth as people congregated and noted the time. He studied the dendritic patterns worked into the underside of the 'Cinth's arching roof, but soon gave up trying to keep himself occupied. An eerie calm permeated the 'Cinth, as though every commuter had their breath sucked out of their bodies.

Shineshift glitches: he had heard about them from Setona, but this was his first time experiencing one. A faint breeze, perfumed by ozone, blew down the main track as he sat on a large girder protruding through the floor of the platform like the spine of a dragon, the huge black rivets running along its length like scales. The visible sections of indigo sky in the roof flashed as if light was cracking through the firmament.

Then he realised: Cabuchon must've given the order at last. He imagined the autonomous Demarcation satellites breaking out of their tight formation in the circumstellar disc around Gachala. They would amass in orbit around Chatoyance, like a beautiful canopy that admitted nothing in and out. Marsh ran to the nearest highlights column seeking more information or reassurance. The highlights remained oblivious to his alarm; the strips twitched and pulsated before they were shed en masse to refresh the newsfeed.

Marsh tore off a fresh strip of highlight as soon as the column generated it:

## TIER DWELLER SCION FATALLY INJURED IN FREAK DANCE ACCIDENT

The highlights that followed gave the story top coverage but the news was only speculation and noise. It was murder, no suspects had been arrested yet. Marsh dropped the highlights on the station floor.

The tannoy buzzed to life. "Await official Shineshift change announcements. Remain calm and go about your business. Do not look towards the sky. Do not listen to rumours for guidance."

People remained quiet, but not calm. Marsh read their faces—well, the ones that were not covered with filter veils or implants, the unaugmented eyes wide with trepidation. As for the people whose eyes he couldn't read, he noticed their jaws set in tension. Everyone was caught between anticipating calamity and contemplating the welcome relief it would bring from Chatoyance's incessant activity—but not release, for that would take generations of unlearning.

Their delayed response calmed Marsh, but he recognised how typically Cabuchoner it was to assume the worst. He crushed the discarded highlights underfoot and returned to the girder.

He recalled telling a story to a group of Chatoyant children on a platform at the 'Cinth. It had been his first time experiencing a transport delay on Chatoyance. He began by telling it to himself, as a way to relieve the tedium of waiting for signal failures and track faults to be repaired on the Subaltern's Parade. With a few embellishments and gestures, he recited the version he had read many times as a child; and before long, a small curious audience had gathered around Marsh.

*Long ago, the Overseers abducted people from Home System and took them to a vast world of mineral wealth hidden underground. The slaves dug and dug until they could see no more.*

*Look closer, the Overseers said. Go deeper.*

*They removed the eyes of their slaves and in their place inserted eyes of the Overseers' own making. They scattered the slaves' old eyes across the sky where they shone together with the other stars. The slaves were forced to see with new eyes that could only pick out minute details of rock and stone in the total darkness of the mines.*

*Over time, some of the slaves' eyes disintegrated into clouds of dust and vapour. When it rained, the slaves bathed in the rainwater and the water coated their eyes, restoring some semblance of normal* sight. Over time, the old eyes fell from the sky into forests where their former owners retrieved them. These slaves tried to remove the Overseers' eyes but they could not, so in utter desperation they gouged out one eye and crammed their original eye into the bloodied empty socket. This combination allowed them to see to the horizon, into space as well as the microcosm.

Keeping their newfound sight a secret from their masters, the slaves bided their time. With patience they dug deeper to extend the mine shafts and hollowed out hidden chambers in strategic positions. With their new sight they honed weapons out of their tools and made new ones.

The Overseers had grown neglectful and complacent in their watch and so mistook the increased activity of the slaves for enthusiasm or subservience as the Day of Falling Dust approached. The slaves had to strike soon or else there was going to be no chance, after the Overseers sealed the mines with explosives and transported the slaves to other worlds.

On the eve of the Day of Falling Dust, the Overseers stood gloating over the open pits and shafts of the mines as they had done so many times before. The slaves greeted their masters with news of a new discovery. The slaves also suggested that the closure of the mines had to wait.

Lax and slothful over the years, the Overseers indulged the slaves. Blinded by greed and complacence they believed the exhausted mines still contained an untapped seam of riches.

"Where is it?" demanded the Overseers, straining to see in the darkness.

"Look closer," replied the slaves, as the Masters had always told them.

The Overseers screamed their impatience and their voices shook the tunnels. They pounded the walls of the shafts. Dirt rained down on them.

"We cannot see these new gems!"

"Go deeper," the slaves said, in the Masters' words.

"Enough of this!" roared the Overseers. "We are leaving!"

And the slaves replied with silence, which terrified the Overseers for the first time in their lives. They were not used to being in the dark tunnels for so long.

"All of you are not leaving these mines." The slaves spoke again, voices ringing out in bitter triumph. "Our homes are now your graves."

The Overseers barely had time to understand when the tunnels shook and the roofs collapsed. Quickly the slaves fell upon the Overseers, wielding their new weapons. With their sharpened tools the slaves cut out the eyes of their masters and scattered them deep in the earth.

Now chained together, the Overseers stopped screeching in agony and began pleading for mercy.

"All of you wanted to see new treasures in the

mine?" The slaves addressed their former masters. "Now your eyes are the gems. Your bodies will join them!"

The Day of Falling Dust went ahead as the slaves sealed off the mines for good and fled the planet in the Overseers' ships. The Overseers still thrashed and cried out in their subterranean prison, fading into silence as time went by. Their bodies changed into valuable gems and their eyes the most valuable of all.

But, it is said, not all of the Overseers perished on the Day of Falling Dust. Some clawed their way out of the mines and swore vengeance on their escaped slaves, no matter how long it took. To this day the Overseers are still searching.

With perfect timing, the tannoy in the 'Cinth had emitted an audio mishmash of static and breaking news as soon as Marsh ended the story, and Marsh had joined the throng heading down into the T-Cars. After his performance he clung onto a pole in the next T-Car, taken aback at how easily he remembered the story. It was one of many collected in various children's books; he had never had reason to inquire into its authorship. Those books claimed the Overseers story had originated from the expansion phase of Home System, accumulating details over time.

It was an odd choice of tale for children. Definitely not a comforting bedtime story. Marsh figured it started out as a mnemonic, evoking a bygone age of fraught pioneer exploration beyond the Kuiper Belt. He felt such history held little meaning now for the Archer's Ring, since Home System was mostly abandoned, except for the Jovian and Saturnian moons.

The story had to be based on some real incident or incidents, or else it would not have persisted. Cynical of his people, Marsh saw a good reason for its subsequent decades of retelling: it fed into the fortress mentality of most Cabuchoners.

Marsh hated to admit that the Doyen was right. Standards were slipping indeed. The Doyen, like his companion Tier Dwellers, recognised and feared the first signs of Cabuchon's inertia.

ON THE MORNING after the Doyen's visit, Setona waved to Marsh from inside the dimness of the stock room. By accident he snapped in half another flimsy pair of vending-machine chopsticks and made a gesture in SignalPose: [dabbing at his lips with his forefinger]. It meant, "Not now. Having my lunch."

"Since when do you eat lunch?" Setona was selecting a leash for the display leopard from a rack on the wall. "Don't think I don't see you nibbling at lumps of potch opals in the storeroom or hiding slivers of Desert Rose under your tongue."

Marsh didn't reply. He splayed and wiggled the fingers of his right hand, trying to recall what 'pica' in SignalPose was. Instead, he mimed hacking at an imaginary rock face with his left arm.

"Don't confuse Chatoyant Industrial SignalPose with

Modrani SignalPose—we're much more elaborate. It's what we're paid for."

She stepped out of the stock room and showed him the modrani gesture for 'miner', using two knuckles of both hands to graze her cheeks to represent smudges of dirt.

In reply, Marsh made the gestures for 'cravings' [index finger and thumb held like a pincer and placing morsels of invisible food into mouth].

A genetic predisposition towards pica was common among Cabuchoners from earlier Waves, but a widespread stigma still existed to the extent that March had learned to not say the word aloud when he was growing up. The innocuous combination of hard consonants and ending open vowel suggested the name of a close friend or a relative rather than a condition. Mineral deficiencies, the doctors had said, and prescribed iron and zinc supplements, but Marsh finished his doses quickly and resumed eating blades of grass and pinches of sand from the garden, much to the dismay of his parents.

His parents were both senior members of the Corund and didn't talk about his pica; they even found a measure of tolerance for it. For older Cabuchoners, pica was a genetic adaptation, a remnant of the less romantic side of the tentative Home System expeditions and the First Wave of migration before the Kuiper Belt opened up. Those first ships had been carrying sleepers while their skeleton crews faced the attendant risks of plunging into the void. Stories emerged of rationing, and malnutrition leading to starvation, and reports of mutiny and cannibalism. To acknowledge this unsavoury part of their history was to contradict the glorious narrative of the Archer's Ring, ceaselessly expanded and foisted upon subsequent generations like Marsh's.

Still, Marsh liked augmenting narratives of his own. He took out a pendant from under the counter: a long shard of Europan sea jade, dangling from a platinum chain. The jade was irradiated in sub-zero waters exposed to Jupiter's magnetic field and super-compressed by water pressure; the shard's vivid sheen was an interplay of swirling kingfisher greens and yellows shot through with fine black threads of chromium. He loved staring into its depths. No matter where gemstones originate, they always transported him far away.

"My great-grandmother spent five years operating a remote crawler on the ocean floor of Europa with thousands of other prospectors, trawling for slag that would yield treasures. Like this fragment of Europan sea jade. She made her fortune and repaid her passage to Jupiter. Perhaps this fragment once passed through her hands."

"Not very likely. It's rumoured this piece is cursed. The provenance card states the shard has drawn Tier Dweller blood," muttered Setona, reaching out to run a slender finger along the delicate sharp edge. Her fingertip came away with freshly drawn blood.

"The pendant should be in a Constabulary evidence vault," Marsh said and looked up the provenance card in the stockroom records. Unsurprising, the information provided was by turns specific and vague: the jade was certified to be of Europan marine origin, not a clever imitation grown from an artificial seabed simulated in an industry geolab.

"Don't you know? Evidence vaults have big leaks. And places like the Back-Bazaars soak up the leaks, at least most of the time." Setona smiled at Marsh's naivety. "No wonder you got arrested for art theft back home, poor innocent boy."

"*Possession* of stolen art." Marsh scowled. "Someone I knew thought I had connections and when he found out I had none he wanted, he turned me in." He didn't get a chance to mention his pica to Setona during his brief interview. She had glanced through his employment history and was hardly ruffled about the type of trouble he had been involved in. Then again, Setona would never find a Chatoyant willing to work for 20,000 uta a month. "And what about the provenance of offworld gems mined by Chatoyance and its subsidies?"

"I'd rather trust a Back-Bazaar merchant who lays everything out—wares *and* provenance, if you're discreet—on one of their tarpaulin stalls than suppliers and dealers in compliance under the Ninclarsaen Procedure. Its integrity is supposed to be infallible, but it's about as secure as the roof of the old 'Cinth station."

Marsh asked, "The scope is too wide to control?"

"The Procedure lets anything in. Worse still, it lets the same things in all the time. Blood gems from conflict zones, and greasy gems bought with stolen funds."

Marsh looked at the counter. "I've been wondering why only secondhand pieces and curios are on display."

"Blood comes with grease. You can disguise either

one, but not a mess of both. That never ever comes off. I relinquished all of my gifts of jewellery." Setona added, "Unless I've left a few stuck on the display leopard."

"*The pendant's former ownership allegedly involved an undisclosed Pre-Downturn crime of passion...*" Marsh started reading aloud from the provenance card and then stopped to ask, "Aren't Chatoyant crimes involving Tier Dwellers mostly crimes of passion?"

"You have *no* idea," replied Setona with a finality intending to close off the subject.

Marsh remained unfazed and set down the pendant on a tray. The waters of Europa receded and sublimated as he imagined the shard thrust into an eye socket or lodged between the spiked vertebrae of a Doyen's articulated spine.

"Prices keep fluctuating, so let's see which story sells it faster: a personal connection to my family or a high society murder."

"The murder," insisted Setona, sucking on her finger with theatrical relish. She daubed some more blood on her lips to save on reapplying gloss. "Chatoyants pay more attention to the glint of knives in dark alleyways than changing Shineshift lights..." She was suddenly distracted by something outside the windows.

Setona hurried outside as Marsh went to the doorway and surveyed the piazza. The fountain jets still accompanied the sculpted horses on their gallop to nowhere, but a crowd now gathered around the fountain's wide, deep basin.

Marsh stepped outside, hit a switch set in the doorframe

to power up the crowning-shield and walked in the direction of the fountain. The crowd's attention was focused on the body of a young woman in the water. Both of her arms were carelessly thrown over the edge of the basin, as if the woman had passed out drunk. Encircling the wrist of one of the arms was a familiar-looking keloid scar.

Marah shoved his way through the crowd, past Setona and over to the wide edge of the fountain's basin. He lifted the woman out of the fountain, oblivious to the icy jets of water and the murmuring crowd and placed her on the paving. She coughed up some fluid and passed out again.

Setona stood over Marsh and the shadows cast by the horse sculptures obscured the question she asked in frantic SignalPose:

[Who is she?]

[I don't know] Marsh replied.

It felt strange to tell her so because it was not exactly a lie.

# CHAPTER TWELVE

SENIOR INVESTIGATOR DUMORTIER stood outside the doors of the Sunlight Corridor. Through the interlocking triangular panes of gold- and indigo-tinted glass, he made out the silhouette of his superior Lieutenant Soni Katyal.

He touched his fingertip to the crowning-shield to test it. As he predicted, it barely yielded to the slight pressure. The glass was for the aesthetic, but the crowning-shield did the actual work. Constabulary versions did not hum or vibrate like the ones used by civilians. It was a misconception that a crowning-shield was a 'forcefield': it was a physical thing, a shield of nanoparticles that could be set to any spatial configuration: doorways, buildings or vehicles. The particles bumped up against surrounding air molecules and dust, creating the crowning-shield's trademark shimmer, and Dumortier watched this interplay for a minute as a meditation. People persisted in believing that crowning-shields were *completely* invisible to the naked eye; but this being Chatoyance, where half the population sported optical implants, most people had no idea what the naked eye was capable of.

"Ma'am, our queen is in the crowd," he blurted as soon as the glass panes parted before him.

Katyal kept her back to him and her attention on the Chatoyance skyline, as though she failed to hear him or recognise his quaint use of outdated code. Dumortier had long ceased feeling self-conscious about it. When working on Tier Dweller cases, it was prudent to plug all possible boltholes in case of moles within Constabulary departments. The code was obscure enough to be impenetrable to all but Dumortier and his superiors.

"Ma'am, the queen—"

Katyal beckoned him inside. Dumortier hesitated before entering the Sunlight Corridor, mesmerised by the illusion: every hexagonal arch along the corridor receded away from him until the farthest arch nearly disappeared. This was no drab, overcooled utilitarian conduit linking the twin blocks of Constabulary Headquarters and jutting out of the buildings like an exposed rib. The Sunlight Corridor connected both sprawling roofs in an elaborate undulating ribbon. The long, bright and almost sacred space, reserved for superiors and their investigators, facilitated discreet yet open communication. It announced to all personnel and reassured them that "We harbour no secrets here."

*No official ones, anyway.*

"Slow down on the Gia Aront case," Katyal told him.

Dumortier glanced behind him in case she was talking to someone else standing outside the doors.

No such luck.

"Apply the brakes now? Tyro Pleo Tanza has been spotted in Temple Plaza. She may have been granted sanctuary."

"The Temple does not grant sanctuary under any circumstances—"

This was either a very recent directive or he had fallen well behind on religious matters.

"—and its committee wouldn't want the Temple turning into a magnet for undesirables, harboured by nuns and priestesses. We wade through enough legal morass every second of every day."

"Do we apply normal surveillance or lockstep levels to Tyro Pleo Tanza in the interim?"

"Watch her, but don't impede or detain. She can swim the entire canal network or camp out in Khrysobe Spaceport as long as she doesn't make it off Chatoyance. There's nowhere she can hide. But if she's spooked, she will start running here and there, exhausting her energy and ours. Don't pick her up until I give that order."

Dumortier's enthusiasm abated. He did not appreciate being summoned at such short notice and for apparently nothing more than to have his previous orders rescinded. The choice of venue was undoubtedly deliberate on Katyal's part. Still, every Constabulary officer dreamed of their visit to the Sunlight Corridor. Not many were granted this honour.

An instinct left over from his officer days told him to

linger in the presence of superiors and not rush off when dismissed. Make the most of your moment, even if it turns out nothing is required of you. He suppressed it.

"May I go? I need to get back to Canal Police."

"Drop the disappearance case for now as well, Dumortier. This concerns the biggest fish that ever landed in our laps."

Tier Dweller cases were Dumortier's remit, hence nothing much was ever required of him. He relied on his aesthetic to shoulder most of his work, cutting an austere figure yet elegant and charming enough to blend in at functions and special events. If you moved with fluid ease within their circles, they opened up to you like clams at high tide. Even VIPs and officials from Cabuchon and Anium felt comfortable in his presence—until he switched off the charm, flash freezing his targets like liquid nitrogen.

A sequence of low clicks punctured the air, followed by a whirring from the smooth white floor between him and Katyal. A sleek conference table and matching chairs rose between them. He took a seat at the end closest to him and Katyal sat at the other. A real-time satellite map image of Chatoyance appeared in the table's surface.

"This Pleo Tanza, does she have any priors?"

"Nothing too serious. Caused a public disturbance a month or so ago. Officers were called to the community hall in Blue Taro and Boxthorn."

Katyal's gaze flicked downwards and she read aloud from the report readout on the table. "Protesting a then-proposed training initiative..."

"An initiative which was subsequently implemented," Dumortier informed her. "Experimental lapidary implants."

"Says here, in the endnotes, that the experimental implants were 'under review' at the time of writing." For Katyal no detail was too minor.

"You and I both know 'under review' can mean anything when it comes to Chatoyant institutions."

Katyal regarded him with mild exasperation. She didn't need the reminder.

"Polyteknical carried out the initiative," Dumortier added. "Forty students outfitted with implants and under observation."

Katyal closed the report. "Misguided heroics tend to attract attention."

"Too early to speculate if Gia Aront's death is another one of Pleo Tanza's heroics."

"Bring Pleo Tanza in now and I can't guarantee the Aronts won't try to bury her."

"Who asked you to bring me in on Gia Aront?"

"Is it relevant?"

Dumortier looked around at his suroundings. "Both of us are in the Sunlight Corridor, so yes."

"Patriarch Aront requested you. I agreed. But only after discussion with Sakamoto."

"Ahh," breathed Dumortier in a way that meant, *Say no more.*

"So, to an outsider it looks like a fantastic embarrassing accident. But that's Polyteknical's interpretation—we take a different view."

"The Tier Dwellers purloin so much from the good people of the Archer's Ring that they've resorted to cannibalising each other?" Dumortier sucked on his teeth. "I never thought I'd live long enough to see that."

"Gia Aront was always the most attractive target."

"Much too obvious," replied Dumortier. "Who'd dare try? Until now."

Things occasionally pierced the blanket of corruption: scandals, land swaps, allegations of blackmail. No one had expected to discover an actual corpse lying underneath; it was a fortuitous collision of factors. Tyro Pleo Tanza may as well have stabbed Gia Aront on board an Aront luxury barge and pushed her body dead smack into the path of a Canal Newt.

"I'm aware. But by right she should be placed into protection."

Dumortier described a spiral in the air in front of him with his finger, to illustrate that he'd gone over the problem many times since he was assigned to the case yesterday. "Tyro Pleo Tanza is the daughter of Idilman Tanza, the sole survivor of the Forty. Might as well strap an advertisement beacon to her head."

"Also, there's a high possibility of wetwork."

Dumortier wanted to laugh. "The Inner Council? Over one dead Aront scion?"

"So the question now is: safe houses or flats?" Katyal asked.

"I have to treat existing ones as all compromised." His spiral in the air shrunk like the strategic options he had considered in the last day. "Besides, if we take the initiative to fake her disappearance, it'll look like the Aronts paid us or extorted us into doing it for real."

Katyal drummed her fingers on the table, making the map flicker.

"Don't underestimate the Tier Dwellers' talent at damage control," said Dumortier. "The Aronts haven't made any public statements or given interviews. Likely a delaying tactic; they can't control damage if they don't know the full extent of it."

"For now," conceded Katyal. "This is where we flow into the gap created."

Dumortier nodded, although he agreed with her only in theory.

This could go either way. A high profile case solved to his—and Constabulary's—credit, and Katyal finally makes a significant breakthrough against the Aronts. Both results achieved without any more wasted effort on the few minor Tier Dweller cases Dumortier was chasing. Cue ceremonies and speeches before the Lieutenant-Colonel pinned medals on both their chests.

Or Gia Aront could cause him more than a little trouble, incurring the displeasure of those with vested interests in the Aronts and their fortune. Dumortier then foresaw different metal on his chest; shrapnel from an IED fixed to the underside of a parked Shirpen.

"Once the Aronts have their justice, even you won't be allowed to take another look, not even with my permission and clearance."

Dumortier inclined his head in agreement. It happened often enough in the past that Dumortier's predecessors had acknowledged it as standard operating procedure, simply the cost of conducting an investigation: an extra-legality which could be enough to tie Constabulary's hands.

Gachala's verdant disc peaked above the horizon, scattering violet, teal and orange hues across the sky. The calmest period in the day was during the reset of the Shineshift cycle. Transfixed, Dumortier had never watched the sunrise from the roof of Constabulary HQ before. He never had reason to come up here and was glad the view did not disappoint. Gachala lived up to its gemstone namesake.

"When I started watching from up here I noticed the rays never hit the same places twice. It was like Gachala was showing me new details and secrets every day."

Dumortier was not in a mood to offer opinions on the scenery. "If you say so, ma'am."

"That's when I realised we should stop fumbling around in our own jurisdiction. The Downturn left us a city-sized mess. *We* are vigilant, but that is never enough."

Whenever Katyal was frustrated with Constabulary— which meant most of the time—she employed the royal 'we.' Its current overuse told Dumortier how Katyal was on edge, wrestling with the potential opportunities Gia Aront's death had unexpectedly brought.

"I do what I can, ma'am. Each case is unique, but happily they yield much useful information. I learnt very early on that it's important to not disrupt the ecosystem. It's all part of the long game."

"All you investigators and your 'long games.'" Katyal

stared balefully at the table's surface as though she was looking at his fellow investigators. "Data and intelligence collected must translate into action."

"Take down the Tier Dwellers, their partners, their networks? Drain the canals? Shut down Khrysobe?" Dumortier tried not to snort out of respect. A noble aim, but it remained merely an intellectual exercise.

"That's Constabulary's wider game, not yours—for now. Our slowness to act is compounded by the Tier Dwellers, so we end up immobile, like carvings on the Temple walls. The Tier Dwellers know this too well and exploit it."

"They continue to mistake investigators' patience for slowness or absence of action. Ma'am, I recommend not dispelling that useful illusion."

The windows of the corridor suddenly flashed and then dimmed, as if in response to his statement. Even at this distance, from behind specialised glass, Dumortier still looked away when Gachala's rays hit the roof of the Temple. Katyal did not flinch as she stared directly at it. She was not wearing shades.

"That glare," he muttered. "Doesn't any city ordinance forbid this daily health and safety hazard?"

"The Temple nuns told the city elders the roof is to help 'shock awareness back into people.' Something about—" Katyal took a deep breath and quoted: "'The light of Gachala is not benevolent or life-giving glory, but harsh and unwavering. A strict but impartial teacher.'"

"Bullshit." Dumortier turned his chair away from the view while rubbing his eyes. "A fancy roof helps the Temple sell its new religion. A roof courtesy of overgenerous Tier Dwellers on the committee who must've had final but very questionable say in its design. Fingers crossed they don't build an extension."

Katyal turned around and smiled at him without mirth. "You know them so well."

"I assume that's why I was assigned, ma'am."

"Your unique perspective would also make you a wonderful Chatoyance tour guide."

"I wouldn't last long—much too honest. Too many precious tourist illusions will be shattered. Ever been to the New Areas?"

"Where asteroid miners live?"

Dumortier shook his head and pointed at the Lonely Heron Bridge, its metallic parabola leaping up in the distance. "*Those* asteroid miners."

"The Forty?"

"The conditions of the New Areas would count as disaster tourism, without the tourists."

"They've been provided for, all according to mining labour laws. It takes money to manage the New Areas: even the shittier ones like Blue Taro and Boxthorn possess very decent facilities and infrastructure. Chatoyance Industrial and Mining have done well by them. Or else the inhabitants would riot."

"But the New Areas are originally Aront land. Chatoyance is trying to fob off the miners' families and bury the tragedy." Dumortier pulled up a grid map in the lower pane of the window and magnified a satellite view of the Lonely Heron Bridge. He circled a rough oval next to it. "Look. The New Areas are not marked."

Katyal frowned and checked the satellite timestamp in the top right corner of the map. "This says it's up to date."

"They're not marked because it's unofficial."

"It's not your concern if the land is unofficially occupied, albeit for reasons of charity."

"This area was intended as a water treatment plant by Aront Corporation before it became a 15-acre wasteland, a reminder of the Downturn. Now it's a reminder of Kerte Yurgi—which is much more recent and painful. Relocating the residents now will take years of legal wrangling. Some people would very much prefer to make Aront Corp rescind its ownership of the New Areas. And then Chatoyants would like Kerte Yurgi to fade from public consciousness."

Katyal remained unmoved. "Proceed as you would a normal accident investigation."

"Ma'am, it isn't normal, or an accident."

Katyal asked, "What's your theory?"

"Someone wants the land back from Chatoyance Industrial."

"So they murder Gia Aront in an accident-not-accident? Does that sound absurd?"

"Hell knows? The Aronts, their rivals and their rivals's rivals"—Dumortier shrugged—"double, triple and quadruple crossings. Disputes over refinery contracts, moon bases or the mineral rights of asteroids floating between gas giants. The land can be a new research facility, canal wharf or another barracks for their House guards. Nothing's impossible."

"I assume nothing about our chances," said Katyal. "Everyday I've been searching for a fault or crack in the Aront floodgate that we can concentrate on, something we can wedge open: scandals, corruption, affairs. Now we have the ultimate murder. This moment in time is crucial. We may never have an opportunity like this again. Do you understand?"

Another voice interrupted from behind Dumortier.

"They're vulnerable, which means they'll make mistakes in judgment."

He glanced back down the length of the corridor and saw a silhouette with perfect posture approaching the conference table. It resolved itself into the figure of Lieutenant Sakamoto. How long had she been listening in? She walked in with both hands clasped behind her back, as if she was still on a parade ground.

"Pleo Tanza is reckless." Sakamoto seemed confident. "If she acted alone. Don't underestimate that."

"Autopilot," Dumortier muttered as he rose from the table. His spiral had vanished. "She bides her time for a chance to hit back at those who failed her father and her community at Kerte Yurgi."

Sakamoto glanced at Dumortier dismissively. "I heard the Aronts requested you. Specifically," she said.

"My reputation precedes me," replied Dumortier, and gauging from Sakamoto's stiff posture she did not like his answer. "Are you surprised they didn't go with one of their private sniffer hounds?"

"I don't appreciate your tone—although not unwarranted, given most of your cases concern Tier

174

Dwellers. At least *pretend* you're pleased by their request. Patriarch Aront's only child is dead. He calls it outrageous that an accident like this could occur and he wants a name and face he can trust."

Dumortier was relieved to hear that Patriarch Aront himself viewed his daughter's death as accidental. No need to reconstruct Gia Aront's final hours and minutes, map out her relationships or document mundane details of her daily routine to retraumatise her parents.

Katyal frowned. "Do you want this handed over to Aront outliers? That'll happen, if you delay for long."

"Not a chance," he replied quickly, unsure if it was with pride or folly—perhaps both. "I've summoned a Detainment unit to bring in Saurebaras."

"Call that off too."

"But she's still in Polyteknical."

"Bring in Saurebaras now and we risk our chances. I can't guarantee her safety, or that of our personnel." Katyal's voice had sing-song cadence of someone who had been repeating herself for a long time. She sounded tired.

"Saurebaras has undergone intensive somatic reconditioning," Sakamoto said.

"In the more extreme sense of the term." Dumortier sighed theatrically, then went to the wall console and traced out the command on the pad. "Does the Patriarch know my less-than-stellar record? I don't want him to suddenly change his mind about me halfway through the case."

"Don't sell yourself short," said Katyal. "The Aronts know your experience when it comes to Tier Dweller cases."

"Doesn't he love oversinging our praises?" Dumortier muttered to the tiled floor. "Especially when he needs us. Or wants us to think he does."

"At the moment, we can exploit the Aronts' dependence on us," Sakamoto said. Her conversational style reminded Dumortier of old Pre-Downturn Constabulary training films—short bursts of exposition and observation followed by silence.

"So, carry on, but don't try and bring in Saurebaras or Tanza," observed Dumortier dryly. "Have I missed anything?"

"That's it," replied Katyal. "Dismissed."

Dumortier reached the door of the Sunlight Corridor when Katyal spoke up again.

"One more thing, Dumortier."

"Yes, ma'am?"

"Why do you call Tyro Pleo Tanza 'queen'? That codeword was only ever used on Tier Dweller suspects."

"Ma'am, she has presence even when sitting in a cell."

# CHAPTER THIRTEEN

DUMORTIER PARKED THE Shirpen under the elevated T-Car track. The vehicle was standard issue, but the dents were all his, as he liked to joke from time to time. He gave himself ten minutes to hurl a packet of stale coffee granules down his throat before opening the butterfly wing door. The familiar odour of urine, stale algae coffee, and recycled oil wafted towards the Shirpen from various stalls and cubby-hole eateries.

As soon as he locked and left the Shirpen, a T-Car creaked into the platform overhead and discharged its latest throng of commuters. People flowed onto Polyteknical Station concourse, brandishing their fare tokens and discarding highlights.

It had been three years since Dumortier had been anywhere near the school, and yet the place drew him back today. He remembered getting lost in the overhanging maze of walkways. Back then the Polyteknical had set itself apart from the flow of grimy streets and buildings, like a military base in a civilian area. Today, the college merged with its cleaned-up surroundings until any distinctions between pavement and prestige broke down. And yet the streets still reeked of frying food and piss.

A shimmering golden mist of nanoscale machines coalesced above the street to track all movements, including his own. Just as Katyal and Sakamoto had informed him, the new Mias surveillance network was already up and running without any teething problems. Dumortier remained skeptical—if Mias did not turn out to be a hindrance like its predecessor Oias, he would be surprised.

He slipped away from the main street into a dingy alley to avoid any chance recognition by street vendors. He recalled using the Polyteknical delivery entrance which, by some administrative miracle or oversight, still existed.

He picked his way along a dim winding passage, shuffling past storerooms of discarded equipment and furniture. The heady scent of syringa greeted him before he emerged into Polyteknical's Garden of Contemplation, still well-maintained despite an obvious absence of horticulture servitors. A student, eyes closed, sat in quiet contemplation inside the cross-section of a boulder-sized geode of powder blue agate. Other bisected geodes had supplanted much of the grass, their collective weight inducing fine cracks in the flagstones and abutting the precisely-arranged bonsai. A meditation pool spread at the foot of a wall, fed by a fine turquoise waterfall.

The trickling of the water on the wall evoked a gentle tropical shower, but didn't quite drown out the persistent hum of Polyteknical's surveillance system. He had been given a choice when he was promoted to investigator: optical or audio enhancements. Most of his colleagues opted for optical enhancements such as night vision. Ever the contrarian, he had gone for audio enhancements, and he paid the price ever since in the form of headaches when his cochlea was overloaded.

Dumortier passed through an archway and located the free-standing staircase on the far side of the garden, the hexagonal tempered glass steps winding around a central support pillar of polished malachite. He broke into a fast stride, stopping at the top of the stairs to let a dozen students file past him. Like a stranger at a wedding, he ignored their whispers and curious glances.

He paused before he found his way to the multipurpose hall, staring at the five perforations in the pillar as if they were a puzzle which had eluded him for years. But he knew their origins—they could have so easily been five perforations in his skull instead.

The multihall and the corridor leading up to it was still off limits. The Spinel guards interposed themselves in front of the doors as a signal for Dumortier to identify himself, but immediately moved aside to admit him when he showed them the *paiza* tattoo set below his collarbone: three broken horizontal lines of gold filament set on a scarlet square. Paizas gave select Constabulary officers and investigators unhindered access, and overrode most Chatoyance authority. The guards were to render

Dumortier any assistance and protection as may be necessary.

The guards opened the doors to admit him, but Dumortier remained outside for a moment, not wishing to immediately disturb a recent crime scene. The hall was no longer the flamboyant place of interior design it had been three years ago.

A beep from his proximity sensor sounded in his left ear, but Dumortier had already sensed Saurebaras approach him from behind and activated the recording stud set into his collarbone. He tensed, remembering what happened at the demonstration three years ago and touched his splinter heart gun in the holster under his coat.

The reconditioning appeared to be holding up. "They sent *you*—how depressingly predictable," he heard Saurebaras mutter, unaware he could hear her. Then she added, more loudly, "Auditions and recreational classes have ended for this term. Come back next year."

His presence today did not seem to surprise her. Maybe she was expecting it. After all this time she was expecting nothing less. Her voice was equal parts velvet and impish surprise. The officious choice of her words underscored the contempt beneath them.

"I don't dance," replied Dumortier.

"So I won't keep you here. I'm sure you have a waiting list of suspects to rough up."

"I don't shatter my knuckles during interrogation anymore. We outsource that sort of treatment now. Harder to trace."

A faint vein stood out on Saurebaras's forehead as she asked, "Still an officer?"

"Senior investigator," corrected Dumortier.

She moved past him and rested her hands on the balustrade overlooking the garden.

"Congratulations on the promotion, but you haven't gone up in the world."

The prospect of investigation was not fazing her, but something else was playing on her nerves, making her censor her answers before vocalising them, so that she wavered between flintiness and palpable relief. She kept her back to him.

"And you're still here," said Dumortier. He tried appealing to her professional pride. "What a pity. This art they make you teach in Polyteknical isn't the real you. It's the foam riding on a tsunami."

"Better than clearing out the dead for the Tiers," said Saurebaras.

"Gia Aront was unfortunate," said Dumortier.

"You believe that?"

"Who wouldn't mind swapping places to be sole heir to the Aront business empire for a day?" Dumortier gazed at the sky, as if it was part of the Aront empire.

"Her father must not be all that upset, or else he'd shut down Polyteknical instead of sending a single investigator." Saurebaras drummed her fingers on the balustrade. Doves cooed from the garden below.

"I don't doubt that, but how her parents feel is not my concern here. Can you think of why Tyro Pleo Tanza would try to kill Gia Aront?"

"She didn't try to kill Gia."

"You sound very sure."

"Of course. It happened in front of me and twelve other students."

"Isn't it an odd coincidence that a sparring session spun out of control yesterday? Up until then, you had a spotless record. Less people die or get injured around you than ought to, given your history."

"It's rare to get injured during recreational striking or training," agreed Saurebaras. "A responsible instructor won't let you spar before six to twelve months. By this time, you've learned impulse control. Unless you're training to compete, you should have next to no risk of severe or fatal injury."

"So tell me what happened."

"But you're insinuating that I set it up? Or perhaps let an accident occur."

"No, I'm not. You haven't been charged with negligence—yet. A warrant needs evidence of malfeasance, or nonfeasance."

"I don't come to your canton and insult *you*, investigator."

"I'm going inside the hall. Accompany us, please," Dumortier ordered both guards.

Interesting choice of words, he thought. Constabulary hadn't completely erased what tact was left in him.

The empty hall was dim, but Gachalan light streamed through the ceiling panels, casting sunspots on the floor. A spider web of cord and lines ran down from the ceiling, supporting a tunnel of tents made of translucent sheets.

Yesterday, a team of Constabulary forensic technicians had sectioned off the piste where Gia and Pleo had their bout, and the surrounding area.

The Spinel guards remained at the entrance to the tunnel as Dumortier stepped inside the piste where the fatal bout had happened. A wall screen lit up as the piste sensed his presence, though the ovals remained inactive.

Dumortier raised both arms and watched the figure on the wall screen do the same. Saurebaras called out to him from the other side of the sheet.

"The piste is sensitive to movement inside it, but doesn't completely activate when it detects just one person. It's preparing for a solo."

"What about movement outside it?"

Saurebaras stamped in staccato four times as though Dumortier had just finished sparring. The piste stopped moving and hummed as it powered down.

"The piste responds to me alone, and I've just assessed your performance—mediocre. Vacate the piste."

He did so.

"I was hoping, with the presence of two co-operating Spinels, we'd cease this habitual dance of words. A diversion, I'll admit, that is not unengaging," said Dumortier. He asked again, "Where is Tyro Pleo Tanza?"

As if on cue the Spinel stepped closer to Saurebaras.

"There is no need for that—" she began, pushing past the guard. Dumortier followed her back into the tunnel of sheets.

"It won't be necessary if you cooperate."

Saurebaras shifted her weight from one leg to the other.

"Pleo Tanza was overcome by the effects of mild fan venom and injuries sustained during the sparring. I took her to the infirmary. She lay on a cot, thrashing about." Saurebaras snapped her head and shoulders from side to side in demonstration. "And she was crying out for Cerussa."

"Who?"

"Her twin sister. And the crystal nightingale." The randomness of the second detail threw Dumortier for a moment. When he looked blank at the reference, Saurebaras sighed and hummed a few bars in a soft contralto. "From the song. Quite a popular one from Pre-Downturn."

"I wasn't on Chatoyance back then."

"The lyric ends with lovers kissing in a corner of an abandoned T-Car station."

Music was a time machine for Dumortier, although one with imprecise effects. He recognised the song from the snippet, so evocative it was of the bygone carefree years before the bloat stage of Chatoyance. It had been too abstract for his taste. Specks of bamboo flute, dobro guitar and the titular birdsong dispersed through samples of ambient noises of empty Chatoyance stations at night, supported by an unhurried mid-tempo beat. Apt for listeners to project their own meanings onto, and he had no doubt that most of them did, back in the day. He dismissed the memory and returned to the conversation. "Was she discharged after treatment?"

"Check with the Polyteknical infirmary." Saurebaras tugged on one of the tunnel's support cords as if to test it.

"I did," replied Dumortier. "There is no record for the discharge of Tyro Pleo Tanza."

"Then she died. I've been to the infirmary often. It's more like a holding area for a morgue."

"No record of her death. Unlikely she gave you and two Spinels the slip?" It occurred to Dumortier that she was skirting around some dangerous issue. Who or what was she protecting? "In fact, your negligence in failing to follow up with her and her being at large incriminates you. This is still an ongoing accident investigation."

"Isn't that easier in one of the reinforced station cells?"

Dumortier blinked. "Kindly cooperate with Constabulary, madame. Don't make me remind you of your... professional history. It won't automatically waive your right to silence and counsel, but it won't be easy on you."

"What, for failing to report an accident within the statutory six hours?" Saurebaras said with a small laugh. She made her way out of the tunnel and back into the bright light of the hall.

"It puzzles me as to how a senior and experienced instructor suddenly loses control over a sparring session."

Saurebaras shrugged melodramatically. "Read the report and view the footage."

"I have."

"I'll answer to Polyteknical."

"Injuries occur—murder, even—but not this. Where is Tyro Pleo Tanza?"

"I took her to the infirmary. Exhaustion. And she had sustained some injuries."

"There is no record of her discharge. Or admittance."

As if on cue the Spinel stepped closer to Saurebaras. "For obstructing an investigation I could throw you into a quintuple-reinforced holding cell without—"

"Laboradoresence," mumbled Saurebaras.

Dumortier's experience told him to expect a fight about now. If Saurebaras resisted—and it would be three against one—there would be thirty seconds or a minute of a struggle until he placed the restraints on her.

He blocked her on route to the double doors, and she responded with a sudden wave of her arm as though to dismiss him, then spun around 180 degrees and planted a kick in his chest. Gasping more out of surprise than pain, he fell on the floor and clutched at his heart.

So much for experience.

He saw his shock reflected in the Spinel guards' faces.

"That was a controlled kick," said Saurebaras. "A goodwill gesture. Now get out of my way."

The Spinel charged at her. Saurebaras held one end of her fla-tessen shawl and cracked it like a bullwhip, making the other end wrap itself around the guard's neck like a python. She reeled in the guard like a dog on a leash, who was struggling to pull the scarf off.

"Listen to me, Dumortier."

He reached for his splinter heart, although this wasn't a good time or place to discharge it: too many variables, and all of them with lethal or incapacitating outcomes. The second Spinel was already brandishing her standard issue flanged club. "Let her go first."

Saurebaras immediately obeyed, much to Dumortier's surprise. The shawl relaxed its grip, although it remained around the Spinel's neck.

"Allow me to make your investigation easier. Gia's so-called accident was no accident. Have you asked yourself why you were assigned to an accident investigation?"

Dumortier didn't respond as he slowly climbed to his feet.

"And involving *me*, who nearly killed you three years ago?"

"Go on, then. Why?"

"You assume Tier Dwellers love their children."

"I don't have time for non sequiturs."

"Could you entertain the possibility that the Aronts actually *did not* love their only child?"

"I can," he replied, to keep Saurebaras talking. "But how is it relevant here?"

"Matriarch Aront paid me a visit before her daughter's death."

"Checking on Gia's academic or artistic progress?"

"She doesn't *pay* anyone a visit—she deems you worthy of what valuable time she has to spare. And the Matriarch also gifted me with this." Saurebaras reached into the fold of her skirt, took out a small pale object and held it out: a flower made of dog claws.

Blood rushing to Dumortier's ears drowned out the far-off birdsong from the garden. The words 'conspiracy to murder' filled his mind. To receive the Aront's unique calling card was to be marked for death.

Dumortier felt for the cicada stud set into his collarbone and the muted electro-pulses of the device told him it was still in recording mode. The gesture did not go unnoticed by the Spinels, or by Saurebaras.

"Her mother wanted Gia out of the way."

"That's a very serious accusation." He worked one of the studs off his sleeve and tossed it into the piste, immediately activating the screen. If he was going to get seriously injured or die here, at least he'd have footage.

Saurebaras chose that moment to become shimmering chaos. The shawl unraveled with a fibrous snap as it separated the Spinel's vertebrae. The red armour clattered as she tumbled in a limp pile, and the helmet skittered across the floor to stop at Dumortier's feet.

Saurebaras held her skirt out to one side and curtseyed at Dumortier as though for applause. Her fla-tessen fan slipped from the skirt's folds, opening before it landed on the floor, a matte black wedge that began to spin on its own. It veered and shot towards the other Spinel and embedded in her calf, white spikes penetrating the armour plating.

Saurebaras kept her head raised and her gaze on the screen. Her hand trembled as it held onto her skirt. Dumortier recognised from her rapidly blinking eyes and lips pressed tight that she was in a kind of trance but under increasing strain.

"I want to thank you in advance, Dumortier, for helping me create a little spectacle. Your presence today sets another stage for me."

Saurebaras gathered her shawl, sprang up and headed towards the doors. Dumortier noticed her characteristic unwavering glide was now unsteady, but didn't place too much hope in it. The injured Spinel was taking no chances, remotely shutting the hall doors.

He reached into his coat and felt for the holster. Time to deploy the splinter heart.

"No guns permitted in Polyteknical and in its surroundings," the Spinel reminded Dumortier. Her voice wavered when she laid eyes on the weapon glinting under the hall lights. It was a more gun-*shape* than gun, a melding of barrel, muzzle and grip wrought by organic processes.

"I'll worry about regulations later. This isn't a gun in the usual sense," he replied in all seriousness as he checked the sights. Dumortier had discharged his splinter heart many times before and knew there were to be no clean angles. Via processes he never pretended to understand, the weapon inflicted subtle yet extensive damage on flesh and bone. Its glossy membranous cartridges burst open like seed pods from Hell, releasing tiny flechettes with large payoff.

He took aim and felt the recoil jolting his arm. The splinter heart shot out a cluster of fine grey composite shards—lab-grown to pierce flesh and keep going through bone upon impact. Too late: Saurebaras executed a running leap and the shards missed her. They tumbled to the floor like metallic hail and she slipped through the narrowing gap between the doors.

"Don't touch it," he told the Spinel, who was trying to pull off the fan. He whipped a forensic sac over the fan and prised it off. Blood seeped out of the wound. Despite the sac's hermetic seal, he still felt the fan releasing more spikes under the translucent coating, and threw it onto the floor.

The Spinel had made it to the door, grabbed both handles and wrenched them open. Dumortier activated the other stud and fastened it to his collarbone, calling for any backup patrol teams, even walkarounds on their beat. He would need a distraction, to buy some time before they arrived. The corridor better be empty now, he prayed as he stepped out of the fla-tessen hall.

To his chagrin a group of students and staff was gathering around the malachite pillar. A glimpse of billowing shawl and pale hands caught his attention; Saurebaras was perched like a raven, low on the balustrade overlooking the garden. She fluttered one hand, then the other as she picked her way along the railing.

He found her movements bizarre. It was almost ugly how random and chaotic they were. But they were enchanting, almost hypnotic, and he couldn't look away. Dumortier was compelled to see her routine to its end, together with the other students and staff.

*They think she's putting on a performance.* He had to dispel the notion now. It wouldn't matter what the crowd thought Saurebaras was doing if she decided to use them as a shield. As he manoeuvred towards her, Dumortier set the splinter heart to fire single shots, cursing as the slide bit into the skin between his forefinger and thumb. "All of you move! Stay down!" he yelled at the students.

The command was unnecessary: the throng was parting at the sight of the approaching Spinel, with blood trickling down her leg and mace at the ready. He kept the splinter heart trained on Saurebaras, raising discordant screams from the crowd. The students nearest to him raised their hands and sleeves to protect their implants. Three Polyteknical staff tried to keep order and marshal the students away from the pillar and along the corridor.

"She finally snaps and they send *one* Constabulary officer?" the staff member nearest to Dumortier asked, lowering her bejeweled white mask to reveal intricate meshwork embedded into the skin around her eyes, their golden irises rotating as they focused on him. In brutal contrast, a deep scar ran across one of her cheeks.

So, the rumours weren't true—the masks were removable. He focused on her lower face and forehead, the untouched segments of her humanity.

"I warned the Central Education Committee of Saurebaras's potential recidivism," the staff member continued. "In typical fashion, they just said 'no personal complaints were received by them, but they will pass mine on to the relevant body—'"

"All of your students are at risk. I can't guarantee their safety if they remain here," Dumortier interrupted her.

"My charges. I don't just see them as students," she corrected. "No excuses, how refreshing."

"And all of your implants." Dumortier tried another tack as he prepared to take another shot. Saurebaras should be weakening by now. Calculating quickly, he went for higher ground and vaulted on top of the agate geode, lining up his shot.

The Spinel was about to the swing the mace at Saurebaras, still moving erratically on the balcony rail. Her shawl split into four strands at its other end: one struck the guard's head like a flail, knocking off her helmet. The Spinel's head jerked back as Dumortier's splinter heart shards caught in her throat, and she collapsed onto the floor.

"Listen, Dumortier!" He thought he detected the strain in Saurebaras's voice—not of exertion, but of urgency.

Before he could take another shot, Saurebaras looked back and hurled a small black object at him. It flew towards him and knocked the splinter heart out of his grip, falling into the fountain below. His hand went numb, then started hurting all the way up to his elbow. Blood dropped from his fingers. He examined his hand and discovered five perforations in his palm. The fla-tessen caltrop had sunk its spikes into the skin and flesh before retracting.

The end of the shawl wrapped itself around his wrist. Dumortier tumbled headfirst over the balustrade, but retained enough presence of mind to brace himself for the fall. With a splash he landed in the uppermost tier of the fountain and was about to right himself when Saurebaras gave the fla-tessen shawl another yank. He fell forward again, hitting the water of the next tier, and Saurebaras dragged him down the entire length of the fountain until he landed on his side, soaking wet, in the grass. Something gave way in his hip with a palpable crunch, and suddenly he could not feel his legs through the agony. It was worse than getting shot.

His sodden coat weighed him down and he felt water seeping into the grass beneath him. His ear stud crackled, but it still picked up Saurebaras running to his side. She was welcome to finish him off; his body was too damned broken and heavy to do any fighting back. She tugged on the shawl, but Dumortier grasped it tenaciously. Weakened by its recent use, it tore off at his wrist, and he tightened his fist around the scrap of evidence.

Renegade instructor and runaway student. Despite the pain, ideas and connections were already forming in Dumortier's mind, slowly at first but definitely coalescing into a whole. Saurebaras had been waiting for a chance to act, for a breach in the dyke she had played a role in fortifying over the years.

*Hold off on the tyro*, he recalled Katyal's order.

Invariably the frustration swelled up again, almost blocking out the fire from his hip. Saurebaras was untouchable because the Aronts still were.

His ear stud crackled into life. Miraculously it was still working after his ordeal.

"Nightingale," muttered Dumortier to the garden, like a curse. Despite the recent commotion and onlookers milling around the edges, the Garden of Contemplation's serenity remained intact. No one came to help him— although he did not blame them, after what they had just witnessed. It felt like he was dying.

When the paramedics arrived and loaded him onto a stretcher, they heard him humming the snatch of song over and over again.

# CHAPTER FOURTEEN

THE PENDANT OF Europan sea jade was obviously cursed. When the next potential customer insisted on proof of provenance, Setona decided she would tell them about the girl turning up in the fountain and ending up in her shop.

Setona pressed her hand to her chest, where her real heart used to be during her modrani days, and took a very deep breath. She drew on a career's worth of modrani experience in remaining poised under pressure:

1. *Focus on immediate details.*

At this moment they were not reassuring: streaks of dried blood around the girl's lips, dyed hair shorn off at a weird angle. Her eyes would be very striking if they weren't glazed over like an addict's.

2. *Make a short list of them.*

Eyes, blood, hair, lips....

3. *Repeat this list, like a mantra.*

Eyesbloodhairlips... eyesbloodhairlips...

The relaxation technique ceased to be effective when a small crowd began lining the edges of the piazza to watch her and Marsh. She flashed them her best wild-eyed smile; the Crocodile, she had called it. Used whenever a product launch got too frenzied, it contained both a threat and an invitation to stick around. Her gamble worked, at least for now. Unnerved by the triptych of incongruous figures arranged before the fountain, they gradually dispersed.

"Don't bring her inside my—" Setona began. Too late: the Cabuchoner had picked the girl up and set off before she finished speaking. He had other concerns on his mind, or he could afford kindness. Setona resented and admired that flexibility in him, but for now, she had other worries. An accident or murder victim would turn her shop into a crime scene. What if the girl lashed out and injured her or Marsh, because of the drugs still in her system? During these past years Setona had worked so hard to remain forgotten.

Along with the rest of her peers, Setona had had a brilliant Act I; unlike them, she had eschewed a second one in talent management, or in outright rejection of the industry. If this move had earned her a reputation for being unambitious or directionless, she could live with her choice. She believed in the old modrani warning against post-career hubris: "Never let your ego empty your bank accounts."

Retail Sector 12 on Chatoyance had been perfect for her business. She had found its exuberance charming, enhanced by the piazza and the fountain. This animation had not curtailed her initial dread in opening her small business: the welling anxiety in the first month, the premature elation of the first quarter of sales, the torture of casual browsers who eventually decided not to come in, and the grim sinking feeling that she had made a mistake. Her ego had not emptied her bank accounts (which were assuredly full for years to come), but had sapped her spirit.

But old habits and nostalgia still wouldn't let her go. Setona had set up an undersea fantasy in a large tank in the window display. Neon-hued fish darted back and forth over a jagged bed of sand and coral fragments. The fish would be flash-frozen for storage at Shineshift and the water drained off. Marsh was more than welcome to eat the remaining sand with the coral. She grimaced at her choice of costume she had laid out on the platform earlier that morning: a shimmering mermaid's tail made from the latest air-textiles, a wig of waist-length lilac hair, and a pair of scallop shells.

*Silicone... tacky... shell bikini and wig... much tackier.*

Setona shut the shop door, kicked the costume away and stepped onto the platform. She took a deep breath, grasped the tank's edges and tipped herself in, head first. She must allow the tank be her sanctuary for now. Water buoyed her extremities and stilled her mind, taking the strain off posing for too long. Startled fish darted around her as she righted herself and clasped her hands over her diaphragm, another gesture from her modrani days. She closed her eyes; to an observer she may have appeared to be praying or centring herself, but she was in fact eliminating possible conflict and career-ruining actions. After all, you can't slap or punch someone with clasped hands.

A knock on the window side of the tank. Startled, Setona opened her eyes and saw three teenage girls jump back: one of them had her hand still half-raised to tap on the glass again.

*Get away from here,* Setona mouthed as she pressed her face against the glass. *Unless you want to end up in this tank with me.*

All three girls yelped and scurried away in their transparent raincoats, worn over patchwork A-line dresses. Wearing *what passes for fashion*. It irked her to recall the Doyen's words, but they were not untrue. It helped to think of him as such, because she was not sure what he was now, less organic and more whirring parts.

Setona floated over to the interior-facing side of the tank and surfaced, watching Marsh lay the girl on the counter. She splashed water at the door protected by the crowning-shield and the water drops bounced across the shop and wet the back of Marsh's neck. He turned around with a pained expression.

"Leave her where you found her."

"She's not dead."

Setona kicked a piece of coral so hard it pierced the sole

of her foot. Her brief relaxation in the tank had done nothing to suppress her frustration.

"I'd feed you to the display leopard if it could eat," she fumed as she clambered out of the tank and limped off the platform, dripping. Her modrani skin and hair were manufactured to repel water and she was dry in a minute.

"Cerussa!" the girl suddenly gasped.

"Why is she calling out the names of minerals?" asked Setona, massaging her temple. Such randomness was too much to deal with right now.

Marsh shrugged. "She's a Polyteknical student and—"

"Ma?" A weak voice interrupted both of them.

Setona heard the girl lying on the counter mumble again before she coughed up cloudy fluid onto the counter, and her body strained upward before she passed out again. In response, Marsh placed his folded coat under her head, turned her head to one side, and searched around for a spare rag.

"Are you sure you don't know her?" Setona asked him again.

"I know she exists—I see her on the same T-Car as me every morning, on the way to Polyteknical station. She writes her life story on the walls of the T-Car. I think Cerussa is a close relation."

"But *still*," insisted Setona, "how do you know she's a Polyteknical student?"

"Look at her hands."

Marsh held one hand up for Setona's scrutiny— the closed fingers were knobbly and calloused. Blood under the nails told Setona the girl had been in a fight.

She coughed again and stirred. Setona watched with fascination as the girl's hand unclenched and a bone-white forcep slid out from under the index fingernail.

"Grafted tools of profession," said Setona, trying to sound unimpressed while various scenarios played out in her head. She went back into the stockroom and came out with a tube of epitheliax for the girl's leg. "I've seen them before. Most people in the lapidary and gem assessment lines acquire them over the course of a career. Of course, there're always exceptions; some modrani get fitted out with them for novelty's sake. The darling Doyen is nothing but a support system for them."

"Compared to the work done on her, *he's* a heap of outdated equipment bent in the form of a human," replied Marsh. He tried to examine the forcep, but it quickly retracted. "Did you see that? The reflex is so exquisite, these implanted tools are so seamless, so—"

"Valuable. And patented—and shot through with serial numbers."

When these facts did not dispel Marsh's admiration, Setona continued, "Such traceability is deterrent enough for most street-level criminal elements."

"Still, why does Polyteknical let its students walk around with these implants?"

"Polyteknical is smart not to draw unwanted attention to the implants. If they act like they're normal mundane tools of profession, no one would know otherwise."

She put enough edge in her voice to make him put down the girl's hand, but Setona saw the idea germinating in his mind and she knew what would be worse than turning her boutique into a crime scene: turning it into a chop shop. Serial numbers never *entirely* put the dealers and middlemen off.

She ought to dismiss him right now to forestall that eventuality. But he was the only hiree that had stuck around for longer than a few months. Setona had run background checks on Marsh through her modrani networks, the secret handshakes and connections that ensured the safety of modranis before accepting a job with a client. It was a force of habit; in practice, Setona took a perverse delight in unpredictability. She was testing the water with Marsh— and Marsh, who had told her of his need to lay low, was similarly up for testing the water with Setona.

What she discovered about Marsh did not faze her. He had stolen art and jewellery from the family vault owned by the Lascaris, a family with senior members in the Corund.

"Stealing for money is stupid," Marsh had told her. "There are less risky ways to get it."

"You did it for the thrill?"

"I was smitten." He tried to sound vague.

With the thrill of stealing those pieces, or with Nina Lascaris, or her brother? Setona had not asked.

Unprompted, Marsh continued. "Beauty for beauty's sake, and all that bullshit... No one was hurt and there were no victims. People like the Lascaris can't be victims of theft. There's nothing they lack, nothing they don't already own and nothing they desire."

Mysteriously, the charges were dropped, and no further action taken. No victims indeed. Apparently, Marsh had been telling the truth.

If Setona stared hard enough at the four stallion statues of the fountain they started galloping towards her. Maybe they were display animals, waiting to be activated during an emergency.

"Those serial numbers will be the end of me. And you. Get rid of the Polyteknical girl before Shineshift. She shouldn't be here."

"I have the feeling she didn't choose to end up in the fountain."

The girl stirred and rolled onto her side. Her grey eyes were wide open and the cloudiness in them had faded. She propped herself up on one elbow.

"Hey, take it easy." Marsh stepped in front of her. "You've had a shock."

At the sound of his voice, the girl's eyes darted to and fro, focussing on something neither Setona or Marsh could see. She bent forward and put her hands on her thighs as though she was about to vomit. Concerned about the floor, Setona moved to redirect her to the storeroom where there was a washbasin.

The girl lashed out and stabbed Marsh in the shoulder with her forceps. With a yell he let go of her.

And it happened so fast. Out of five forceps that went in; four came out. Setona saw the girl wince when she pulled them out, and in a curious move she reached out to him again as if to retrieve the forcep, but then shook her head by way of apology. The girl left Marsh clutching his shoulder while she ran out of the shop door, half-stumbling away from the fountain and down a side street before Setona could react.

Setona helped Marsh up and onto the work bench behind the counter.

"I was naïve," he admitted.

"You *are* naïve," she said. "But not in the ways that count."

Setona went into the stockroom and returned with a vial of milky fluid. She cracked it open and poured the contents directly onto Marsh's wounds.

"Watch out, it'll sting."

Marsh sucked his breath through his teeth.

"Epithelialix paste with collagen serum," Setona told him. "A modrani trade secret. Contrary to popular belief, our jobs can be quite dangerous."

Marsh felt his shoulder and was surprised to feel uninjured skin where his wounds were located. The bleeding had stopped.

"It looks much better, but the injuries are still there."

"Will it help with scarring?"

Setona shook her head. "That's up to you."

# CHAPTER FIFTEEN

*Temple of Gachala Visitor Information and Rules*
*Kindly observe the following for your safety and to*
*enhance your time here*

Enter the east gate and make your way to the west gate. The central courtyard is off limits during the day due to the strong reflective properties of the temple roof.

DO NOT CROSS the heat shield boundary surrounding the central courtyard. It is there for your protection. The Temple, its committee, and its affiliates will not be responsible for any accidents, injury, damage to personal property or death arising from or during your visit.

Do not hesitate to join the nuns and worshippers in the main Hall of Radiance. Your presence will never be deemed intrusive or heretical. The All-Encompassing Solar Palace of Gachala welcomes all those with authentic purpose.

\* \* \*

AT NIGHT THE temple was at rest, all its spiritual duties on hold until sunrise. By extension, Temple Plaza was quieter than a museum after midnight. Pleo bent over one of the numerous public drinking fountains, gulping down handfuls of water. When her thirst had been quenched, she admired the serene beauty of the cantilevered teal roof stretching over the sloped glass facade. The architecture was something out of a dream, an alien sky over a geometric iceberg.

The scene before her renewed Pleo's hope for sanctuary, her most urgent need for now and—fingers crossed—within reach. She couldn't remember much after getting carried out of the infirmary by Saurebaras: a fracas with a medical bot, a grimy ceiling moving above her, possibly a tunnel, and her mind weaving in and out of consciousness. Dull, heavy pain came on in waves, then dissipated to a sudden floatiness. She had woken up in a shop full of gemstones, a tall beautiful woman with glittering arms and eyes, and the man she had seen in the same T-Car every morning on the way to Polyteknical. Then she had run.

The crowning-shield barrier covering the east gate of the plaza was turned off. Hopeful, she went up to the bolted grid and shook the gate. The heavy metallic creaks echoed through the plaza's expanse, amplified by the laminar granite flagstones and Gachalan sun discs set into each one.

Dawn was still far, not for another six hours. Pleo never came here at night: no one ever did. There was no reason to visit a temple dedicated to the sun when the sun wasn't shining. But it did not mean no one was watching.

"Reverend sisters! Help me please!"

The high gate remained shut to her pleas, so she let go of it. Sanctuary was definitely off-limits, and her fate already decided by the nuns who were watching her now and taking in her audacity. Last year she was a scrappy miner's daughter who had stopped going to temple. Now she was a wanted fugitive with a missing implant.

The burgundy wood grain of the inner door looked familiar. She reached in and traced all forceps of her right hand over it, although the almond scent of fresh oil told her the door was a very recent addition. Her analysis revealed it was petrified Catru teak. Pleo was dismayed that her mother's donation of fifty uta a week went towards this.

A shape stepped inside the other side of the plaza, directly opposite the east gate. Pleo thought the Temple had sent a nun out to see to her. The hooded figure remained still. Apart from herself it was the only other presence in the plaza.

Was it a Gachalan nun still begging for alms at this time of night? Impossible, their sermon hours were from sunrise to sunset and their robes were not such an unnerving light-swallowing black. And it couldn't be a Charon, a disposer of the dead. This would make it the second time she encountered a Charon—a statistical impossibility. More so than other Chatoyants, who if pressed neither denied nor acknowledged their very existence.

She couldn't make out a face, only metallic glints where

its face should be. The figure stood very still and looked at Pleo—or in her direction, as much as a being with no visible face could ever look at anyone.

But she had committed the taboo of looking back at a Charon when she had left Cerussa at Leroi Minor. Now this figure was here to claim its due. Its continued silence spoke to Pleo, as if to say, *why, in spite of the warnings laid out in the ritual, did you look back?*

Now it glided towards, reminding her of Saurebaras.

Fear rose within her. It froze her to the spot, but she marshalled all of her willpower at the last second before it came too close.

"Who are you?"

No answer. For a second she tried to convince herself it was an illusion, or a hallucination she had conjured up. It had marked Pleo and would keep going, whether through her or by her—but when it had carried out its purpose it would disappear, or return to wherever it came from.

The figure passed through the beam of a flickering street lamp, throwing shadows on the flagstones. It must be real, but Pleo drew no comfort from the discovery. It did not matter what was after her.

*If this thing really was Cerussa it'd tell you to leave and return home.*

Pleo held on to that thought as she backed away from it and retreated further inside Temple Plaza and to the Sun Canal. She ran the rest of the way. She was pissed off that she couldn't even think of her safety in this situation without Cerussa haunting her.

She went down the steps of the flooded canal bank,

wading into the chilly water until it was at knee height. Pleo sensed micro life and other animals stirred up and fleeing at her intrusion. They were more than welcome to consume her body if that hooded thing killed her. Much more dignity in dying that way. Not to be retrieved by Polyteknical, stripped of her implants, hair and eyes before being sewn up like a doll.

She sloshed her way along the bank, periodically checking the bank steps as they bobbed and receded behind her. The hooded thing was nowhere to be seen, and Pleo slowed down out of relief. Like a vampire of ancient lore, it dared not cross running water. Now all she had to do was find the next set of steps, climb up them and onto the long thoroughfare of Gachala Avenue.

When Pleo glimpsed the darkened steps, she forgot about being tired and soaking wet. As she approached, the water in front of her churned and the hooded thing rose out of the water in front of her, straight-backed as if rising from a coffin. Water dripped off its robes, now plastered to a body that was eerily thin.

Pleo screamed and dodged the thing's outstretched arm. It managed to grab her shoulder and clamp one sodden, fabric-wrapped hand across her mouth. With her remaining forceps she slashed at the hand, tearing off matted threads. She jammed her elbow spur into the side of the thing, feeling the spike drive through more layers of cloth. The hooded thing didn't cry out or give any indication that it felt pain.

Despite the silence, the elbow spur proved effective, making the thing loosen its grip, and Pleo broke free, towards the steps. She grabbed the railing and clambered out and halfway up the steps. The hooded thing half-floated, half-walked to the bottom of the steps. Pleo extended her arm towards it, her forceps held like claws.

"Show yourself!" Pleo swiped at the hooded thing's face. The tips of her forceps caught and dragged across rough metal. She intuited iron oxide, steel, and aluminium from the tactile feedback, but drew back her hand, startled by the unexpected sensation. When the fabric tore away she knew why—a tight rusted metal mesh concealed the face of the thing. She heard a muffled gurgling from where the throat was supposed to be, as if exposing its masked face had affected its breathing.

Pleo saw a chance and took it. She climbed a few more steps, hoping gravity was on her side when she hit the unhooded thing in the chest area with a fla-tessen hand strike. It fell back into the water with a soft splash. She ran up the stairs and stopped to check that the thing was not following her. She saw it float away from her before drifting to the opposite bank.

Satisfied with the distance put between her and the thing, Pleo hurried towards Gachala Avenue before a Canal Newt spotted her. Going back to her dorm or home was now out of the question. Whoever had sent that hooded thing would send more.

The next best option was a room that had belonged to the late Gia Aront.

Pleo wished the temple had admitted her—crossing the heatshield boundary into the courtyard was less risky.

# CHAPTER SIXTEEN

*WHAT'S WORSE THAN getting pieced back together?*

Dumortier heard his urine trickling through a catheter and into a bag. He wasn't aware of waking up; instead, he regained consciousness in several drawn-out stages, each step accompanied by an increasing sensation that he was floating.

*Getting pieced back in the wrong order.*

He tried to make a fist with his injured hand. So far still functional, but he winced when he tried doing so with the other. Shards from the broken splinter heart were still embedded in his wrist and palm, the raw wounds visible through the clear membranes of collagen dressing. He could not feel his lower body, but he was relieved to see the cast of self-mending plaster encasing his hips and legs when he craned his neck downwards.

Still in one piece—fractured and bloodied, but that was good enough for now.

As the full-body harness creaked and swayed, his gaze focused on a section of ceiling above his face. It turned out he was not wrong about the floating. The minimalist high-ceilinged room was too quiet and spacious for a Constabulary ward. He was sure his basic insurance didn't cover the harness suspended from the ceiling or the birdsong piped in through the pair of loudspeakers, styled to resemble dandelion clocks, floating above his head.

A medical hexapod servitor scuttled into Dumortier's hospital room with characteristic urgency. It held up a tray as soon as he craned in his head to see.

He saw five malachite fragments along with his regular coffee vial, arranged on a slotted tray borne by the hexapod's rotating sixth leg. Each fragment was suspended in a slice of clear synthamber as though snatched from freefall, and labelled with the same case number and date.

The hexapod placed the tray on a floating tabletop and spun around on its rear legs and on to its next delivery destination in the hospital wards, leaving Dumortier with his recent memories on the same tray as his coffee and a dish of grey paste.

*There must be better-tasting ways to poison me.*

It occurred to him the hospital suite was a way of preparing him or softening him for an incoming blow.

*To serve as an Ocelot is to pray your services are never required.*

But Senior Investigator Dumortier's services and experience as an Ocelot were required—twice in his career so far, and by the same people. The first time was three years ago.

The second time, he anticipated with disappointment, was today.

The malachite fragments were a message, and a reminder. They matched a specific cluster of perforations made in the malachite column outside the hall three years ago, the last time he'd done this duty.

It had been a demonstration for military contracts, invariably behind closed doors and top secret. But Constabluary had requested special access from Cabuchon and the reply had been clear: admission restricted to officers with highest clearance.

"A dirty trick." Sakamoto had briefed him before authorising his Ocelot paiza and directing him to where he could collect a new dress uniform. "Cabuchon believes we're so understaffed as to have none."

The uniform was stiff but he felt better for wearing it. On that day he was only meant to be an observer, leaving him in position to see who was entering the hall or who was hanging around outside. The voices of the guests were abstract yet intimate. Too preoccupied with exchanging gossip and messages before they suddenly noticed his presence.

Saurebaras had stood across from him, basking in the afterglow of accomplishment with Ignazia and Patriarch Madrugal. He made his round of the hall and passed them.

In that moment, Saurebaras coalesced: the hint of a curtsey to him, unnecessary given the importance of the people milling around and jockeying for her attention. Even he picked up the start of a flirtation. Dumortier was uncertain what to make of it, but he didn't get to his current position by being like those three target practice dummies set up on the floor. He opted to nod back at her: *Flattered, but I'm on duty.*

Before the demonstration began, all unauthorised personnel had to leave. The Tagmats backed off when he showed them his paiza. He remained at a safe distance from the floor.

She had a set of fla-tessen fans, and was demonstrating the possible damage they could do to a human body on the dummies. Applause was followed by Ignazia presenting the caltrops, one of which had ended up in a Tagmat guard's forehead.

"My art is not for the highest bidder!" he had heard Saurebaras yell.

Saurebaras had not been trying to distract him—she had thrown down a challenge. He'd chased her outside to the corridor. She'd turned around in mid-run and hurled the caltrop at him; he'd ducked behind the malachite pillar...

Dumortier's hands suddenly trembled, his palms slicked with perspiration when he remembered how easily it could have been five fragments of scalp and bone sheared off his skull, and how he wouldn't be hanging from the ceiling, staring at a vial of coffee. His skull fragments and brain matter would be cocooned in slices of gel synthamber, used for biological and DNA evidence, and his body cremated because he had no known next of kin to claim it.

"—you were right. That look in his eyes, the elevated heart rate. He still remembers."

"—you can lay to rest any fears of amnesia."

He felt helpless, like a child eavesdropping on adult conversation. The pair of figures stood directly below him, talking to each other, but their words were all out of context. When they came into gradual focus, he recognised them as Gachalan nuns in flowing emerald green robes. Maybe Saurebaras's venom was more lethal than he thought. If he was going to die soon, he appreciated receiving a bit more ceremony than the average investigator.

"Are you waiting to hear my prayers, reverend sisters? Don't bother to take a seat, I have none."

Both figures flipped back their hoods, revealing the faces of Lieutenants Katyal and Sakamoto gazing up at him with concerned but serious expressions.

"I'd prefer that you're in a better condition to consider our proposal." Katyal stepped closer to the spica. "But there's no time, even with accelerated healing."

Dumortier suppressed a groan, expecting news of his imminent dismissal or a sudden unexplained transfer to some shot-to-hell backwater settlement outside the Corona. Yet neither woman was clad in their gold-and-indigoes—they were off-duty, officially.

"No surveillance in here," Sakamoto said, although she still double-swept the room with an ex-field operative's experienced movements. "So the hospital staff think Katyal and I are reverend sisters administering your final rites."

"With all due respect, is this an interrogation or a debriefing?"

"Think about what both of us have to say for a few moments. If you agree to it, it's a promotion." Dumortier did not trust Katyal's neutral tone—it was both a reassuring pat on the shoulder and a kick in the face.

Unable to shake his head or nod because of the spica, Dumortier raised his hand in the affirmative and then shifted his torso from side to side to signal the opposite. Sensing his struggle, the spica lowered itself to floor level with a soft hum.

"I was sloppy and too preoccupied with getting something out of Saurebaras," said Dumortier. "If you want my resignation, you have it now."

"The Tier Dwellers left us a mess that needs to be cleaned up as discreetly as possible."

"They always leave a mess." However, Dumortier was grateful they didn't say *you've* left us a mess.

"Don't blame yourself for what you couldn't prevent." Sakamoto pulled up his medical chart and winced when she read through it. "We're glad you're alive."

"Enough with the secrecy." Dumortier tried to angle himself in the spica so that he could look both of his superiors in the eye. "Tell me: why does one Tier Dweller scion—dead by accident, apparently—warrant a pissing contest like this? Since when are we suddenly so involved? Polyteknical has its own investigation department—let them handle this."

"The problem is everyone wants to try being a hero to Tier Dwellers," said Sakamoto. "'Everyone' including the three of us in this room, at some point."

"When one group has enough power all other authorities look the other way," Katyal said with a shrug. "Even Constabulary, which has stopped examining itself."

"We do more reacting than acting," Sakamoto added. "They mock us when they flout the law. We're a packet of nerves, a twitching organism, not an organisation."

"And now," concluded Katyal, smiling, "we finally get our chance."

Gachala's bright green disk dipped behind a passing cloud bank, and the room dimmed for a split second. Everything about Katyal and Sakamoto told him *We are relying on you. Constabulary needs this.*

"How many other investigators are also Ocelots?" he asked.

"None," said Katyal. "However, as for *senior* investigators, let's just say you're enough for now."

"You're asking me to join your covert parallel force—"

"We both are," emphasised Sakamoto.

"Look at my condition now. Get somebody else," said Dumortier.

"If there was somebody, we wouldn't ask you." Sakamoto checked the medical chart again. "And we could leave you alone to mend a fractured hip."

"I should have known."

Twice he'd been called to Ocelot duty, and both times had involved Polyteknical and Saurebaras. Last time, a couple of minor houses had been involved; now it was the Aronts themselves.

This should, he determined, mean no dramatic change to how he conducted his job, but he could not convince himself of it. *Too late.* This was over his head, over the heads of Constabulary command and the rest of Chatoyance. It went all the way up in the clouds, and specifically on the lavish Aront Tier, where someone had already made a decision to involve Dumortier. From the conversation on the bridge to now, Katyal and Sakamoto were just expediting it.

Dumortier had started out at the stations, docks and spaceport, handling pimps, pushers, black market traders and suppliers before moving up through the ranks. He lasted in Canal Police for 48 hours due to an undetected health issue (or so he was told to state for the record), but that was a different matter.

They didn't select Dumortier for Ocelot work because he was dirty: to the contrary, he was chosen for his scrupulous reputation. It made a perverse kind of sense: dirty officers were not discreet, and they became more careless the more they became involved. Ocelot investigators usually started out by going after small targets, and Dumortier preferred working alone during the early hours of the morning, when the Shineshifts were over and skeleton crews ran the T-Car network.

He suspected a few possible individuals who had the wherewithal to break procedure and regulations at such short notice and order the retrieval of the fragments from the evidence vaults. If they were tampering with the logs, it was a new low.

Was Gia Aront's body still in the morgue? He'd checked: a media embargo was currently in effect. Only the highest Constabulary and SeForTec clearances could access case details and stats.

*Fish rots from the head*, according to the old saying.

Dumortier had always thought Chatoyance—the cat's

eye—was misnamed. Chatoyance was not a eye, not a single organ, but a whole organism. A once-prized fish, its gleaming scales, patterns and lateral lines were the canals and T-Car lines. The worst rot was to be found in the guts: although in his opinion the fish was rotten from the start, all that mattered was which stage of decomposition it was in. The Archer's Ring and its rival systems had long passed through the incipient stages, regressing from a golden age of prosperity—which had attracted new arrivals to the mining and fracking settlements—to the turbulence of the Downturn.

The bloat stage of Chatoyance's prosperity and excess had long passed: womb-like arcades, floating biomes of flora and fauna, new stations and lines with fanciful names. Genuine coffee from orbital greenhouses, not this vile algae-derivative shit dyed a suspicious uniform black. Now Chatoyance had entered Stage 3—a gradual yet active decay, with the rot seeping out of various orifices. Arcades were shut down and sealed off and the biomes abandoned after their Corund sponsors and their business partners cleared out, leaving behind an undercurrent of tension and despair.

In such a climate, Dumortier did not blame anyone who still applied to Polyteknical, or the children of the Forty who tolerated those experimental implants. The tragedy had marked them out, taken them out of the race.

Tier Dwellers also valued Ocelot investigators for their discretion.

*An Ocelot's first directive is containment and damage control. To never allow Tier Dweller shit to flow downwards to the streets and taint the rest of us, or Constabulary and its officers will be nothing more than sewer workers in their employ.*

More urine dripped out of Dumortier and flowed through the catheter, snapping him back into the hospital room with his superiors.

"You think all Chatoyance needs are a few knocks to right itself? Like an old-fashioned neon light?"

"You're an investigator," said Katyal kindly, "not an omnipresent deity. What happened with Saurebaras is not your fault."

"This is not a controlled lab experiment," added Sakamoto. "Constabulary calculates the outcome but not the interplay."

Katyal twisted her sleeve, betraying her apprehension. Dumortier was perversely pleased.

"You will not be going it alone." Sakamoto's expression brightened, like she'd been waiting for a chance to announce some good news. "Nadira Morad, landing name Gaspard, will be assisting you."

Dumortier paused for a few seconds, unsure if he had heard right. Gaspard was Constabulary's most senior and eminent SeForTec. "This case does not warrant the skill set and experience of Nadira Morad Gaspard."

"You worked with her before?"

"I know her by reputation. She handles the most major of cases."

"Your high opinion of her is duly noted—but our order stands."

"Why not get hold of Deputy Hitei?"

"She is still in vitro until next week."

"I'll be in this spica, also out of action, until next month at the very least."

"We have access to advanced healing techniques," Katyal cut in. "It will not be that long." She pressed a discreet button on the wall.

A birdlike orderly entered the room and went through his medical chart. "Seventy hours to repair the patient's hip fractures," it confirmed in its thin metallic voice. It was designed to emulate a soothing bedside manner, but unfortunately came across as eerie. The predicted duration was all Dumortier needed to know for now. He heard the procedure explained to his two superiors and got lost in the jargon: *bone matrix, suspension, amniotic fluid, body temperature...*

"Officially both of you will treat your Aront house call as a 'courtesy visit,'" Katyal said briskly as the orderly left. "Saurebaras was a regrettable oversight, and you're taking the blame and taking charge of the mess. Powerful people act less guarded when they believe you have less power than them."

"Courtesy visit, courtesy visit," Dumortier mumbled as if consigning it to memory. At least he could try to play along with the euphemism.

# CHAPTER SEVENTEEN

AFTER SEVENTY HOURS and half a day in intense physiotherapy, Dumortier was discharged and deemed fit again for light duty. Via another Shirpen, Dumortier arrived at the Constabulary shooting range, located deep in the Catacombs of Excellent Precision. He had never really appreciated the wry humour behind the name before. Its anonymous benefactor, a long-deceased Chatoyant official, had donated an abandoned hospital to Constabulary and they had left the inscription on each of the flagstones leading up to the foyer: "Enter in the spirit of pure inquiry or do not enter at all."

He stepped into the old hospital foyer and was greeted by an empty reception desk set into a wall of faded Egyptian hieroglyphics and imagery. The pantheon of ancient gods and goddesses were inlaid with coloured mica and flanked by engraved water lilies flowing out towards the edges. After the sparkling eyes of an ibis-headed sculpture scanned the security credentials on his paiza, Dumortier made his way down a stairwell to a wide, high-ceilinged tunnel. It lit up in sporadic bursts of flickering blue track lights, so intense it made Dumortier think of radiation bursts. The hospital had been out of bounds for decades; maybe it *was* radioactive, and a whole lot more.

But Dumortier was not here for a history tour. Disorientated and irritated by the lights, he relied on his enhanced hearing to find the chamber described in Nadira Morad (landing name: Gaspard)'s message. He picked his way along another passage that veered off the main tunnel before retracing his steps and finally locating the chamber. It must have been one of the older ones: the soundproofing had deteriorated.

*Thwack!* He heard an object thrown at a target practice dummy.

*Thwack!* A second time.

"Stay where you are," ordered a woman's voice, assured, as though from countless years of experience. The slow cadence and clipped diction punctuated and spaced each word like a highlights column printing out the news.

He obeyed without question. SeForTec Nadira Morad Gaspard had a way of making a person feel as though she was speaking directly to their subconscious.

"Enter now," she said a minute later without turning to greet Dumortier.

He did so, but hung back in the shooter's area until his eyes got used to the harsh lighting inside the chamber. He picked up the unexpected tang of salt.

Three target practice dummies stood at the far end.

Dumortier observed Nadira pick up a fla-tessen fan from a steel basin with a gloved hand, shake off the excess brine and steady herself before aiming the fan at the head of the centre dummy. She kept her arm extended at the end of the throw, her long fingers splayed.

The fan missed the head of the target dummy by a frustrating centimetre—and not for the first time, as Dumortier observed from her frown.

"It's much harder than it looks," commented Nadira as she bent down to retrieve the fan.

"Maybe remove your gloves?"

Nadira straightened up and returned to the other side of the chamber to try again, taking off her gloves. She lifted her chest and dropped her shoulder blades, angling her torso at the target dummy before drawing back her arm. This time, the fan hit the dummy in its chest. Dumortier did not refrain from applauding. The scene played out in that grey space between performance art and documentary footage.

"Engaging artform," Nadira said, more to herself than to him. "I should take it up in my downtime."

"That being said," replied Dumortier, "can Forensics pay a few Adepts to test these fans—of course, in the strictest confidence?"

"Even with our combined Ocelot and Senior SeForTec clearance, we don't have the time."

Dumortier nodded. "Students need months of practice to get a feel for the fan. And during the same time, the fan has to become familiar with you. I'm not sure how it is with training fans."

"The ones I have now have membranes grown to adapt more quickly to new users. But it greatly reduces the strength of their venom. At least half of the fan needs to be submerged in the solution. It takes an hour or two."

Dropping the fan back into its basin, Nadira reached into the neighbouring one to pick up another fan lying at the bottom. Dumortier peered inside: the fan was different from the others. It was familiar in its minimalism; the lacquer work on the ribs was sparser, done with a stencil depicting entwined coils like DNA strands, and it lacked the membranous black lace of the training fans.

"We obtained Saurebaras's personal fan," Nadira observed, reaching into the basin. "Watch this." At the moment Nadira's fingers brushed the membranes of the fan it snapped shut in the solution. "But priority first: I must show you Gia Aront."

"Isn't she supposed to stay in the morgue?"

"Formally, this place qualifies," Nadira said as she walked out of the gallery. "I had Gia transferred here in case someone tried to tamper with her body. Please pardon the use of the forensic sarcophagus."

"What do you want to show me?"

"See for yourself—I insist on it."

Back in the main tunnel, the lights had stopped flickering. Dumortier felt the floor slope downwards as he followed her to another chamber.

It was bigger than the ballistics range. A pair of junior technicians wearing red surgical veils stood facing each other in the centre of the chamber. Dumortier took reassurance from the reverence with which these newer

SeForTecs treated their positions: in his early days as an officer, they'd always been brusque and impersonal. Upon Nadira's order, one of them gestured at the black oblong defined in the floor in front of him. His hands described an elaborate geometric sequence in the air, and the other technician mirrored him for confirmation like an elaborate magician's trick. Eight clicks instantly followed. Minute latches were released at each of the oblong's vertices—four visible to Dumortier, the other four below floor level.

The forensic sarcophagus rose like a periscope and stopped at waist-height. Dumortier realised the oblong was the lid of the sarcophagus.

"Leave us," Nadira told the technicians. They left in silence.

*Gia won't get a better coffin than a forensic one*: he considered telling her father that in all honesty. He was afraid to touch it in case of accidentally contaminating it: an absurd notion. The transparent panel below the lid had been hermetically sealed.

Her mouth was closed, her lips purplish. One eye was still open and clouded over; her other eye was a clearly defined cross-shaped hole where the fan had penetrated it. Her fingernails were grubby and her palms calloused, not pink and soft like the Tier Dweller cadavers of his previous cases. Was practical work harsh and strenuous in those labs and seminars? The notion of Gia Aront doing menial chores and hard academic work was laughable.

Dumortier peered closer. Gia Aront's head was lying at a strange angle, loose at the base of her neck, as though her skull had been yanked too far back and now only the skin of her neck attached her head to her body. It had been realigned with care as she was placed in the sarcophagus.

He tapped the panel over Gia's neck. "Did this happen at any time during processing?"

"My SeForTecs recovered Gia Aront *in situ* with her neck in that condition."

"I thought the fan through the eye killed her?"

"The trauma to her eye was not the cause of death," Nadira said. "The penetration of the periorbital socket was not deep enough."

"It would've only blinded her. And you and I wouldn't be having this discussion right now." Dumortier started pacing the floor in front of the sarcophagus.

"Serotonin levels were found to be elevated around neck area. The cause of death was dislocation." Nadira cupped the back of her head and jerked up her chin to demonstrate. "Hyperextension of the C2 vertebrae. An avulsion."

It was a common enough cause of death among suicide and murder victims. Dumortier recognised what Nadira was saying, but wasn't sure he believed it.

"A hangman's fracture? In the middle of a fla-tessen piste?"

"Yes, apparently that's what happened."

Dumortier was now pacing up and down the chamber. Threads were unraveling and reweaving themselves in his mind. "Pull up the sparring footage."

Nadira nodded and touched a control panel. A screen flickered to life on the wall facing the sarcophagus. Gia

Aront and Pleo moved within their intersecting pistes, their arms blurred. Pleo raised her liddicoate shawl to shield her face. Dumortier thought the shawl had deflected Gia's fan, but she had not thrown it yet; it looked like she had used a castanet.

"The fla-tessen piste is highly sensitive," he said. "I've had a demonstration of its capabilities. It detects anomalies and it activated when I threw a mite inside it. You can't even spit on it without it reacting."

Nadira said in mild irritation, "The footage quality emphasises the shadows."

"That isn't a shadow." Dumortier traced a fingertip around Gia's head and a slightly darker area behind her, in the vague shape of an upper body. "It looks like three people were inside that piste."

"Two *people*," said Nadira, then, "and one more presence."

Dumortier noticed wry satisfaction in her expression; he'd just passed a test. "That's what you wanted me to see?"

"Yes."

"What sort of presence? As in a rogue training simulation?"

Nadira pointed at Gia Aront's head and neck on screen. "Fla-tessen never uses training simulations. And training simulations don't dislocate vertebrae."

Dumortier forwarded the footage to the moment the fan went into Gia Aront's eye. He had seen many types of physical trauma in his time, but even he had to look away for a second. He had little stomach for eye injuries.

"Perfect clean hit," he said.

"According to Pleo Tanza's progress reports, fla-tessen is not her strong point."

"So it's a fluke. Total beginner's luck. "

"Or was set up to look like one," countered Nadira.

He remembered Saurebaras in the hall: *They sent you— how predictable.*

Dumortier pulled up the recorded excerpt taken from his collarbone stud. "Enhance and increase volume by 70 percent." It played on a loop, over and over again. On the fifth replay Dumortier heard another voice speaking just below Saurebaras's voice, denatured yet unmistakable.

"There was something talking to you then, in the loosest sense," acknowledged Nadira. "Enough to create air pressure and vibrate air molecules."

"If this presence can talk, then it can manipulate objects. Her shawl moved by itself when she attacked me and the Spinels, both inside and outside the fla-tessen hall. I don't discount it; I've heard of telekinesis, maybe tested by rumoured Cabuchon military units. "

"Tulpa, not telekinesis," said Nadira, "and what Cabuchon military do are not rumours. Trust me, I'm privy to such information."

"Sure, but it doesn't help us with anything to this case."

"It should," said Nadira. "A tulpa is a thoughtform."

"Tulpas and thoughtforms are a myth." Dumortier sounded sure of it, until he saw Nadira's face.

"Something inexplicable attacked you, but in Saurebaras's presence?"

"It was *of* Saurebaras and yet not her." He was reluctant

to say it, but it was true.

"We'll dub it an 'un-person,'" said Nadira, "for the purpose of our discussions."

Dumortier replayed the footage. "And this un-person was in the piste, and at the moment when the fan went into Gia Aront's eye, it pulled and snapped her neck."

"Yes," said Nadira. "The somatic reconditioning Saurebaras underwent has some side effects, but not all of them known."

"Saurebaras framed Pleo Tanza." Dumortier felt the air in the chamber getting lighter at this breakthrough. "No one outside of Constabulary must know what both of us have discovered."

"I concur," said Nadira.

"When putting someone in prison, don't give them access to a weapon. And make sure they themselves aren't also weaponlike."

"Saurebaras found a way to work around the reconditioning," said Nadira. "Thus the reconditioning cheated Chatoyance and Polyteknical; they believed it was infallible. Since there's nothing else to follow up from the discovery of the body, let's start tomorrow by going to the Aronts and questioning Gia's parents. We leave out the part about the tulpa."

"Sakamoto believes it's all a waste of time."

"You don't agree?"

He shrugged. "I know Katyal when it comes to the Tier Dwellers. To her nothing will be a waste of time."

"Look at how the accident happened, the position of the body in the piste, and that injury to her neck... it all

seems so *personal*. There are so many possible threads."
Nadira peered at the footage again.

"Well, let's weave them together. See if they make up a rope."

"All links and symbols need to be decoded. The question is whether Gia was an opportunity kill, whether it could have been anyone—something on which to hang a murderer's plan, perhaps—or if it had to be her, of all people."

"It's already started with her," he said. "Who she was. What she might have been to someone else. That's the only starting point we have so far. And what Saurebaras tried to tell me."

"It doesn't make sense."

"No, it makes perfect sense."

"Before you leave, I have something to present to you."
She led him back to the range. The Constabulary quartermaster was already waiting there, a bright-eyed woman with salt-and-pepper hair clad in creased indigos, who seemed very much at home in the chamber.

She held out a weapons case and uniform to Dumortier. "Ocelot issue."

Nadira took the case from the quartermaster and set it down on the worktable. Inside the case was a gun Dumortier had only seen in arms and ammunition training footage. A shrapnel heart.

"Senior SeForTec's privilege," informed the quartermaster, presenting Dumortier and Nadira with eye and ear protective gear. "She gets to test it out before you."

Nadira put on the gear, picked up the shrapnel heart,

checked the serial number and racked the slim slide on top. She took aim at a new test dummy and fired. The recoil kicked but Nadira did not flinch, compensating with the extensive weapons experience of her previous transfusions. Dumortier had never seen a shrapnel heart in action before and what he saw demonstrated was quite impressive. It fired darts of compacted rock salt instead of bio-flechettes. The salt darts were a far cry from the organic barbs of the splinter heart, longer and more jagged around the tips.

Dumortier glimpsed the worn and pitted back wall of the test chamber through four ragged holes in the dummy's torso.

"We like to say that splinter hearts whisper, while shrapnel hearts curse the air," said the quartermaster with a measure of pride in her work, "but glass hearts shatter everything."

Nadira finished with the splinter heart and gave the gun a final check. "All yours, Ocelot Investigator."

Dumortier took the shrapnel heart from Nadira. He was pleased that there was no slide that bit into his skin. He felt its sturdy weight and her trust in him when she released her grip on the weapon. This gesture reassured him for now.

"Pleo Tanza was last seen in Retail Sector 12," Nadira told him. "An incident at the jewellery shop there. Should we send someone to question the owner?"

Dumortier shook his head. "Katyal doesn't want the net closing too tight around Pleo Tanza until further orders from her or Sakamoto."

"Time is being lost."

"Not for now. The owner of that shop is known to my unit. An ex-modrani called Jean-Ling Setona who used to frequent the Tiers. *She* can keep a secret."

BACK INSIDE THE Shirpen, Dumortier ran a check on Jean-Ling Setona and noted the name of her latest employee. He ran that through another background check which yielded brief yet more revealing information. Setona could keep a secret, but not the person working for her. Dumortier wondered if the Mias network had overcome its teething problems by now, and could get a lock on this employee. Ocelot clearance, it seemed, made accessing Mias a pleasant experience.

# CHAPTER EIGHTEEN

MARSH STARTED OUT of a light sleep and almost rolled off the public bench. An approaching sound reminded him of his brush with the law back home, setting off alarms in his subconscious. His entire body tensed; unsurprising, given the events back in Setona's shop earlier that day. Now it was after midnight and he had stayed out of his nanoapartment as an extra precaution.

A vibration hummed in the air around him. The sound came again, this time louder and next to him at ground level. Four pairs of heavy grey boots, capped with metal, hit the paving in perfect sync as four guards trooped past him on the Subaltern's Parade. It was the last thing he wanted to hear after encountering the tyro.

Despite its name, the Parade had fallen out of use as a ceremonial route. Now it was a nocturnal park lined with victory cedars, frequented by marble doves and people walking off excess energy after Shineshift. The

Parade exuded gravitas in what, according to the visitor information screens, was a too-little-too-late tribute to an unnamed Tagmat subaltern wrongfully accused of desertion, according to visitor information displayed on screens hanging from the cedars' branches.

These guards were not clad in the cardinal reds of the Spinels. Marsh saw their bone-white uniforms, covered with textured armour plates that were grooved like insect carapaces. Jagged spikes lined their gauntlets, giving the Aront house guards their Dogtooth moniker—and a hint of overkill. But these Dogtooths were too far from their homebase; the Tiers were across town. Marsh could see their lights twinkling in the distance.

Perhaps in unconscious solidarity with the historic subaltern, the people along the Parade shrank from these mercenary enforcers of Aront will and power. Behind Marsh's bench, an elderly Chatoyant couple stared and muttered their disapproval, then retreated inside the main pergola that flowed along the Parade. Marsh forced himself to stay still; running would have looked too suspicious.

The Dogtooths' figures receded and a recreational mood was restored to the Parade. Marsh hoped they were only conducting a training exercise, but the visit had soured his mood. He headed back to the glare of the Subaltern's Parade station. Someone would be searching for the Polyteknical woman who injured him, but hopefully not for him.

According to Setona, Constabulary or similar bodies always came after people during working hours. So at least for today, Marsh was safe; Setona had closed up in time for Shineshift. He was also glad she was going to pay him late this month; less uta flowing into his account meant less activity and less chance of anyone tracing his movements.

He glanced at the back of the queue he had just joined, but there was no sign of any Dogtooths in the station. One by one the sentry turnstiles admitted commuters. Marsh hesitated for a moment—he was almost sure no one was tracking him—then by impulse, broke away from them to walk across the station's utilitarian hall and to reach the other enclosed escalator which led up to the T-Car line.

A man stood at the foot of the escalator; there was no reaching the T-Car platform without passing him. He wore an all-weather translucent overcoat over a brushed steel-grey suit: according to Setona, the outfit issued to plainclothes officers.

He must have observed Marsh abruptly leaving the first queue; to return to it now would generate more suspicion.

"This station is a long way from home, Cabuchoner," said the not-officer in a casual voice, as if he and Marsh were in a spaceport waiting lounge. "Your identification, please."

Marsh complied, showing his work permit, but he bristled at being singled out. "You're not in your indigos."

"Don't wear them." He sounded amused. "My name is Dumortier. What are you doing here on Chatoyance?"

Marsh shrugged. "I guess I'm lost."

"Lost enough to work here?" The man squinted at the permit.

"My employer renewed my pass last month."

"Yes, I know Jean-Ling Setona well." The Constabulary officer waved the permit away. Marsh's leave to stay was not the issue at this moment. "You're lucky I've found you in time. Alias—John CaMarr-Schist, but your landing name is Zynclave." The not-officer paused to check Marsh's reaction—Marsh bit the inside of his cheek to ensure his face remained expressionless. "Great-grandparents were administrators for ice settlements on Europan frozen seas. Family in high places. Chatoyance is a long way down from Corund, my friend. A cargo squirrel's existence must be so exhausting."

Dumortier saw the blank look on Marsh's face and laughed. "Cargo squirrels? No one knows how they came about. Possibly a type of rat and another type of rodent were desperate and horny. Found them in grain stores on supply frigates when I was working in Khrysobe Spaceport. Ordered to shoot them on sight. Could never bring myself to shoot one."

"Why?"

"My supe called me sentimental. I'm not, but I recognised kindred spirits. Plucky little things. All survivors."

"Why are you telling me this?"

"You're like a cargo squirrel—too small to fathom the true scale and nature of the grain you're living off. Here's some free advice: go back to where you're now staying before the next Shineshift." He pointed at the Dogtooths passing by the station entrance and added, "Or you won't go home to Cabuchon at all. These Tier Dwellers' guards are like gnats—they land on anyone and draw blood.

They're recruited from Anium. They have no connection to Chatoyance and no obligation to play fair. Dogtooths tend to like non-Chatoyant blood. My superior made me watch as my teammates clubbed cargo squirrels' brains out with sawn-off pipes. I don't want it to come down to that with you."

He waved Marsh onto the escalator. Maybe it was the end of his shift and he did not want trouble.

IF MARSH HAD hoped to catch some shuteye inside the Parade station when Shineshift wound down, he was out of luck. An out-of-service T-Car hung underneath the platform and commuters were waiting as they caught up with the highlights or sent messages back and forth.

Marsh hung back at the top of the escalator and waited for a few minutes, then descended into the T-Car when it was activated. The cool empty carriage offered welcome respite from the strain of holding himself together while Dumortier had spoken to him. A klaxon blared, and another T-Car passed by on the opposite track, the rumble of its passage dopplering out. Marsh's nervousness dissipated like the afternoon haze. His left shoulder still throbbed, five parallel slashes of muted pain that kept him company for the remainder of the journey. He reached out for the carriage pole, favouring his right arm, but stifled a yelp as the faulty pole hoisted him up with a series of jerks.

The Canal That Quenches All Thirst ran through the old Hospital Quarter, connecting both death and commerce, yet the lives of the people living on opposite ends appeared aeons apart. On Lantern Street, posters still hung onto the ornate lampposts. Marsh read fragments of old advertisements sloughing off in reverse chronological order in the breeze: *Ancient Streets, Modern Amenities. Exhibition of PostTransit Society Sculpture, Plenary Hall 7, Pupil Convenient Centre. Towards A Post-Transit Society; Canal Mouth Development: Office and Retail Units now available*. Marsh still did not know what any of it meant; their context was lost long before he started living there.

The retrofitted display block loomed over Marsh, reminding him of the counters he spent his working hours attending to or standing behind. As a precaution he counted the storeys to locate his nanoapartment at mid-level, and saw no strange shadows moving in the window. He passed through the once-vermillion entrance gates, now faded to terracotta over the years.

A cluster of sparks lit up the row of windows above the main door, accompanied by a sporadic hissing and crackling that died off. The cheap crowning-shield reinforcing the walls was struggling to connect to the main power grid. As a secondary precaution before making his way inside, Marsh picked up a pebble and hurled it against the wall facing him, where the grimy vertical panels bumped up against the worn moulded slabs on the ground. With a pop, the pebble bounced off the crowning-shield, shot past his legs and landed next to one of the gate posts. At least the block wasn't collapsing tonight. Somewhat reassured, he retrieved the pebble and went inside.

He ducked to avoid the crisis-crossing lines of laundry hanging overhead and picked his way through the corridors, too narrow for residential living. On the upper floors, most of his neighbours' doors were open, letting out warm air, aromas of cooking and glimpses of domestic life: steam whistling out of retrofitted samovars, stoves crowded with trays and pans. On the worn dining table lay an assemblage of auspicious objects left over from the New Year's festival: a string of firecrackers to ward off evil, and oranges and pomegranates to represent the wish for wealth, honour and many descendants in other settlements. Over a mother-of-pearl-inlaid table a wallscreen blared, a rerun of a soap opera on Khtn-3—the channel broadcasting from Anul, the largest shepherd moon, and part-owned by various Cabuchoner entrepreneurs. Two children standing in their doorways eyed him with casual disinterest and an old man squeezed past him and mumbled profanities, as though Marsh could avoid brushing up against him in the tight space. *The feeling is mutual*, Marsh often felt like yelling back.

Marsh's nanoapartment was dim and sparse, but it suited him since he was out for most of the day. "Flea boxes" was the more familiar term among their denizens. Sliding screens attached to tracks hung from the ceiling allowed him to convert the tiny space into different rooms, convenient for the few occasions when he had taken a lover. Right now he was too exhausted to bother with the routine of compartmentalising. The only clue to his background was a poster of the Cedar Avenue back on Cabuchon, facing his cot. He missed the public parks of

Zen-like stillness, containing oases encompassed in larger oases resting on terraformed acres of land. Works of art were displayed on cultivated victory cedars; the tree was both a symbol and pride of Cabuchon. For 20 juta an augury vendor on the avenue would tell your fortune by consulting the cedar leaf oracle: choose a leaf at random from a bunch of sixty leaves, repeat six times and take note of the results.

Six months before he left Cabuchon the oracle had warned him of a shock in the near future which would shake him out of his current stagnation, and now he saw the truth in its message for the first time. Today, instead of tossing his carrier onto the worn floor next to his dirty clothes, he set the bag down by the door and stood in front of a mirror hanging next to it, gingerly taking off his shirt to inspect his injuries.

He was very impressed with the healing—Setona hadn't been overselling the properties of the epithelialix paste she had applied on him. The bleeding had stopped and the paste had reduced the swelling. There was minimal risk of infection if he kept the wounds covered for another day. Pain still throbbed under the skin of his shoulder, but the epithelialix concealed the wounds too well. The gouges did not show through the thick layer and his shoulder appeared normal and uninjured in the mirror. In disbelief he rubbed hard, feeling the fresh scabs under the seal.

*The woman on my T-Car every morning, the one I found at the fountain, has marked me*, he thought, and felt strangely honoured with this connection.

As he reached out to pick up his carrier Marsh felt one gouge split open and something jut out from under the skin. Repulsed and scared in equal measures, he steeled himself to reach for his shoulder and his fingers brushed over a slender foreign object. He returned to look in the mirror: the object was as long as his ring finger and it gleamed white despite the dimly lit nanoapartment. A forcep: it must have broken off when she had stabbed him earlier and become embedded in his shoulder.

Marsh gritted his teeth, grasped the tip of the forcep where it poked out from his scapula, and tugged twice. The result was an agonising split-second of resistance before the tender skin gave way in a ragged shiny strip. Blood quickly refilled the wound and trickled down his back, cold air rushing over exposed tissue. He worked a fingernail under the edge of the epitheliax seal and peeled it back, one sticky piece at a time.

When he had finished the five parallel gouges reappeared on his shoulder. The wounds tingled.

Due to space constraints Marsh lacked the full range of gem identification equipment, but he still made the best of it. He had fixed a lamp under the sorting pad which doubled as a desk, and now sat on a high stool, donned his eye loupe and held the forcep under the light. It was almost weightless, like fish bone, and dazzling white. Marsh bent it in all directions between his fingers and it sprang back with a defiant strength.

He picked up the finest diamond scribe from his opened toolkit and ran its tip over the length of the forcep, but it resisted his attempts to score its surface. Switching to dark field illumination, he made out minute filaments at the tip of the forcep, probably for holding mineral samples via sub-molecular tension, like the toe pads of a gecko. Most of the forcep was intact; whatever had attached the forcep to the sheath had broken instead— there was grey discolouration at the base where the forcep had broken off. Marsh adjusted the loupe to the highest possible magnification to examine the rough cross section. A grainy pattern, alternating dark and faint chevrons intersecting in narrowly spaced arcs against the grey, resolved into focus.

He wrenched away the loupe and set it on a tray, rubbing his eyes in disbelief. Then as though in a trance he put the loupe on again. Marsh stared at the image until his eyes blurred with the strain after two minutes of examination. He readjusted the magnification, searching the length of the forcep for other signs of inlaid hardware such as grid patterns or serial numbers but found none.

It was not possible for Schreger lines to be present for they only manifested in organics such as ivory and dentine. His discovery meant the forceps were organic, or at least comprised of an organic matrix.

Fifty-seven bones in the human hand. These students had five more, in the form of teeth in their fingers.

But since when? Up until now, stolen Polyteknical implants had all be made of foreign materials, albeit compatible with surrounding body tissues. The DryWare Market was the only place to confirm his discovery. Finding a Bio-equipper unmoved by palm-greasing and not caught up in internecine protection rackets in that tangle of side streets and making it out alive was like getting a definite answer from the cedar leaf oracle—impossible. Most of the traders had a covert taskforce of goons under their command, who murdered clients with valuable finds. Was his tentative protection deal with the 555 Triumvirate still valid? The satellite markets were slightly less risky and outside known gang turfs. He went through a mental roster of contingency plans in case the DryWare and WetWare Markets turned out to be unworkable. Art and jewel theft were suddenly so insignificant and yet so much safer.

Marsh went to the window, ready to hurl the forcep out, listen to it hit the short-circuiting crowning-shield and sizzle into charred specks. The portion of night sky visible to him through the window lit up with lightning. Cabuchon winked at him, a fine bead out of reach.

*Return the forcep to her as it was part of her. Do right by her.*

But not before a thorough evaluation. Here was his big chance to make it off Chatoyance.

The forcep was as slender as a cedar leaf and now imbued with greater significance. Marsh saw a line of cedar trees stretching out to a distant vanishing point that was his future. He recalled the rest of his reading: *It's not that the wind is blowing, it's what the wind blows.*

His skin itched, trying to heal and restore itself. He had promised that he wouldn't return to what he used to be. But if it helped him get off Chatoyance?

He decided not to wait for the next Shineshift. The intermittent darkness was pregnant with possibilities and

Marsh was going to exploit it. He placed the forcep in an airtight sheath and strapped it to his arm, then left his flea box. Outside, the crowning-shield glitched and sent him off with a volley of sparks.

# CHAPTER NINETEEN

Nadira Morad (landing name: Gaspard) was both salamander and human. To what extent she was more of each, she still was not sure.

When she was ten years old, she had modest dreams of living forever in the Anium canton on the edge of the Signet System. She would own a thriving aquaculture farm and tend to it in perpetuity—aided by the best immortality treatments, of course.

Years later, she got her wish in the guise of SeForTec transfusions. She heard the term used by the medical technicians as they rattled off details from their charts the first time they had revived her:

"—personnel name: Nadira Morad (landing name: Gaspard)."

"—pulse is 64 bpm. Level with baseline."

"—all vitals are stable."

"—all extremities intact and functioning."

She had sat up too hastily in the recovery tray and coughed up a bedpan's worth of warm briny synthetic amniotic fluid.

"Transfusion complete."

Nadira had managed a weak laugh at the way the technicians used the word; it sounded so understated and straightforward. They called it a transfusion, yet she felt like a newborn.

A technician's freezing gloved hand patted her on the shoulder—the gesture was a cue to get out of the bedpan.

She had stood on the observation deck suspended above the rows of SeForTec vats extending as far as she could see in the storage facility. Banks of maintenance and life-sign monitors scanned and hummed in the background. The faint outlines of her colleagues and ex-colleagues— past, present and future—were visible in the translucent vats. It had been a reassuring sight; only a few empty vats per row, suggesting no backlog of cases. Bodies and limbs floated in the translucent vats, all labelled with names, dates, designations, and case numbers.

Back in her early days, they all slept easy.

A woman's voice had called out to her from the opposite walkway. "Welcome back, Salamander."

She saluted in return. "Thank you, Cicada. Rest well until you're needed again."

Nadira and her colleagues had long discovered camaraderie in the examination of cadavers and crime scenes, and assigned each other epithets chosen from assorted symbols of new life, energy and resurrection. 'Salamander' was for the recently activated, 'cicada' for those off-duty and about to enter or reenter suspension, to replace lost or depleted components before going back into circulation.

The rigorous SeForTec reconditioning was an essential bulwark against bleedover: the risk of past memories overwhelming her at any time. Reports and firsthand accounts varied about the nature of bleedover: it was not exactly flashbacks, because the memories remain vivid without the sensory experience. Nadira tended to give more weight to the accounts. She had heard anecdotes about SeForTecs locked into silence by memories from their previous manifestations: to speak of those experiences was to relive them. Others experienced narcolepsy, PTSD or dysmorphia.

She was able to remember without it affecting her current state. Somatic therapy helped, as did cortical reorganisation to improve motor control, in extreme cases. Under controlled conditions, SeForTecs were permitted moments of catharsis. At night, or when off duty, she would lie in her cot and allow the seismic pressure of past memories to build up under her body for a glorious, disorientating minute. With years of practice, the pressure always receded.

"Consider your accumulated memories as though they were documentaries. The subject of all of them is you, of course."

When Nadira first heard those words of advice, they had rung out across the hammered sheet-metal floor of a makeshift auditorium.

Everything was makeshift back in those early days,

including advice. Easy to say when it was difficult to discern between what was you, and what an imperfect memory. But it was not always about her, Nadira realised over her first four transfusions (not 'incarnations' and nothing as crude as was denoted by 'decantations'; the rest of the interdepartmental staff liked to use those terms interchangeably). Constabulary went to work by channeling her into the same vessel indefinitely, as long as her mind was still viable.

Old software into new wetware. New wetware equipped with new dryware. Transfer and transfuse. Repeat until the physical broke down or became irreplaceable. Reassignment or resignation—Constabulary always gave a SeForTech the choice between the two.

Nadira had rejected both from the beginning. She secretly hoped to remain in stasis until Constabulary came up with another alternative.

NADIRA AND DUMORTIER were ahead of schedule as they made their way into the Orchard sector. Orchard was built on a small artificial mesa and Nadira had to steer the Shirpen onto a steep ramp, cruising past the base of the Aront Tier. The particulate-rich morning haze pushed the vehicle's filter-visor to its limit. She switched it off and slowed down the vehicle, squinting at the Aront Tier in wonder as if it had sprung up overnight.

A giant mushroom.

No doubt it was continuously watered and fertilised by ill-gotten wealth. If she stayed to watch the Tier at night she might see it emanate clouds of poisonous spores that merged with Chatoyance's haze. The Tiers, and their residents, seeding the atmosphere with largesse—or with sanctioned corruption (both were the same these days), if she wanted to be facetious. But she couldn't afford to be; she was an avatar of Constabulary and she executed its will.

The Aront Tier also reminded her of a command centre, sentinel-like as it waited for its next set of orders. She had been up on most of the other Tiers but the Aront Tier was not exactly the most graceful collection of angles. It lacked the glamour and the cliched touches to convey wealth and superficial status—as if the Aronts considered themselves beyond all of that. No glass lift cars ascending and descending on tracks laid into the support columns, which also lacked heraldic patterns in unique colour schemes. It could be charitably dubbed 'militant luxury.'

In an unexpected touch of whimsy, the Aront residential tier's resemblance was closer to a parasol, casting large shadows over the ground directly below it. A parasol to be carried into battle, she guessed as she picked out a few security features on the rim: floodlights, guard posts, and fortified surfacing. All sent the same message to potential intruders and attackers: *It's not worth the effort.*

She had little doubt the Tier Dwellers were deliberate architects of their own prisons, a design resulting from both hubris and desperation.

"You think the others already have Tyro Pleo Tanza?" Dumortier watched a cluster of purple dots pulsate over a section of the Orchard covered in blue gridlines in the windscreen display.

"That activity is on the Madrugal Tier—not likely." Nadira glanced over. "Looks concentrated."

"It's either a party or a funeral. For Tier Dwellers there's often no difference." Dumortier killed the display. "If the Aronts put a price on her head, they'll save you and me a landfill's worth of paperwork."

"You wouldn't need me either," said Nadira. "You'd be riding with Detainment."

The Shirpen turned into a concourse and settled into a discreet docking enclave behind nine hulking Dogtooth vehicles. Nadira and Dumortier waited for a guard escort to greet them before they got out of the Shirpen.

"Did they tell you that joining Constabulary would give you a front row seat to the greatest show in the Archer's Ring?" Dumortier asked as they waited.

"Academy warned us during the first week," replied Nadira.

"Give up your seat—now we're going behind the scenes."

"I've been to the other Tiers before."

"Not the Aront Tier?"

"Never been called there. I'm actually quite surprised."

"Sure?" Dumortier narrowed his eyes in disbelief.

"They were very much after my time."

Dumortier adjusted his sleeves. "Not that I presume to advise you, but I'm reminding you: a direct question is an affront to their sensibilities. They prefer to dance around."

"I'll be tactful."

"But bluntness has its uses with difficult witnesses and suspects. Provoking a reaction can give a more telling answer." He blew out his cheeks. "Got anything for nerves?"

*He shouldn't* have *nerves*, Nadira thought as she drew her jacket around her, patting her pockets for magnesium citrate tablets. She found the last one, half melted in its tiny clamshell packet. Dumortier accepted and extracted the tablet.

The Aront security detail did not disappoint. Like a torpedo, the lift did not so much as open as *discharge* five Dogtooths. The guards filed out and motioned Dumortier and Nadira to step into the lift to the main habitat. The lift ascended like an arrow, passed through the concourse roof and stopped after a few minutes.

Nadira was expecting a more detailed glimpse into the workings of House Aront security: banks of surveillance equipment, barracks, chattering comms equipment, all infused with that trademark Aront grandiosity found in their public infrastructure projects. Size was money. But the martial feel of the ground level docking bay and upper concourse had already vanished, replaced by a checkpoint as mundane as the ones in a Khrysobe Spaceport.

"Leave all weapons here. Collect them on your way out," ordered a Dogtooth as soon as they stepped out of the lift.

Dumortier reached under his overcoat, unclipped his ancillary mace from his belt and tossed it over to the nearest Dogtooth, who was holding a tray. The mace landed in it with a thud.

"Final reminder to turn off all augmentations," said the Dogtooth as he placed the tray into a wall slot.

Nadira touched both of her temples in an exaggerated show of compliance, although her SeForTec clearance made her exempt from the visitor procedures of Tier Dwellers. Earning their trust was vital. She noticed that Dumortier did not remove or disable his ear stud: he pressed it twice and then three times in a coded sequence. The stud's tiny light stopped pulsing green and turned white. He was gambling on the chance that analogue mode was obsolete enough not to be detected by security.

"Security tightened up since my last visit," murmured Dumortier.

"It seems very crude to me; I see no counterintrusion measures except for these guards."

"If the guards are effective, security is not crude," he drawled. "Keep in mind what we just discussed regarding tact and bluntness; there's no telling which face the Aronts will wear for us today."

After the checkpoint the lift's ascent sped up, and the g-forces made Nadira place both hands on the glass pane in front of her for support.

The doors slid open onto an observation platform, a wide torus hugging the circumference of the Tier's shaft. Nadira and Dumortier stepped out. She stepped up to the windows, entranced by the panoramic view of Chatoyance. Up here the city settlement was laid out splendid, like a mythic realm. The Temple to Gachala was a blue flame and the canals glimmered in the light, the bridges like essential stitches in an intricate pattern. Sweeping up from the ground in an immense organic wave, the roof of the 'Cinth enclosed the daily hubbub within it. The New Areas of Blue Taro and Boxthorn were no longer a haphazard afterthought, but dendritic in its arrangement.

A recorded woman's voice crackled to life over the speakers, her dulcet tones drawing attention to the horseshoe bend of Aront Major Canal. The outline of a drained canal, bone white in the window glass, highlighted the latest completed project.

Dumortier tapped her on the shoulder and she suddenly felt conscious of him observing her enthrallment. But that wasn't what he was drawing her attention to—a third person had stepped onto the platform.

Patriarch Aront looked older and gaunter than the PR-approved images Nadira had seen all over the news. He exuded grace and practised authority, giving off the air that he was serving an administration—his own—which did the outlandish for the very sake of it. He crossed the platform to shake their hands.

"Senior Investigator Dumortier, it's been a while," he said with convincing familiarity.

"Can't argue with that."

Nadira pretended to admire the view again while studying the interaction between the men. Patriarch Aront's familiarity with Dumortier was genuine, and it made Dumortier uncomfortable.

"A slow and steady rise is the best," said Patriarch Aront, slowly taking a seat in the middle of an open-back white sofa with sloping armrests. "It means you didn't use or abuse any helpful connections."

Dumortier hesitated—a second too long—before pointedly replying, "The same could be said of how you achieved your empire."

Patriarch Aront laughed like a parent surprised at his child's budding wit. Touché, but Nadira saw Dumortier hold his hands by his sides, one of them squeezing and releasing a fistful of overcoat. He should have taken two tablets.

"It's lunchtime, my sincere apologies." Patriarch Aront resumed host duties as though the previous exchange had never happened. "How about refreshments?"

He tapped one of the sofa's armrests, and an aide carried in a tray and set it on a side table. The tray bore loaded black obsidian plates and a square cut bottle of garnet-hued wine. Nadira read the brand label engraved on it: *Catru Estate: 3325. Sparkling. Finest quality guaranteed.* Thick glass, and a large cork.

Patriarch Aront went to pour himself a full glass and knocked it back. This was not the Patriarch's first bottle of the day, Nadira figured. Nor the morning. If he was not talking, he was drinking.

"Please." Patriarch Aront gestured to the food. "Perhaps not the Catru wine. It occurs to me both of you are still on duty."

Nadira wanted to tell him she never ate much. She thought of the bitter yet restorative colour-coded drinks issued to SeForTecs, brimming with nutrient-laden jelly spheres in suspension. Dumortier inclined his head at the plates in a gesture that said: *Some hospitality won't kill you. Accept a little to expedite this meeting.*

She picked up a golden wafer of sorghum, topped with magenta caviar from strange crossbreeds of fish engineered to produce whatever colour was in vogue this year. It was rich, briny and creamy, with an incongruous hint of plum. Her dreams of owning an aquaculture farm resurfaced for a split second. Next to her, Dumortier took a quick bite of a plain wafer as a formality and touched the recording stud in his collarbone.

Her aquaculture farm sank back under the tide of duty. Time to begin the session.

Patriarch Aront held up the glass of wine as a toast to Dumortier and Nadira: "We, up here, live in equal parts dread and gratitude of our fine city's Senior Investigators and SeForTecs. Propitious that *both* should have reason to step onto a Tier."

"I wish the circumstances were better," replied Nadira.

Patriarch Aront turned back to Dumortier and remarked sotto voce, "Your assistant has picked up your light touch."

Dumortier coughed twice. "Nadira Morad is Constabulary's most senior SeForTec. Expect nothing less than exemplary from her and her team."

"Most of Chatoyance already knows about our tragedy."

Neither a question or a statement. Nadira decided to go for for honesty. "I'll personally see that Constabulary renews the media embargo on your daughter's death with immediate effect. The news outlets are very irresponsible."

"Very much appreciated, but not if it could hinder

your investigation. In any case, please don't tread around my wife and me. For the sake of Gia, you don't have to protect our sensibilities."

Nadira kept an eye on the bottle of wine—it was still two-thirds full. If he finished this one and called the aide for more, the visit could stretch well past Shineshift.

"Sometimes," he continued, "Matriarch Aront and I have to accept that our image is more powerful than us. We've been philanthropists, industrialists, and tycoons. First and foremost we're still spouses, parents. It's so unbelievable all the roles we need to assume in public! I've stopped being shocked and disappointed when people call us corrupt and unfeeling. It may surprise you to learn that I wish that miner's daughter is not involved. Her parents have to suffer with that."

"We're here regarding Gia." Dumortier sounded unimpressed with Aront's grandstanding.

"Gia, ahh, yes. And we ensured she had the same awareness of public opinion," he added with the fatigue of somebody who has wasted too much time and breath justifying their behaviour to idiots. "Murder attempts and sabotage come with the success, unfortunately."

"It won't help to start cooking up theories," Durmortier soothed in a priestly tone Nadira suspected he exclusively reserved for the recently bereaved.

"It won't be necessary anyway. That miner's daughter did it. Are Saurebaras and the tyro girl still at large?" Aront took several shallow breaths, as if trying to control himself. "You should have both of them in Constabulary cells as we speak."

"Patriarch, an investigation takes time," said Dumortier.

"Proper channels are too slow."

"Do you see progress when you look down there?" asked Dumortier. "I see more ruin than anything else. Call me a realist. Unless I'm actually looking at a ruin in slow-motion."

The Patriarch stared at him for a moment. "If not for the likes of us, all of you"—he jutted his chin at the window, dismissing all Chatoyants living below the Tier—"would suffer in an industrial purgatory."

Nadira noticed the Gachalan disk set high into the wall, its teal and gold pattern an exact match for the temple roof.

"My wife acquired religion this year, I think. Just a little too late to save Gia."

"Do you really believe so, *my husband?*" Matriarch Aront called out from a lift door as it opened onto the observation deck. Her perfume entered the room before her.

"No, no, sorry. My grief getting the better of me. It's not too late at all," soothed Patriarch Aront.

"Have you caught the tyro yet?"

Nadira looked at Dumortier and he shook his head. *Don't answer.*

"Soon," replied Dumortier.

"'Soon'? There's nothing worse than 'soon.'" She went to pour herself some wine. "But when you do, you will deliver her here? I want her head. If you can get me that dance instructor's head too, so much the better. I want to turn them into carbon and encase what's left. I blame both of them for what happened to Gia." She said it with a flick of a hand, as if she was beyond the concerns of others.

Dumortier did not reply.

"Satisfaction," said Nadira as though she was simplifying a philosophical concept for the Matriarch's benefit. "You demand it for Gia, but it's not anyone's to give. What you're asking is illegal, but in light of your loss, Dumortier and I are willing to overlook it."

"Do you know what it's like to lose children?" The glass of wine was drained with haste. "I don't suppose you do, because you spent half your life in a vat! Gia is dead. Satisfaction is my due."

"Swibi," Patriarch Aront put an arm around her shoulders. "Don't get yourself upset. These two are on our side."

He now addressed Dumortier with a cut glass, all-business tone of voice. "Should my Dogtooths have to supplement you in order to find one girl?"

"Of course not."

"Then leave us. And return with better news."

Dumortier performed a slight bow, and Nadira followed him into the lift in silence.

# CHAPTER TWENTY

A DOT OF fern green light pulsated at the corner of the Shirpen's windscreen where Dumortier sat in the passenger seat. Seconds later he still had not responded: he always found these notification lights soothing in their tweaked colour palettes, modified for ocular comfort. But the windscreen always noticed his delay, which danced on the edge of flouting at least three on-air protocols. He could no longer ignore it when it began emitting shriller, more insistent beeps than the ones used in his ear stud. Beeps that could be telling him anything: signs of life or signs of life ending.

"This is Dumortier," he finally responded.

"Trooper Devinez transferred to Canal Police last year. No subsequent sightings or body reported or found since then."

Or signs of life that ultimately signified a dead end.

"Who made the Missing Officer report?"

"Name declined. Report submitted to Sergeant Morin of Canal Police, sir."

"Over and out."

Another dot of light, burgundy replacing the fern green. Katyal's voice, just as strident over the comms channel as it was in person. "I understand and commend your commitment to all aspects of your investigations, but Constabulary is overwhelmed."

"I'm just concerned that one of us has gone missing and—"

Katyal interrupted. "At this time it could be anything."

Dumortier muttered, "Sure, she may have been crushed by a malfunctioning Canal Newt." Then, louder, he said, "Understood."

When Katyal signed off, Dumortier sighed and tapped the Shirpen's windscreen to darken it, scanning the stretch of Guanna Avenue ahead as it was overlaid with grid lines, then touched his side of the Shirpen's windscreen to restore it to full driving view. It lightened to normal transparency, allowing him to scan Gachala Avenue. It was the longest of the seven avenues radiating from the blockaded site that was to be The Monument To The Falcons, a new set of cenotaphs, yet to be unveiled but officially announced a week ago.

"So... I couldn't help but overhearing..." Nadira said after a minute.

Dumortier shook his head. "It's a loose end. Quite a major one from the case I had to drop before Gia Aront."

"Katyal and Sakamoto are like every superior I've seen over the years; they concern themselves with the bones and muscles. They forget that investigators and SeForTecs still have to pick at the connective tissue."

"Hmm," replied Dumortier. "'Connective tissue.' I like that."

"But I could help you, once Gia Aront's case is over."

"Thanks, I'll let you know," he replied, grateful but a little distrustful of Nadira's sudden generosity. But that was a concern for another time.

As straight as a spear, a newly built—still waterless—canal ran alongside the Shirpen. Dumortier checked the name on the canal network map, which proved oddly nondescript: North-South Canal.

Dumortier motioned for Nadira to slow the Shirpen down, and she pulled over at the barrier. They both got out of the Shirpen, and Dumortier stared down at the empty channel for a minute, then he tossed his cylinder of lolo paste over the barrier. It bounced once off the geomembrane canal lining, rolled away from Dumortier and Nadira, and continued in a straight line along the canal bed.

"The bed is tilted," said Nadira as soon as the cylinder was out of sight. "Incline not steep, yet considerable. I'd say five to ten degrees."

"It ensures the water flows in one direction." Dumortier pointed straight ahead down the canal.

"Where to?"

"A topographical or waterways map will have the answer. We need to check them."

They climbed back into the Shirpen.

Nadira insisted on carrying out the check. Her eyes performed a string of rapid saccades as she parsed the topographical data flowing over the console, her field of vision flooded with informatics. Dumortier had seen similar reflexes when she was testing the fans and shrapnel heart back at the shooting range, and wondered if all SeForTecs were as fast at processing.

"There it is." She reached out and placed a fingertip on the display, freezing a section of waterway map.

The new North-South Canal originated from the Harp Reservoirs in the northernmost sector of Chatoyance, flowed directly to the south sector and terminated in the Jare Artificial Lake. In doing so, it bisected the centre of Chatoyance—known as the Pupil—and formed a cross with the Aront Canal running east to west from the Temple of Gachala.

Dumortier tsked. "One thing's for sure: it will be scenic, when it's filled. Perfect for cruises and floating palaces."

Nadira circled the Temple site with her fingertip. "All those tourists and devotees swarming here and outwards. More uta for Arontcorp."

"The revenue from them won't be as much as the mooring fees collected from 7.6 miles of canal." Dumortier dragged the map to show this distance from Harp Reservoirs to Aront Canal. "And the North-South flows in one direction to encourage the traffic towards Aront Canal, which is three miles long but near the Pupil. Imagine the total fees to be collected."

"Chatoyance Government approved this? How do they justify it?"

"On paper," replied Dumortier. "For all the uta passed under the table and a cut of the mooring fees, the city gets a new canal. No one will question the necessity, because the Aronts play the part most beloved by old money: altrustic developers."

"A new canal that stinks before it opens," said Nadira.

She restarted the Shirpen and drove it back onto Gachala Avenue. Her insistence on manual driving reassured him, as if she too inherently mistrusted automation despite, or because of, her long years of service. She had not spoken much since they had left the Aront Tier. Dumortier assumed she was deep in analysis, turning the encounter over in her mind.

After fifteen minutes of driving, she said, "I, too, need a diversion."

"All right." Dumortier checked the time; seven hours to the next Shineshift. Both of them could use an hour or two of decompression after meeting the Aronts.

"I want you to see something. For and with me."

"Regarding the case?"

"Indirectly, yes. But it's strictly off-record."

"Why?"

"It also concerns an event before your time. Come with me to the new monument."

"Let's go," said Dumortier. SeForTecs were privy to all sorts of information and his curiosity trumped his need for decompression.

He talked to fill the silence as Nadira drove. "Cabuchon used to hold military parades every year during the Festival of Gachala. Troops, banners and vehicles streaming along the avenue. And then they stopped after the Downturn. Poor taste, they said. I say there was not enough uta."

"There's enough uta these days," Nadira said. "Just not from Cabuchon."

"Which annoys them to no end. I wonder if they'll feel the need to restart the parades, to remind us that Cabuchon commands more than enough Tagmat regiments and firepower to handle the alien thugs who kidnapped and murdered forty miners."

Constabulary clearance got them nearer to the construction site of the monument than the other vehicles on the avenue. Nadira eased the Shirpen towards four looming shapes draped in swathes of heavy duty orange fabric, tied down with an intricate system of cables and pulleys. Under the cloth, they looked like a rock formation tamed by humans. The cloaked structure was illuminated by footlights, even though it was daytime.

Dumortier had never seen the intended monument at ground level. In truth, without the grandeur granted by wide-angle hummingbird drone shots, it was underwhelming. Were they obelisks, needles or shafts piercing the clouds, or hulking monoliths? All would be revealed on the big day.

He picked out a wide area beneath the shortest shape, covered by more orange fabric, and guessed it was marking out a new plaza on top of a subterranean mall. Nadira offered to show him the artist's impression, but he declined, already seeing in his mind's eye the plaza lined with meteorite terrazzo, victory cedars and geometric sculptures. The space could be put to better use.

She circled the construction site and guided the Shirpen to a purring stop beneath the largest shape. A strong breeze made the draped fabrics flutter: the diamond of the Aront corporate logo was emblazoned on them.

"This, right here, is the site of the first landing."

"But isn't this the Monument To The Forty Miners?"

Nadira shook her head. "It is—it'll be dedicated to the Forty—but something else happened on this site."

"I didn't know your ascendants go back that far."

"Farther back—and I'm not referring to the pacts signed by all systems."

"The Corundum's establishment?"

"No."

Much farther back? Dumortier tried to visualise a planetoid orbiting Gachala over seventy years ago. A threadbare atmosphere and desolate landscape before the terraformers and atmospheric processors did their work. A large ship, in his imagination, an old Terran System workhorse. And it had landed on a regolith-strewn planetary surface...

Whistling in disbelief, he said the name of the ship very slowly. "*The Thousand Echoes*?"

Dumortier had a detailed knowledge of Archer's Ring history drummed into him during his time at the academy. Why had Chatoyance greenlit the private construction of a monument *here*?

The site might be undergoing rehabilitation, but this did not mean that the event itself had been cancelled. Far from it. If tragedies arose from misfortune, how pernicious misfortune must be, and how capricious. Well beyond the power of Gachala to intervene. So the memory of such events, past and recent, must be combined, and their histories eternally commemorated but also warned against.

"It's surreal for me to hear you say that name," said Nadira. "I've only ever said it to myself all this time. But... yes. The first ever landing on this rock was a crash landing, back when Chatoyance was still an exploratory outpost."

Dumortier replied, "I didn't know—no one does, not even now—about how exactly *The Thousand Echoes* met its end."

"You could have. It was made known via the Open Information Act, a few years ago. It didn't really make the headlines. But no, up till then, no one knew it was a crash landing."

"Chatoyance and Cabuchon were founded on an accident." Dumortier nodded slowly at the monument in progress. "That makes perfect but unbelievable sense."

"Significant pieces of the original wreckage were salvaged at the time. Fuselage, and parts from the bridge. I believe it has already been commemorated in the monument." She pointed at the largest draped installation. "I'm guessing in there. Maybe it's going to be preserved in synthamber."

"And your descendants?" asked Dumortier. "Where are they? Do they know about the monument?"

"I can't speak for them, because I have none."

He waited for Nadira to elaborate further. When he realised she was not going to, he said, "I think I can understand how that came to be."

"No, you don't."

Dumortier flinched in his seat: not at Nadira's tone of

voice, but from the emotion in it. "I'm sorry," he began. "I shouldn't have assumed things."

"Forget that. What difference does it make?" Nadira sighed. "I never wanted to be singled out as a poor child of Archer's Ring history. I'll leave my SeForTec work as my legacy."

"Memory is a very tricky beast. But you don't need me to remind you of that."

"It traps you," replied Nadira. "Or it releases you. The vital question for my colleagues—past and present—and me is, is it worse to be haunted by something you remember, or by something you don't?"

"Which one is it for you?"

"Neither. I stay out of memory's reach."

Nadira restarted the Shirpen and drove away at slightly over the speed limit. A warning light flashed orange on the windscreen. Dumortier wanted to ask whether SeForTec clearance extended to traffic regulations, but let the question die in his throat when he saw the intense look on her face.

A glowing red dot replaced the orange onscreen, and this one was definitely not meant to be ignored.

"SeForTec Morad LN/Gaspard here. Come in."

"Incident in Southwest Sector. Code 10."

Code 10: bomb detonated. Dumortier reached out to access relevant transmissions, but Nadira was quicker than him. With a few more saccades she accessed the satellite map of Southwest Sector, with a bright white dot marking the site.

"Dry Market, how typical," said Dumortier.

"You two are the closest personnel we have. Dispatch over and out."

"What's going on?" Dumortier asked as he put the Shirpen into autodrive. "Gia Aront dies, we go up to the Tiers and the city below starts falling apart."

The highlights would be going crazy with this. Dumortier wondered how the T-Car network would cope.

"Connective tissue," replied Nadira. "It's inflamed and now demands our urgent attention."

"I hope you're wrong—this time."

"Same here."

# CHAPTER TWENTY-ONE

CHARRED SUGAR, CHEAP oil, frying dough, and synthetic vanilla overpowering burnt coffee—thanks to this olfactory melange, Marsh had located the DryWare Market without much difficulty. He avoided Constabulary presence on the T-Cars by taking the footpath running alongside The Canal That Quenches All Thirst until his nanoapartment block had shrunk to obscurity. Ten minutes after crossing the canal lock, he entered the southwestern sector of Chatoyance where the streets were less of a network and more like clusters of knots, like obscure botanical structures.

Faced with such organic disarray, he let his nose and ears guide him.

The aromas wafting around the DryWare Market camouflaged its nature and purpose. The hungry would stop for a bite and not venture farther until Shineshift or the traders packed up and moved on; or the smells would induce nausea in the desperate who already lacked appetite.

Marsh was neither hungry nor desperate, but tamping down on a rising anxiety. There was safety in the DryWare Market, but only to a degree. He was what marketspeak called "Devoid"—of implants and augmentations. Thus he was not worth the effort to extract or cut implants and tools out of him unless he wandered too far west, into the WetWare Market. The forcep was wrapped in a sheaf of sterile first-aid foam, strapped to his left forearm and covered by his sleeve. His push dagger was sheathed in his other sleeve. Despite the layers of concealment, he still felt like the forcep was giving off heat. He had to remind himself to walk like he was carrying nothing of value.

The crowd retained their cohesion around him. It was mid-morning, and still possible to navigate the wide street without brushing against another person. A few people scurried around hoisting poles across their shoulders, setting up makeshift stalls. Traders kept to themselves and none of them looked directly at one another unless it was necessary. Marsh took this as a positive sign: Wet and DryWare vendors relied on networks of informants. No recent news or scrutiny from guards or Constabulary had tipped them off—yet.

DryWare was well-adapted to the fluidity of demand and supply; with almost no organic detritus to clean up its activity was less fraught. The arrangement and layouts of WetWare and DryWare stalls changed at random after each Shineshift. If he missed a given vendor today, he could have to wait for another week or month.

"You buying or selling?"

"Looking for a friend," lied Marsh.

Chit-chat was more than a standard opening: it allowed both parties to size each other up. The trader chewed on his lower lip while he shoved a sleeved hand inside his jacket. The treated red leather garment was bartered or stolen—more likely stolen, as the fine tailoring was at least two sizes too big for him. Marsh saw the trader's fingers pat an object under the fabric.

"Hey, don't you think it's too early in the trading day for that?" Marsh protested, raising his hands.

The trader scowled back at him and removed his closed hand from inside his jacket. Marsh saw the filament wiring of a small comms device poking out from between his fingers.

Shouts erupted from the street up ahead, warning everyone to run away *now*. He started back the way he came, briefly considering selling one of his eyes at WetWare because it'd be less trouble.

Double explosions, one after the other, almost festive in their brevity, as though the sound were cut off. As the screaming started and people scattered, Marsh threw himself to the ground between two stalls, covering his head with his jacket. Pyrotechnic flashes lit up the inside of his eyelids. He recalled an instruction from a security drill: When you suspect the use of an unconventional incendiary device and are unable to get to a safe distance or area, protect your eyes and ears and hold your breath.

Someone must have followed him or knew he was coming. But it made little sense to create a disruption like this to get a hold of him. Maybe, this morning, he was just unlucky; getting caught in a flare-up of gang rivalry, a turf war spilling over. Minutes passed, until Marsh's knees and elbows ached from lying facedown on the street, and voices started to rise around him. He uncovered his head and was relieved that his ears were not ringing. He sniffed the air and blinked; at least the perpetrators had not used toxic gas.

"Urtic!" The word cut through the commotion, generating more outrage than fear. Cursing followed, soiling the air around him in multiple languages. "Two devices!"

Trichome bombs modelled on plant seed distribution; that explained the short pops. Fine needles—urtic—or scales were expelled from a metal casing all around. Once, a trichome had been set off outside a school back on Cabuchon: Not as large scale as a conventional bomb, but definitely as nasty. There were some lines even the DryWare and WetWare gangs did not cross during their turf wars.

Another voice asked, "Who did this?"

"Scum who want to shut the Cat's Eye for ever," replied a woman's voice muffled by an air filter. "It's all falling apart as I speak. And it's about time, if you ask me."

"No one's asking you," rejoined another woman, and Marsh heard her mutter, "Gachala's teeth, these doomsayers are everywhere all of a sudden."

Encouraged by the commotion, he staggered upright and stumbled out of the alley, hesitating before he stepped back into the market. People hurled crates and containers onto transports, tents and stalls dismantled in anticipation of pacification and clean-up drones. They would fly in along with their Constabulary handlers, and seal off the area before the trading day was over

Countless tiny pits had been blasted out of the street, scattering fragments of stone in a rough torus. Stink of burnt almonds and tar. Marsh saw sunlight glinting off urtic needles embedded in the wall behind him and in the discarded plastic sheets used to cover merchandise. Five bystanders sat on the ground tending to the injured, two of whom had lacerations across their faces.

"—Should we move them?"

"—Can you walk?"

A rough hand grabbed his elbow and spun Marsh around. "You a medic?"

The hand's owner was a burly man in clothes dusted with pulverised street and sporting a bleeding nose. Marsh jerked away from his grip. "No, I'm actually—"

"Out of the way, then! They need help, not an audience!"

He made his way out of the range of the bomb and further into the market. The stalls were less densely packed at the end of the narrow lanes, and beggars, with their trademark silver scarves over their mouths, gathered in the cul-de-sacs beyond them. Men and women hawked assorted scraps of discarded technology and vehicle components arranged on mats. Marsh recognised prosthetics improvised from spare parts, broken handrails and stanchions from T-Cars bundled together and stacked like the gathering of a surreal harvest. The ibis head of a sentry turnstile, now retrofitted as an empty-eyed desk ornament, lay next to a set of brass measuring scales.

He sensed that they were exaggerating their business-as-usual demeanours after the bombing.

"Heard you're looking for your friend?"

A woman and a girl seated under a wall covered with cracked plate glass and disused signage.

The question did not surprise Marsh: it really had been a comms device inside the trader's jacket.

"Looking for something *for* a friend."

"Nothing here catches your eye?" She waved her hand over the wares and sounded insulted at his indifference.

Might as well be direct. He didn't want to get corralled by arriving officers and cleanup crews. "My friend requires a valuation."

"Of what?"

"A procured item."

"Procured by what means?"

"It was an accident." Marsh hoped the truth was sufficiently convincing for her.

"Size?"

Marsh held the tips of his thumb and forefinger ten centimetres apart.

"Provenance?"

"The serial number is embedded in the item." It was the truth.

"If it's biological, you're really in the wrong place." She waved in the general direction of Wetware.

"It's not purely biological."

"Put the item in here."

With her curiosity sufficiently piqued, the woman held out her arm for Marsh to slip his hand inside the long grubby sleeve of her coat. Sensing a scam—or, worse, a trap for severing limbs—he backed away.

The woman burst out laughing.

"He thinks something will bite off his hand." She nudged her neighbour in the side, a girl with a smudged face swathed in a cloak of faded red wool over a brown slacken vest, who was not listening in particular. "Relax, my dear, I don't want it, you're not in WetWare. Whatever you're carrying, you need the Arcades."

Marsh swore and went back to the thoroughfare. He ducked behind a discarded water tanker, where he heard the squawking of headsets. Glimpsing a pair of Constabulary indigo uniforms up ahead, he remained crouched. The narrow streets and lanes did not permit access to Shirpens, but the uniforms were trickling in, precursors to the cleanup crew.

An unexpected draft kicked up and blew cool musty air from behind him. He turned around and found what he had mistaken for a doorway was in fact a parabolic archway sealed up by hoarding: the expensive camouflage kind used by Chatoyance Municipal that mimicked various types of walls. Red light glowed in the gap beneath the hoarding. He pushed on the edge of the weathered panel and peered through the gap. Daylight from the street skimmed over a row of arches, identical to the one outside, and a mosaic floor in a faded pink and black.

It was old, and built to a still-older design, a nod to nostalgia. Marsh let the section of panel fall back into place, as if he was guarding a newfound secret.

The woman and the girl had followed him out of the narrow lane and were edging towards him, more curious than suspicious. Marsh could feel them willing him to step inside, almost pressing on his back.

The evaluators who worked in the Arcades were in there, behind the hoarding: it was the only explanation for their behaviour. For a moment he found himself wishing he was back behind the faulty crowning-shield of the display counter, picking at pomegranate seeds.

His ticket off Chatoyance was not in Retail Sector 12. It might yet be found in the Arcades.

# CHAPTER TWENTY-TWO

HARD CURRENCY BLOCKS exist for only one reason.

Pleo heard this reason through the walls—a group session in rowdy progress a few rooms away, while the ventilation system laboured to remove the olfactory evidence.

In damp clothes still reeking of canal water, she stood in Gia's rented room in the hard currency block, taking it in with a newly dispassionate eye, although she had been here before. Conditions were better than in her room in the Polyteknical accommodation node: the plumbing worked, and the sound insulation and carpet were replaced on a regular basis. Maintenance happened; the room was still registered under whatever alias Gia Aront had been using. Rent was directly debited until Gia's trust fund ran out or was withdrawn, which meant not soon. Pleo could lie low here for now. In an unexpected turn of events, Gia's patronage of this block vouched for Pleo's refuge. But even now, Pleo was uneasy. The room had been unused for a fortnight—much too long for a hard currency block.

Three high-backed white leather chairs faced the bed in an interrogatory arrangement. The bed saw little signs of wear and tear. It was new although expensive to replace, being of the type that had no legs; its only means of support was a chromed platform fixed to a bulky headboard, giving the illusion that the bed was floating. The occupants, whether sleeping or having sex, were above the floor and dirt in all senses.

Someone born into that much wealth possessed a measure of entrepreneurial sense by default. How exactly Gia had channeled this know-how, Pleo had decided, was none of her business. But the thrill of slumming it must have worn thin very early on. Pleo wondered when Gia had realised that more visceral kicks arose from how dangerously close both of her existences—Aront scion and sub-letter—came to colliding.

And the collision had finally happened when Pleo followed Gia to the hard currency block.

After their spat outside the fla-tessen hall, in front of the mural of Ignazia Madrugal, Pleo had spotted Gia scurrying out of a Polyteknical side door in an asymmetrical black coat and matching boots. Gia was heading towards Polyteknical Station without her security detail, an air filter mask strapped over her mouth. It was uncanny how Pleo had almost missed her: Gia had effortlessly shed her Tier Dweller persona, leaving it in the fla-tessen hall changing rooms. Pleo imagined a translucent moult of

Gia's skin, rolled up and wedged behind the basins, to be retrieved the next day.

A minute later Pleo was tailing Gia as she crossed the bustling concourse of Polyteknical Station. She had thrust her fists into her coat pockets while busily skirting the rank of sentry turnstiles. Pleo kept track, noting that Gia paced back and forth five times as though she was bargaining with the turnstiles, or she didn't know how to take a T-Car. Finally, Gia had reached a decision, pulling a string of fare tokens out of her coat pocket and striding through. Pleo hung back and pretended to study a map of the T-Car network. She let Gia go up to the platform, keeping a distance of twenty metres.

Naturally Pleo had assumed Dogtooths relayed Gia back to her home at the end of a long day in Polyteknical: any Aront offspring would not be slumming it with the riff-raff in the downmarket accommodation nodes. Maybe she found riding a T-Car without trailing a squad of Dogtooths a thrill in itself? Nothing scandalous about that, only foolhardy, but if she rode the T-Car past the 'Cinth and into Exterior Zone 1 she would be tempting fate.

Pleo's curiosity faded when both of them boarded the next T-Car stopping at the platform. She decided to get off at the 'Cinth if Gia did the same. Both of them could lose each other there and Gia would never need to know she had been tailed.

The T-Car had been delayed for a full ten minutes at the 'Cinth before continuing eastwards away from the central zones of Chatoyance. Gia remained in her seat while Pleo swore into her air filter mask, pleading with the idiot Tier Dweller to get off when she still could.

Six stations later Gia stepped down onto the platform of Canal Mouth.

Pleo would have had no reason to stop here; Gia even less so. Canal Mouth was a planned commercial hub that turned out to be an expensive failure. No advertisements overloaded the senses here, selling hair and beauty products or real estate on Cabuchon or Anium—only enclosures of corrugated metal and bare walls. It was not a sector to visit or select from the T-Car map unless you had a good reason. Clusters of vacant purpose-built blocks and warehouses had already attracted businesses of a different sort. The streets still gave off an air of expectancy despite the dead leaves and dogshit piles scattered on the footpaths.

Gia kept to the edge of one of these paths. Pleo gave her due credit for her street smarts. It was obvious Gia was accustomed to being followed—by potential kidnappers, corporate spies, reporters—and Pleo had cast herself in a similar yet undefined role. Gia showed no sign that she knew she was being tailed. Just in case, Pleo followed a footpath to the disused loading bay of the nearest warehouse and watched her from the doorway.

Gia headed for a building that was more glass than walls, supported by interior steel columns. Pleo waited until she went inside before slipping away from her hiding position. She had never been to a hard currency block before, but she recognised the trademark washed-out taupe of the entry steps and door; she didn't know whether to be amused or dismayed that the colour actually matched the taupe of low-intermediary fla-tessen shifts. The paint job was recent, judging by the lingering smell. From the outside, the repurposed office was sterile, unremarkable and, most importantly, anonymous.

She had pushed open the narrow door, expecting bells to ring, garish signs and tattooed thugs barring her entry. Instead an empty lobby, dimly lit by multicoloured lights in the floor, greeted her; and instead of transactional seediness, Pleo saw disuse running its course. In more prosperous pre-Downturn times, there would have been a virtual night manager stationed in front of the panelscreens, and the fountain in the reception area bubbling with dyed water. Now it was dry and filled with detritus.

Gia had disappeared around the panelsceen wall, its dozen inactive glass displays capturing her reflection for an instant. Pleo followed her up a short flight of stairs to an adjoining atrium.

It had been like entering a different realm. Pleo looked up at a dozen chandeliers suspended above the spiral glass staircase, all swaying like giant jellyfish tentacles. Daylight was diffused through a grimy stained-glass roof, built to scroll aside when the weather was good. The scoured synthmarble floor was typical of a place which had changed hands many times, each owner becoming less dedicated to upkeep than the last. The harsh administrative lighting made Pleo feel like she was here to get her off-system visa renewed.

A man and a woman, both clad in shapeless brown faux-suede raincoats, had emerged behind her from the gloom of the lobby. They brushed past Pleo and stopped at a fallen chandelier lying at the foot of the spiral staircase. The man reached out and broke a prism off the ruined fixture, perhaps as a way of recording his anonymous visit for the hard currency block's unseen landlords. Pleo noticed that the chandelier had been stripped of half its crystals and bulbs.

She sat on the bottom step and watched the couple disappear up the stairs. She wondered how long she could sit there without anyone noticing, and to see how hard currency block users and tenants conducted their business.

Laughter drifted down from several floors above, and Pleo recognised the lone familiar voice. Her feet crushed shards of glass as she broke off a prism from the chandelier like the couple had done. As an afterthought, she took another one. It made sense to act like she was more than a regular visitor and the extra prism would make a handy weapon.

She went up the stairs, stopping at each floor. The rooms were arranged in narrow corridors encircling the atrium. The laughter waned but did not die down, drawing her nearer and nearer.

Pleo reached the top floor; the glass roof was more forlorn and dirtier than it had looked from lobby level. Dust, feathers and birdshit smeared the other side of the cracked glass. She set off down the corridor, certain Gia was here. The uppermost floors of most accomodation usually had the best views and most expensive rooms.

Pleo had walked the entire length of the corridor. Most of the doors to the other rooms were kicked in, but one unbroken door had broken prisms piled up outside it. Sounds of furniture moving around mingled with the laughter. She waited, expecting the start of or the conclusion to some debauchery: however, the noises persisted. Pleo didn't find any markings on the door or prisms, and took a wild guess at the security gesture by dropping the broken prism on top of the pile with its siblings. It made a loud clink, and by some crude mechanism the door opened with a drawn-out *click*.

Pleo peered through the gap at the spectacle of Gia Aront putting the room in order. She ran a fingertip over the backs of the chairs to check for dust, her brow furrowed in concentration as if a lab session was in full swing. It was absurd and yet plausible that Gia Aront's life was so cosseted that she had found tidying up a joyous novelty. And that she had to do it in the last place her parents would expect of their only child.

She appeared blissfully ensconced in her own contented bubble. It would be a shame if Pleo punctured it by announcing her arrival.

"Ant."

Without looking up from her task, Gia had casually tossed the word at Pleo by way of greeting.

Fatigued and not prepared to take offence, Pleo sucked on her teeth and turned around to go back down the stairs.

"Wait, wait. You came here alone?" Gia called after her, too quickly, sounding like an apology—as though that word had slipped out due to force of habit. But she remained calm, perhaps relieved and perversely elated at being discovered. "Do what you have to now, make it quick and clean."

"What?"

"You're in the best place to kill me. It's convenient."

Pleo had frozen for a dangerous moment, recalling those mornings on the T-Cars when she went through every fantasy about revenge she ever had since Cerussa died. A few of them involved Gia Aront. There had been talk behind closed doors of retaliation, a fantasy briefly held by the children of the Forty after the Incident. *They knew the risk and let our loved ones die. Their lives for our lives.*

"'Convenient'?" repeated Pleo as if it was the most ridiculous of concepts. The word struck her as redundant. Wasn't Gia's entire life all about convenience? The notion incensed Pleo; how Gia could entertain the thought of her death as a mental exercise? Or on her own terms, as if it was a simple transaction.

"No surveillance inside the private rooms, considerable foot traffic and frequent guest turnover—"

"Ahh," Pleo interrupted. Her fury garbled her voice as she imitated a tabloid newsreader. "'How far will Gia Aront go this week for her kicks? Try: Murder in a Hard Currency Block! Because the wealthier you are, the closer you have to get to the edge for your thrills.'"

Gia blinked and sat on the bed, unprepared for Pleo's vehemence. But there was more in store.

"Kill *yourself*, Aront bitch. Do your own dirty work for once!" Pleo hurled the second chandelier prism at Gia with surprising precision, nearly slicing off her nose and sticking in the headboard. Gia's Adept reflexes had just saved her from disfigurement. Pleo was relieved she had missed, but her anger remained unabated. "Use that. Or I suggest using your forceps to join the Nosebleed club with my sister, but it's probably not *exclusive* enough for you."

"Come in, now. The whole of Canal Mouth heard you," Gia snapped as she got up from the bed. She dragged Pleo into the room and slammed the door.

"I'm no killer," Pleo said.

"If you tried you'd make prisoners of both us. I'd never leave my Tier again, and as for you..." Gia trailed off and left Pleo's fate up in the air. She slumped into one of the three chairs that faced the bed.

Silence fell between them for a while. Pleo's mouth was dry after her outburst. She coughed, ready for the bile still churning in her guts to spew forth again.

"Have you been inside a hydrocarbon mine?" asked Gia, with sudden bright eager curiosity.

"People don't go for the scenery. My sister and I were born in one," Pleo snapped. "No gemstones, only layers of stinking flammable gas compressed by time and gravity. No sparkle, no glitter. People actually die in them."

*Mining scum*, Pleo recalled Gia's words. Who are still living in boxes because they had travelled like cargo. Successive waves of settlers' vessels who opted for the one-way ticket to work in terraforming and mining. Descend into an asteroid hydrocarbon mineshaft and crawl out with crushed dreams.

"I'm aware."

"That people die in mines?"

Gia ignored Pleo's sarcasm and rose from the chair. "You and Cerussa were twins."

"And?"

"I, too, have a twin," she said after some hesitation.

Pleo stepped back in surprise, stumbling into the chairs. Everyone thought Gia was an only child.

"Break one of these chairs and you have to pay for it," said Gia, a second before forcing a laugh and rolling her eyes at Pleo. "Oh, look at your *face!* Sit down. You couldn't afford it anyway. Spit on the chairs if you want— they cost me nothing. The Aront Tier is overflowing with stuff like that."

Pleo's legs sighed in relief after walking for so long. Still reeling from Gia's revelation she managed to ask, "Your twin brother? Sister? Where are they?"

"Oh, he's with me, right inside the bathroom."

Pleo studied the closed bathroom door next to the bed. If anyone was behind it, she preferred them to stay put. Let them listen, she couldn't have handled any more disruption.

"What's his name?"

"It doesn't matter, because he doesn't matter enough to my parents." Gia was holding back, and Pleo wasn't sure whether it was tears or anger. For all the attempted bravado in her voice, her emotions were clear. "When I turned eighteen I stopped being their beloved child—I turned into an inconvenience. My mother's words exactly, along with 'wasted chance.'"

"What did you do?"

"I tried to run away."

"No, I mean, what happened?" Pleo asked. "Why the sudden change in affection?"

Gia raised a perfectly tweezed eyebrow and tsked at her. *Can you be less obvious?* "In the beginning I just ran 'away.' Away from the Aront Tier, from everyone connected with my parents. From my whole cherished existence."

"You still have the means to go anywhere off system," Pleo had reminded her.

"Only on a very long leash."

"Cut yourself off from your family."

Gia fell back on the bed and sighed. "My parents' empire is quicksand. It's *everywhere,* and it all looks like solid ground until you step in it. "

Pleo sucked in her cheeks in mock sympathy. "Freedom. The one thing Gia Aront can't buy."

"Then what would you do—" Gia did not say the second part of the question but Pleo heard it inside her head: *...if you were me?*

Pleo didn't answer that because she could never imagine herself as Gia Aront. "You expect a presentation on how awful the rest of the world is off your Tier?"

"I don't need it." Gia stretched her arms and legs out on the bed. Her bravado had returned. "This place has given me a great view. You can have a genuine conversation here, just like I'm having now. You can have a tryst. Or inject, inhale or shove any shit or drugs into your preferred orifice. I needed to capture that pulse—the Tiers lack so much pulse they're on life support."

"And what does your twin brother think about all of

this?" Pleo indicated the bathroom.

"Nothing," shrugged Gia. "You'd think my parents would be happy that I'd shown initiative and found my own income stream."

"Not what I expected—"

"Everyone says that." She sighed. "It's not 'respectable,' according to them."

"It isn't," Pleo said.

"Too bad it upsets them when I dispense with pretensions of respectability. They think I'm acting out. But for people who love boasting about their 'vision,' they're so shortsighted. I'm merely filling in a niche."

"The clientele who come here; what're they into?"

"Letting off steam. Nothing too deviant or rough."

"Guess that rules you out?"

Gia ignored the jibe. "They can't afford bruises and bites showing on their faces or necks. Or to change or dirty their uniforms too often. And they can't stay long, since they're all on the clock."

"You're talking about your House Guards?"

Gia smirked without mirth. "*All* House Guards: Madrugal, Cizen, Oslis... Even an occasional off-duty Spinel."

"You like watching them?"

"I like to pretend certain people are watching." Gia lifted her head from the bed to look at Pleo. "Three chairs: two for my parents and an extra for a 'friend of the family.' There's always a 'friend of the family' hovering around my home. Attaching themselves onto my parents like barnacles until another one with greater sucking power comes along and dislodges them. Shitty judges of character—both of them."

Pleo felt their presence now: in the over-dismissive tone Gia used, watching their daughter confide in the unlikeliest of people. She wasn't sure what to say, and they sat in silence.

Eventually, Gia said, "A few days ago I received this. One of my mother's personal guards delivered it to me at Polyteknical."

A flower made of dogs claws. Tacky and in bad taste, but Pleo did not understand.

"A message from my mother," Gia told her.

"She sent you this trinket? It's like her idea of a birthday gift?"

"It means I don't have much time. And I don't know if I can run again. You don't know my mother. Be glad you don't."

Pleo shifted in the chair and tried to think of what to say.

"You can make use of this room when I'm gone," Gia said. "The rent on it has been paid for a while."

"I can't accept it."

Gia got up from the bed and looked as though she wanted to hug Pleo. Instead she stood in front of the three chairs.

"Understand, Tanza," she began. "What has happened here between us changes nothing."

"I wasn't expecting any different."

"Indeed. When we next meet in Polyteknical I'll make your time there harder. Understand again, it's necessary;

if anyone in Polyteknical sees us getting too close, my secret here is out. My life is already at risk. You were never supposed to be involved."

INCLUDE ME WITH *your parents for misjudging you,* thought Pleo. She recalled her outbursts at Gia with regret. One never sets out to become a killer—and just like sex, you never forget your first one.

And the parents of Pleo's first kill weren't going to forget about her either.

She pulled the prism out of the headboard and looked at the bathroom door. There was something about the way Gia spoke about her twin brother, dancing on the edge of past tense. There was no one in the bathroom right now, but yet something had to be there. The thought nagged and pestered at her until she could stand it no longer.

# CHAPTER TWENTY-THREE

*HERE'S A MAN who enjoys playing god too much.*

Moonlight and the perfume of jasmine—the garden inside the Madrugal Tier gave off the illusion of a courtyard. Saurebaras watched Madrugal rearrange the Archer's Ring in a sand garden the length and breadth of Polyteknical's driveway. She doubted if he or the late Ignazia had been religious, or even remotely spiritual, but she could not deny the serene order he brought to his creation, a spiral of fine black sand bordered by white pebbles. A polished boulder was half buried in the centre of the spiral. This represented Gachala, and the moss covering the rock approximated the sun's hue, depending on Cabuchon's atmospheric conditions.

Spreading out from the boulder and placed at regular intervals were the other settlements and bodies in orbit. A rough crescent-shaped block of sandstone was Tahel, but did no justice to the streamlined parabola visible on a clear night. On the neighbouring spiral arm lay four rhodochrosite spheres arranged in a square: Synarc, a Tagmat military complex of interlinked bases.

In an inspired improvisation, Madrugal had used quartz pellets for the Demarcation, ever-shifting in its distribution according to the defence of the Archer's Ring.

She stumbled across a violet sphere of amethyst under a bougainvillea bush.

"You've found the Archives!"

A servitor rolled towards the bush, extracted the sphere and restored it to its rightful place. Purple to represent knowledge, and there was plenty of that in the Archives, a repository housed in a hollowed-out moon.

"Could you entertain a personal request?"

"It depends."

"I'm expecting visitors tomorrow night. You'd do me an honour if you danced for them."

"That was my previous life, which ended yesterday."

"But that was only yesterday."

"Yesterday's gone, along with everything else," insisted Saurebaras.

Madrugal scratched his chin thoughtfully. "By next week it'll indeed become your previous life. Indulge me— in Ignazia's memory and for old times' sake?"

"You invite the wrath of the Aronts by letting me stay here."

Madrugal laughed. "Let's pray they're *that* stupid to break the accord. My Sarisses haven't seen action for a while. Here comes one now for a little demonstration."

The Sarisse guard wore moss-green armour trimmed with black.

"Slice the armour," Madrugal told Saurebaras.

She opened a concealed pocket in her skirt and took out her caltrop, and swiped at the guard's chest. Slivers of armour fell away, but the armour was already healing itself.

"This looks like skin." Saurebaras examined the slivers on her caltrop. They fell to the grass like shaved mica.

"Skin is the first armour we wear." Madrugal beamed as he dismissed the guard.

"You'll tell that to your investors?"

"From the outset. The wearer suffers minimal damage when the fibres slough off. Physical force is neutralised or dissipated. Plus, there's almost instantaneous regeneration provided at least eighty percent of the armour is still intact." He coughed. "So, may I repeat my request? Please dance for my guests tomorrow night?"

Refreshed by the calm surroundings, Saurebaras agreed. The Madrugal Tier seemed to have shed its claustrophobic feel since Ignazia had died, and she didn't want to think about next week or month.

He left her in the garden under a trellis decorated with bamboo and leaping carp motifs. The subtle scent of syringa hanging in the night air was undercut by dessert cubes opening in the warm air, with twig-thin carrots called hairpins piled up in a dish next to the cubes. Saurebaras had never liked the sweet fermented paste mashed out of high yield corn.

She retired to the guest room, the embroidered curtains

now faded. A miniature Gachalan disk rested on the family altar. The red femtopaper cutouts reconfigured themselves into phoenixes, dancing around longevity peaches and dragons clutching fiery pearls.

# CHAPTER TWENTY-FOUR

PLEO OPENED THE bathroom door and peered inside. No one was there. Sink, recessed toilet seat, and tub all done over in fashionable black bonded ceramic. The only incongruity was a small cube sitting in the sink.

Pleo reached in, picked up the cube of synthamber and felt a heavy sense of anticlimax. So much grief over the object suspended within it, an apparently mundane sphere of black rock. Synthamber required a specialised converter and a coded sequence to soften it, but she shook the cube anyway, hoping to dislodge its contents.

Gia had been more arduous than Pleo in trying to make the cube give up its secret. Scuff marks and scratches disfigured one side, blurring the view of the object, and a straight crack stretched uninterrupted from one vertex to the sphere of rock within. She turned the cube over and over in her hands like a child's puzzle.

The crack in the cube drew her attention. It was too

straight and wide. Pleo looked closer, and realised Gia had tried to drill through the cube at some point with a large bit. But... if the cube could be scratched, the sythamber could only be imitation. Theory class had taught Pleo that only Constabulary had access to the real stuff. It was durable, but not impenetrable.

Pleo tried the glasscutter-configuration with her forceps, but only succeeded in adding to the tableau of scratches.

She inserted her ring-finger forcep into the hole starting at one of the cube's vertices and pushed through a few millimetres at a time. It was not easy: the hole was coarse and uneven. After an impatient five minutes, the tip of her forcep flicked against the black sphere.

Shock and disbelief at what she detected almost made Pleo drop the cube. She held on and inserted the forcep again.

*Carbon, calcium, keratin... iron.*

Keratin meant the sphere contained vestiges of skin, hair and nails. Iron was present because there were traces of blood.

*My brother is in the bathroom.*

Gorgons turned people to stone, according to ancient myth.

Matriarch Aront had had one of her *children* turned to stone.

Creating memorial gems out of cremated remains was a common practice, but miners shunned it. Expense was no barrier, wearing them on one's person was seen as morbid.

Pleo took a deep breath and put the cube on a nearby shelf. Then she sat on the cleanest area of bathroom floor, thinking about how Gia Aront must have felt at this discovery. Everything rushing away, all vestiges of her existence breaking up. Her vision clouded over with tears. It occurred to Pleo that Gia could have tried to destroy the cube and its contents, and then had second thoughts.

What had Gia done—what was she going to do—with such terrible, dangerous knowledge? Pile dirt onto her parents' reputation? Not that it mattered now, since she was dead.

And Pleo was going to end up like her soon if she did not make a move.

She was certain of one thing. The cube and its contents were coming with her.

Pleo took off her canal-soaked clothes and found a clean set stashed under the sink, along with a sling bag of expensive black leather and the asymmetrical black coat; they had all belonged to Gia. The stiff black sheath dress came up to Pleo's knees: Gia had been shorter than Pleo. The sling bag contained a week's worth of fare tokens and a thick roll of uta.

Then she opened the door of the room and checked the outside corridor. The coast was clear. Pleo ran down the stairs and into the empty lobby, on the lookout for Dogtooths.

Waiting at the bottom of the stairs was a hooded figure.

Pleo stopped in her tracks. *Not again.*

She screamed at it, "You're not Ceri!"

# CHAPTER TWENTY-FIVE

RETAIL ARCADES ON Chatoyance were once built to recreate the womb.

Marsh stepped inside and looked ahead as the hoarding snapped shut behind him. An empty street-within-a-street lay before him. There were various similar projects back on Cabuchon—self-contained and sealed off streets for the elite to wander down and play the flaneur. He was now walking in the idea's failure on Chatoyance. Piles of mortar, steel reinforcement rods and sheet glass lay on both sides of the street.

Something fluttered on the nearest pile of steel rods: an outdated highlight, stirred by the air circulating inside. He picked it up and wondered why it had not already dissolved years ago. Maybe it was made from a substance more durable than insect silk. He read the faded words: *Stop Work Order. Korbuhauss Incorporated.* He recognised the name from Cabuchon. Worse than being within an idea's failure, he was walking in the aftermath of a family's failure.

Something flew past his head, a flash of white against the dimness, and an object landed on the hoarding. It was light and yet it shook the boards. It was also sharp, aerodynamic and lethally star-shaped. But it had missed him.

When he looked back, three hooded figures stood before him on the street.

"State your purpose here before I give you another star," said the centre figure in a woman's voice.

"I need an evaluation," he said to the trio.

"Of what?"

Marsh decided it was better now than later. He took Pleo's forcep out of the sheath strapped to his arm.

"Gachala's teeth," exclaimed the centre figure. "Finally. We were concerned that our diversion had worked too well."

"Killing innocent people in DryWare?" Marsh asked in utter disgust.

"They are not harmed severely. Urtic from trichome bombs dissolves quickly—or is absorbed by the body."

"Wait, who are you?"

The centre and left-hand figures removed their hoods, to reveal a man and a woman. The man's arm bore the copper bands of a Polyteknical instructor, whereas the woman had a blue veil tucked away from her face.

"We are the Charons. We take the unwanted dead and the Nosebleeds, and give them something better than dignity. We imbue them with new purpose."

"What purpose is that?" Marsh felt uncomfortable all of a sudden. Something strong filled the man's gaze and Marsh was not sure if it was serenity or zeal.

"For our crystalline deities," said the woman with similar intensity.

"A new religion to rival the Temple of Gachala?" Marsh asked. When the couple did not reply, he took a step back towards the broken hoarding, and held Pleo Tanza's forcep up in front of him. "Don't you want this? It's worth something. Consider it my donation to your cause and pretend we never met."

"Keep it," said the man.

"It's your connection to Pleo Tanza we want," said the woman. "She's the fulcrum."

That was accurate. His life had been relatively ordered until she turned up. Chatoyance roiled because of what she was involved in.

"You will hear of us again."

Marsh lifted the boards and left. Daylight and the bustling street stirred his heart, glad to see them after the abandoned gloom of the Arcades.

Excerpts from

# COLLECTED NOTES AND OBSERVATIONS ON GACHALAN DEVOTEES

(Volumes 7-9, Year 3444-3445,
private collection, Temple of Gachala
on Chatoyance Archives)

In acknowledgement of the various religions and beliefs brought over by successive Waves, we remain humble and grateful. Without these faiths we would not exist ourselves.

The Temple does not deny that belief in our Emerald Sun and Shield is a new faith. It is a religion set up by committee, and to fulfill a need. Our aims and motivations are continually questioned, but we believe it is vital in these troubled times to rise to the challenge of being more than just a spiritual palliative.

Our practice is kept simple by including the following rules:

First, no birthdays of deities to commemorate. Multitudes of stars are born in fiery splendour across known and unknown space all the time; Gachala is no more special than them.

Second, and by extension, no birthdays of saints are observed, because we do not recognise sainthood when humans possess the potential to transcend sainthood.

Third, our faithful are not compelled to make offerings or donations.

Of late, we Reverend Sisters have noticed a trend in the devotees and visitors to the Temple. More come in greater numbers from Cabuchon to seek out our Sun and Shield, although smaller-scale temples to Gachala were built there before our temple on Chatoyance. We believe our location in the Eye of the Archer's Ring contributes to and enhances the Temple's accessibility and importance as a religious site.

We would be glad of this upsurge under normal circumstances.

But all the Cabuchoners come with the same story.

They speak of the Artisans, telling a tale all heard in childhood. Of how humans overthrew Artisan overseers and fled into deep space. As if brought in by a collective impulse, they ask the nuns if this story has any historical basis, because of the recent events on Kerte Yurgi.

We tell them such a story arose from the need to make sense of or cope with the turbulence that arose during the early years of three systems. We encourage them to gaze skywards to allow the light of Gachala to pierce the shadows of doubt and fear within.

Some resist our advice and even welcome the resurgence of the Artisans. A few have taken our advice too much to heart and broke through the heatshield barrier to the temple courtyard at noon. They wanted Our Emerald Sun and Shield to not only burn away their fears but also their eyes.

An improvised explosive device was found wedged between the ceremonial gongs at the south gate.

The Temple has taken protective measures: we have reinforced the heatshield barrier and Constabulary officers now guard the entrance to the courtyard.

But we try as we might, we cannot reinforce and safeguard the minds of our followers.

## Note

Before her death at the age of 112, Sister Asenju Icro offered her view on the behaviour of the Cabuchon followers and insight into Artisan origins. She was an ex-Tagmat in the Cabuchon military and had seen action against the Artisans during her time.

(Reproduced verbatim from audio of Icro's top secret night lectures, given exclusively to the nuns of the Temple. Original transcript destroyed to safeguard the Temple's security, according to her deathbed request.)

Beauty and brutality... and godlike ancestors. The origins of the Artisans are unknown. Theories abound from many xeno-scientists and study teams in their corresponding xenofields who have examined cadavers and specimens.

But theories are just theories. Thus I'm asking all of you to use your imagination to make sense of them.

Imagine a remnant or an offshoot of an alien species, possibly biologically modified or engineered by another elder alien species. The Artisan homeworld was Earth-like in its geology, as evidenced from the composition of soil samples kept as mementos by inmates at [name redacted] Facility. Carbon, oxygen, nitrogen and hydrogen. A little quartz and feldspar as well.

But why are they humanoid in form and appearance? Xeno-biologists believe this is not evidence of convergent evolution with Terran humans. The Artisans are avatars of another related species in their homeworld, who have been dubbed Overguides, according to the closest translation of their language. These Overguides are dormant subterranean dwellers who have eschewed the burden of individual physical bodies and agendas. They live in city-sized warrens in a kind of hivemind and never emerge, since everything they need is underground.

But emerge they have, in their avatar form, due to human encroachment of their territories. They appear human because they have chosen to do so. Possibly to try and blend in with us for espionage purposes. Perhaps to mock our inferiority to them.

Kerte Yurgi was not humanity's latest encounter with the Artisans. They have hung around the edges of the Kuiper Belt surrounding the old Solar System, watching and biding their time. Fascinated yet provoked by the evolution of humans, they tested the waters by flinging comets into the system, hoping to hit Earth. They did not account for the fortuitous protection of Jupiter's gravitational influences; indeed, they decided Jupiter was the Solar System's first line of defence and retreated in mistaken awe after many failed attempts.

According to xeno-anthropologists, the current Artisans retain none of the godlike technological prowess of their Overguide ancestors, and their present Overguide descendants remain in semi-reclusion underground. The cause of this absence is yet to be established and inmates at [name redacted] Facility were not forthcoming about it. One inmate did make a reference to a geological devastation on the homeworld which nearly destroyed the planet.

This past destruction could explain their expansionist behaviour which, however, is not to be equated with aggression. If they are truly aggressive, we would have been at war before the Downturn. There are small mercies: the Inner Council are in contact with minor dissenter groups within the Artisans who seek to thwart the plans of the majority from succeeding.

It is not known who first coined the name "Artisans." The whimsicality belies the serious observation that *inspired it. Intricate patterns similar to grass script calligraphy were found etched on utensils, and friezes discovered running across sections of cell walls detailing scenes from their mythology.*

*Kerte Yurgi has struck fear into us because it showcases their eons-long patience. Instead of flinging comets at humans, the Artisans have taken the fight to the site of one of our key industries.*

[Audio ends here when the lecture is paused for a recess. The second part of the lecture recording has been lost.]

# CHAPTER TWENTY-SIX

CONSTABULARY FREQUENCIES NEVER failed to surprise Dumortier. Half the time he was surprised they were transmitting at all, and the other half he was surprised he could receive them.

But din, static and chatter were companions to him. Beware of sudden silences. *Loud sounds like explosions are more startling and effective if they're preceded by silence.*

He stood in the middle of DryWare Market, trying to work out when the silence occurred before the trichome bomb had gone off. Had the perpetrators let the tension build, waiting for trading to reach its peak? Or was it fast and brutish? They could have played it either way. It depended on what they wanted to achieve: chaos or distraction.

The bomb cleanup crew were finishing their rounds. There wasn't much else to do after the casualties had been cleared—fourteen of them. Two had lost eyes but the rest were mostly minor injuries. No fatalities. Trichome bombs were more about noise and effect than injury. An old-fashioned nail bomb packed with new organic components, but only harmful to exposed skin.

He examined the pitted section of wall facing him. The blast pattern radiated up and out from ground level in a wide fan shape, and just by studying it he could almost hear the bomb go off. The needle-shaped white urtic had now fallen to the ground and faded to a dull transparency. He granted the bomber full credit for style.

A simple accident during a fla-tessen training session; if only the outcome of this case could be so parochial. He wanted to believe that if it became complicated enough, it'd be taken out of his hands. Now he was nursing some lukewarm algae coffee and a dull headache, along with an ache from his mending hip.

His supervisor at Khrysobe Spaceport would have told him, "Dumortier, yours is a stubbornness I can't dismiss."

Yet he had done so, along with Dumortier.

The Cabuchoner—the cargo squirrel—had come to DryWare, according to the surveillance network along the Canal That Quenches All Thirst. He had been spotted taking the footpath directly to the southwest sector. The surveillance network was often overlooked as clunky and old-fashioned: merely a few canal police officers in plainclothes, positioned along the footpaths and banks.

'Merely' was not how Dumortier would describe them. Their low-key methods were old-fashioned, but like the filters used to treat canal water, the officers funnelled and caught unwanted substances via nothing more elaborate than mechanical efficiency.

But how had they missed Trooper Devinez? A filter cannot filter itself, Dumortier had reasoned after his initial enquiries had gone nowhere.

He forced down the rest of the algae coffee and pocketed the vial, not wishing to contaminate the scene. A mirror-faced cleanup bot, a heavy-duty analogue to Desk Sergeant's model, raised an arm studded with yellow armour plates to give the other officers the all-clear signal.

Dumortier figured the moment of silence occurred in the vicinity of the cargo squirrel, the obvious outsider. DryWare had its share of intergang skirmishes before, but a trichome bomb was downright vulgar to all sides. He trusted them to play with as much fairness as gangs could muster for each other, because navigating rifts was part of their existence.

But no such treatment for the Cabuchoner. A fissure is a line of breakage which occurs as a result of surface tension: his presence here broke that tension.

Dumortier walked away from the blast site and past piles of abandoned wares, now recreating John CaMarr-Schist's morning foray into the market. Being an art thief meant a curator's eye; junk would not interest him. Dumortier did not put it past him to have stolen something from Jean-Ling Setona and be trying to resell it in DryWare.

"The boy from off-Chatoyance was looking for an evaluator," called out a trader.

Know your witness type. The main trick with self-volunteering eye-witnesses was to pretend to be occupied by something happening in the distance—or at least look past their faces, if indoors. Engage directly and they decide you've agreed to accept their information in exchange for something else. Dumortier noticed the man's ill-fitting red leather jacket and knew he wanted a new garment: preferably Dumortier's coat.

"What makes you say that?"

"He had something special, and he was dumb enough to come here with it. He got desperate, went into the old Arcades." The trader wiped his hand on a patch of dried blood under his chin, then pointed at a sealed-up archway in the wall in front of Dumortier. "Not sure if he came out in one piece."

"So what did he have on him?"

The man shrugged and worked his jaw like words were lodged under his tongue. "I told you enough. Constabulary ought to compensate me for losing a day's trading. The bomb was no problem, we can deal with that sort of thing ourselves. It's you indigos showing up with your bots and armoured cars that killed business, for today *and* tomorrow."

Dumortier nodded and, after a second of consideration, took out a roll of uta from his pocket. "Thank you, and take this. You can't have my coat."

The trader whistled in delight: he had not expected hard cash. He grabbed the roll and returned to the remains of DryWare, pace quickening. Clearly his day was not a *total* loss.

The sealed-up archway was nondescript enough.

Dumortier heard wind blowing from behind the hoarding and knocked twice on it. Hollow sounds, followed by furtive movements like footsteps pacing back and forth. Who were these evaluators hiding from, conducting business from inside a failed project? Probably nothing more business savvy than drug pushers or squatters.

He lifted one corner of the hoarding and peered inside. Much as he had expected, although he'd thought the Korbuhauss Incorporated project had never gone past the planning stage. He switched on his recording stud and stepped inside. The hoarding snapped shut behind him.

Dumortier gripped his shrapnel heart but did not take it out of its holster. His enhanced hearing picked up another rush of air, but it was not wind. Two incoming objects. He sidestepped and they hit the hoarding with a pair of thuds. He lifted his gaze and saw stars—but not in the idiomatic sense. Two white, pearlescent five-pointed star-shaped weapons, stuck in the hoarding at face height.

"Is that all?" yelled Dumortier, drawing his shrapnel heart. The dimness in the Arcades concealed as well as it obscured.

A woman stepped out of the shadows, and he kept the shrapnel heart trained on her. The familiarity of her confounded him; the bejewelled white mask covering her eyes, the golden irises.

"Leave," she said with none of the verbose officiousness she had used outside the fla-tessen hall in Polyteknical.

"You attacked first."

Keep her talking: the recording stud was still on.

"I did not," she replied. "The stars are made to attack on their own."

Sudden tapping on the hoarding behind him. Without looking around, Dumortier put his hand on it as though to quell it. It was really to calm himself: the last thing he needed was the attention of people outside.

The woman had vanished, retreating farther into the Arcades.

The stars waved their free arms at him, with the nearest one straining to touch his hand like the predatory sea creatures they resembled. What he had mistaken for tapping were the stars trying to wrench themselves out of the hoarding, making it shake with their attempts. To hell with checking the shrapnel heart's vicinity settings and trying to be discreet. With a mixture of fear and revulsion he fired at them.

The compacted salt darts shattered the hoarding, which collapsed under its own weight, revealing the original archway. Dumortier waited for the fumes to clear before he stepped through. He hoped there were large enough fragments of those stars to analyse, as he called for an available forensic technician to come with extra forensic sacs.

# CHAPTER TWENTY-SEVEN

PLEO GRIPPED THE rusted stair railing so hard a bolt came loose. She felt like she was flying apart or close to collapse. She shut her eyes, opened them, saw the hooded figure still at the bottom of the stairs, and then shut them again.

A draft entered the atrium. The glass prisms quivered and chimed in the chandeliers still hanging from the ceiling. She could bring one of them crashing down onto the figure. But no, putting it out of action wouldn't change the past. Cerussa was dead, that was irrevocable. The hooded figure couldn't be a Charon; they were confined to the canals.

This thing had invaded her daylight and laid siege to the waking realm.

This eidolon. It was an eidolon.

That gradual recognition calmed her somewhat, but did not help her deal with its presence.

Everyone knew the rumours. Tier Dwellers used

eidolons, the animated likenesses of dead people, to strike fear into the hearts of their victims. Destroy one and they send another. And another. Usually, if the Aronts want to kill you, they deliver one of those dog claw flowers. She, a child of miners, was apparently not worth the warning.

She was getting a glimpse of her role in their plans. A symptom of a need that can find no satisfaction via normal outlets. Set up a fla-tessen accident and frame her for Gia's murder, because Gia knew too much about the lie that was her existence.

But Pleo had an advantage over them—with no reputation to safeguard, she did not have to move in secret.

She felt this part of their plan lacked detail. A strand in their web which would compromise the whole. If it came loose, the Aronts had assumed it was of little consequence; they would have found another victim to frame for Gia's murder.

Yet Pleo was proving to be of more than a little consequence. To drive her insane or to suicide, the eidolon sent by the Aronts would have to bear a better resemblance to Cerussa, not wear shapeless hooded garments.

She had to stop recoiling from its presence, go down the stairs and meet it on its terms. In her mind's eye she drew back its hood and demanded answers.

The figure moved a step forward as soon she thought that. She backed away from the railing, but the figure did not advance up the stairs. Pleo watched and waited. The sun light from the ceiling dimmed and, for a second, cast a shadow over the figure.

Pleo averted her gaze and scanned the atrium again. The shadow disappeared as a cloud passed in front of Gachala but another shadow had replaced it. It flitted across the wall of panelscreens, not cast by anything in the atrium she could see. The shadow stayed at the edge of her vision, elusive.

*Thoughtforms,* Saurebaras had told her in the multipurpose hall. ...*you will never possess grace or fluidity. But you are quite,* quite *formidable.*

Pleo tried to recall fla-tessen techniques for deep breathing and improving concentration, but they had no effect on the shadow being. She walked up several stairs to stand under the skylight, in the partially remembered prayer ritual to Gachala.

"Let the light from The Emerald Sun and Shield pierce the darkness of doubt, loss, despair and so on, within you."

The figure moved again, but Pleo saw something resolve and shimmer into focus behind it. Like gazing into the back of a metal spoon, Pleo saw the shadow was now humanoid, a distorted version of herself. She felt no shock or disgust, only a dispassionate acceptance. Like a projector had been turned off, her image went to shadow again.

So here was the trick: visualise light beaming through her body from the head down, see the thoughtform. Look away and it turned to shadow. Repeat as necessary.

"Peel back the hood," ordered Pleo. She knew she didn't have to speak, but it felt right to do so.

As if tugged by an invisible string, the eidolon's hood fell back. Pleo steeled herself to confront a skull or the death mask face of Cerussa. Instead, a metal mesh covered the face. The hair had been shaved, and the skin of its scalp was grey and dry.

This wasn't the same body that went after Pleo in Temple Plaza. Something about its stance nagged at her. Piqued and no longer scared, she went down the stairs to take a closer look at it.

"Who did this to you?" No response, but Pleo was not expecting one. "The Aronts? The other Dwellers?" Then it hit her, stark and blinding as though a rock had smashed through the skylight. "Those vultures have been taking Nosebleeds, bodies from the canals. That's what eidolons are."

Pleo circled the figure and on the nape of its neck was a familiar mark. It had been wine-coloured when she noticed it back in Constabulary's main station. Now it was blue on pale grey with decomposition.

She reached out and touched her index finger to the birthmark, and then extended her forcep. Some layers of skin stuck to the tip, giving lie to the possibility that Trooper Devinez was still alive.

Pleo sounded like a stranger to herself, worn down so much that she was speaking at half-speed. "I killed you, too, officer." She put the hood back over the head as a mark of respect and rested her hand on the shoulder. "I know you'd tell me that it wasn't my fault, but you got dragged into this all because I couldn't shut up. I'm so sorry."

What had been Trooper Devinez stirred under her hand. Pleo put an arm around the waist and tried to lift her. She was heavier than Cerussa.

"You need Constabulary," said Pleo after quick reconsideration. Carrying another body to Leroi Minor Canal was out of the question without the protection of anonymity. "They'd know what to do for you. I can't help, but I'll wait and make sure they collect you."

A light blinked red on the reception counter. She had missed it on her way in. Emergency direct Constabulary line. *All calls are guaranteed anonymous*, said the scratched and peeling label. Pleo was surprised it still worked after all these years. They would send a Walkabout or a junior officer on patrol; someone who'd recognise her but be too flabbergasted to think or act properly. And she could offload the imitation synthamber cube onto them as well, then run off. She flipped the toggle and heard analogue crackles and pops as if the system was waking up after sleeping for a long time.

# CHAPTER TWENTY-EIGHT

THE PARTY WAS an affront to good taste, even more than they usually were. A stylised bust of Iganzia Madrugal carved from pallasite watched over her husband's guests from a pedestal at the entrance. A light fixture of large delicate golden hoops hung from the ceiling. The walls and floors of the party annexe on the Madrugal Tier had been temporarily covered with nacre filler to give the impression the guests were enclosed in a giant oyster. Light diffused off the smooth surfaces but the floor was slippery.

In full swing, the party proclaimed life had to carry on regardless of tragedy. And there was only one tragedy on everyone's lips.

"A terrible thing to happen. Losing an only child."

"She wasn't their daughter."

"Adopted?"

"Much worse—a clone!"

"Only rumours," Madrugal tsked. He was the model of graciousness and expected some back from his guests. "Dismissed domestic staff spread many rumours when they're disgruntled."

Madrugal's party took its guests away from formalities and their cosseted lives and into a place with a different register. Registering a welcome sensation of lassitude, Saurebaras overheard the discussions: a defence of the public parks on Cabuchon against the alleged superior beauty of the vertical gardens on Steris; exchanges of opinions on the merits of reopening the Archives. These details swirled around her, making her temporarily forget about her task at hand.

She studied the guests and so far, was convinced she was intruding on an alien biosphere. Who put this glittering assembly in charge? Talk of politics was absent. She recognised some former members of the Cabuchon Corund.

Under the weight of so much embellishment and excess, the high ceiling of the party annexe had sagged over time. Striations and pockmarks scattered across it where past indoor fireworks had left their marks. Repairs had been carried out—the sort of work that could be done discreetly—but not enough.

The ceiling's condition made Saurebaras suddenly conscious of the energy she had expended in resisting Tier Dweller influences since she arrived on the tier. She could give up hiding and give in to exhaustion, become the resident fla-tessen dancer here. Madrugal would be more than welcoming.

She was perched on the steps to a viewing gallery. She wore a sleeveless black dress mosaiced with tiny white stars to match her fla-tessen caltrop, and a spare red shawl. Her hair was held back with a jewelled lattice of long hairpins. Saurebaras decided to nod back if any guests greeted her. So far there were more nervous glances than hellos.

"Don't be intimidated," someone joked about her presence. Cue a smattering of nervous laughs. Saurebaras stood up, and even that much movement sent a group scurrying for cover behind a row of long tables.

At least Madrugal couldn't say she didn't try to be social. She went to prepare for her dance in the gallery. All awareness had to be set aside when she abandoned her entire self to Flow.

The gallery overlooked Chatoyance, the floor-to-ceiling windows overlooking the 'Cinth and the surrounding canal network. Saurebaras checked her appearance in the windows. The jewels in her hair coalesced with the lights in the distance. She was satisfied she looked quite beautiful and formidable tonight, like a Tagmat warship waiting in dry dock.

*Formidable.* She'd last said the word to Tyro Pleo Tanza. So far Saurebaras had heard nothing about her, which was a relief. No news was good news.

She peered out of the gallery. A dance floor had been set up in the centre of the annexe. Once again she checked the pins in her hair were secure. After all, she was going to leap from the top of the stairs and through the hoops of the light fixture.

Choreography was like trying on a costume, you had to shift around to make it fit your body. There were two ways of going about recycling an old dance routine: the first was step by step, just as it was. Don't let several glasses of Catru Estate wine be your substitute for preparation.

"Ladies and gentlemen, tonight we're all privileged…"

The second way was to make it suit the present you.

*Stating the obvious.* Saurebaras tuned out the rest of Madrugal's speech and introduction.

"In tribute to my late wife…"

That was the cue. There was a round of applause as she took up her starting position at the top of the stairs. She curtseyed twice, once to the guests and once to Ignazia's stone face. Madrugal would appreciate the gesture. She took several steps back and ran at full tilt towards the light fixture.

She leapt through all the suspended hoops without disturbing them, and landed in the centre of the dance floor, her arms wrapped over her chest. She spun around, removed a hairpin and threw it at the peacock ice sculpture, shattering its head.

With chips of ice scattered all over the pearlescent floor, her audience were sufficiently mesmerised. Saurebaras unwrapped the red shawl from her shoulders. She threw it high into the air, away from the kinesphere she visualised around her body as she tapped out a steady rhythm in a spiral pattern.

*Keep it simple and precise; this audience is easily impressed.*

The shawl descended and she caught one end of it, making it billow around her like a red mist. She executed a grand jeté, a long leap to the edge of the dance floor, and stopped right before she stepped off it completely, her body bent back at an unnatural angle.

More applause broke out and she righted herself. Two curtseys from her again. Madrugal crossed the dance floor to kiss her hand. She accepted it graciously, then ran up the stairs again to the viewing gallery to recover.

*At least that's over with.*

She sat at the window and pressed her forehead to the cool glass, and watched the changing Shineshift.

"What are you doing, Madrugal?" Saurebaras heard a man's voice outside the gallery, heavy with exasperation. "Saurebaras... is harboured here?"

Saurebaras crept away from the window to eavesdrop further.

"The Aronts don't know she's here. If they find out, they... can't exactly invade my tier. I'd have to declare a vendetta."

A woman's voice joined in. "Never mind them. As long as they're distracted, it helps our plan. For the sake of their reputation, they can't let a death in the family get in their way. They have to go forward with the North-South Canal."

"On the day of the new monument's unveiling," said Madrugal. "They can't pass up the chance for attention."

Saurebaras reached the doorway and put a hand over her mouth to suppress a gasp of recognition. The copper bands on the arms of the man and woman confirmed they were two of the Polyteknical chief instructors, Nive and Mangolin.

"Thank your crystalline masters for their assistance. The armoured lamellar samples they sent helped with the development of my Sarisse armour."

"*Deities*," corrected Nive.

"Of course," acquiesced Madrugal, unconvincingly.

"There will be no better day than the unveiling of the monument to carry out their will," Nive said smugly. "A spark set off under the full light and heat of Gachala will turn into a blaze."

She turned and went down the stairs, followed by Mangolin.

Saurebaras tried to slip back into the shadow of a support pillar. Too late.

"You're missing a hairpin, Arodasi."

Madrugal blocked her way, holding out the hairpin she had used to destroy the peacock ice sculpture. It was still cold to the touch.

"Welcome to my informal meeting room." He indicated the top of the stairs. "And you've heard quite enough."

New armour or not, Saurebaras could take any number of his guards. But once she got off the tier, the Aronts would be waiting for her.

"I should leave you in the shaft beneath the tier," Madrugal mused. "It's better ventilated than the Little Room of Forgetting, but escape is still impossible."

Saurebaras smiled. "I don't doubt that at all. But I'm expected to appear in front of Chatoyance on the day of unveiling the new monument. A fla-tessen show. My students will perform."

"You're involved in Gia Aront's murder. How can you appear in public?"

"Officially, only Pleo Tanza is a suspect. Polyteknical's investigation has cleared me. If I don't appear on that day, they'll know you made me disappear... I know them; letting me live for now is the easiest option for you."

He inclined his head and applauded sarcastically, but still had to get in the last word before descending the stairs to rejoin his guests. "Performing in front of Chatoyance? Ignazia would be very proud of you."

# CHAPTER TWENTY-NINE

IF DESK SERGEANT had human ears, they would not have believed them when Dispatch put through the call on the old analogue line.

"Location?" asked Nadira. She was waiting for Dumortier to update her before he returned from DryWare.

"Canal Mouth." Desk Sergeant shook their heads in synchronous disbelief. "Trooper Devinez has been found."

"Is she alive?"

Desk Sergeant's silence told Nadira otherwise.

"Don't tell Dumortier. Please. Not yet," Nadira said as she raced past Desk Sergeant to the stairwell leading down to the Shirpen bays.

All of them were in use, but she found a single Zenuss motorcycle in a crosshatched bay. The bike was sleek, had plenty of torque and was supremely manoeuvrable. It would have to do.

\*     \*     \*

THE ZENUSS SERVED her as well as a Shirpen, zipping along the canal banks eastwards towards Canal Mouth.

How was she going to transport a body back for examination on this? Within a few blinks and saccades she had sent advanced word to the technicians in the Catacombs of Excellent Precision, telling them to stand by.

Dumortier must not know, or at least not yet. He'd be fuel to fire once he found out Trooper Devinez had also been tangled up in this web of a case.

She steered the Zenuss onto disused pavements and across parallel footpaths as she approached the hard currency block. A man clad in textured white armour strode into the entrance of the block.

Nadira parked the motorcycle and took out her shrapnel heart. She had seen what sort of employers the Dogtooths had and wasn't above shooting a Dogtooth if one proved troublesome, but she hoped it didn't have to come to that.

She trailed the guard into the dim lobby, noticing the blinking red light of the emergency line. The owners of the block had been savvy; an analogue line of copper wire was impervious to the myriad afflictions of communications technology these days.

The guard stopped in his tracks. Tyro Pleo Tanza, less weary than how she looked in the sparring footage, was sitting on the stairs in the main atrium, apparently waiting after making the call to Constabulary. Her expression tightened at the sight of the guard.

"Came looking for the dead rich bitch's room," he said, "instead I find the one who killed the rich bitch. You—or should I say, those pretty eyes of yours on a tray—will get me a promotion."

He pulled a nasty curved long knife out of his side armour holster. Nadira took cover behind the reception counter and raised her shrapnel heart, checking its vicinity settings.

Pleo showed no sign she was afraid. She stood up and unsheathed her forceps.

"Cat has claws. Meow!" He waved the knife at her.

Nadira decided on a warning shot to break up the fight, and aimed for the floor behind the Dogtooth. But before she could pull the trigger the guard dropped his knife and grabbed his own throat.

Pleo stepped close to the guard with a serene smile.

"What're you doing to me?" he choked out.

Nadira ran out from the reception counter. She knew what was going to happen; the sparring footage has shown her something similar.

Pleo appeared to sink deeper into herself. "Windpipe," she told the Dogtooth by way of answer.

Terror wiped the thuggishness clean off his face, and Nadira glimpsed the fresh recruit he had once been. He did a double-take, as though he knew what was coming but couldn't understand how Pleo was doing it. There was a faint sound of tearing cartilage and a second of warmth on Nadira's cheeks from blood spatter, then the clank and thuds of a heavyset body hitting the atrium floor.

"Freeze!" The shrapnel heart was now aimed at Pleo's face.

"I called because one of your own is here." Pleo pointed to a body that had its upper half covered in a black coat, lying next to a fallen chandelier. "Now let me go."

"You and I know it doesn't work like that. And you killed the Dogtooth."

"He deserved it."

"I've seen this so many times before. Drugs, illegal modifications, pirated implants. You think you're transforming due to your new abilities, but what you're really doing is distorting."

"You have no idea what I've been through."

"You haven't thought this over. I don't know what exactly has been done to you, but come with me, we can get you help." Nadira lowered the shrapnel heart. "We have access to the best treatments. Think of your family."

Pleo's mouth twisted as she spoke. "My sister's dead and my father is a living shell who's better off dead. Mother has gone to Anium for her safety. Not that I blame her."

"I can help you."

"I didn't kill Gia." Then Pleo spoke to the air in front of Nadira. "Hold this officer for me."

"I... believe... you." Nadira began but felt her throat constricting, and her grip on the splinter heart wavered.

Pleo thrust a cube into her free hand. "I've gone over that moment in the fla-tessen piste many times. I didn't know it at first but I tried to protect Gia." She sighed and indicated the cube. "Here is the reason why Gia was killed."

She turned on her heel and strode out of the hard currency block. Gasping, Nadira stumbled backwards onto the stairs as she was released. But when she turned, there was no one else in the lobby; and when she stepped outside, Pleo had vanished.

Too stunned to speak, she hailed her standby team with codes of coloured light.

# CHAPTER THIRTY

SETONA SAW MARSH walk across the piazza from the station to rinse his hands in the fountain. The next Shineshift was not due for another hour, but there were already fewer people in the piazza. She listened for the sounds of Dogtooth boots on the paving stones, but all she heard for now were the automated water pumps.

"Marsh," she called out to him. "Get in the fountain now. Hide."

He looked around him in surprise and stared hard at the horses, as though they were talking to him.

"Look up." She was sitting side-saddle on one of the horse sculptures, her skin the same weather-worn bronze sheen as her steed, and looking very much like part of the sculpture because she did not move. Like most modranis, she could speak and project her voice without moving her lips. "Hide now! Dogtooths are looking for us."

"How do you know?"

"The modrani network told me."

Marsh climbed into the water—its unexpected chill and depth made him gasp—and quickly moved behind a curtain of cascading water and under Setona's steed.

Four white uniforms passed the fountain and streamed into Setona's shop. Setona heard the display leopard snarl at them from the window platform. Gunshots rang out and rolled across the piazza, followed by glass breaking.

The display leopard paced back and forth across the street, blood dripping from its flank; she couldn't tell if it was from a shot or running through the window glass. It finally collapsed on the ground, its tail flicking against the paving.

"Roll out," she heard a Dogtooth say. "The people we want are not here."

She waited until their footsteps died down and an armoured vehicle drove away, then climbed down from the horse and ran to the display leopard's side. She allowed the bronze sheen to fade from her skin, returning to flesh tone.

"Good girl, you guarded well," she said, kneeling next to the big cat.

"We have to leave," said Marsh.

Setona plucked three jewels out of the display leopard's spots. "These are for you: they should cover passage."

He shook his head. "No, madame, you're coming with me."

Setona laughed. "An ex-modrani, a petty Cabuchoner thief and a display leopard trying to leave Chatoyance together? We'll never make it past Khrysobe. And thanks to the new monument opening the day after tomorrow, Khrysobe will be closed. Except for VIP visitors, no ships will be allowed to dock or leave."

"Don't you know all sorts of people in your modrani network who can help?"

"They are resourceful, but there are limits."

Marsh stared at her face as she thought it over.

"Madame, no," he said. "Not the Doyen."

"He's powerful."

"And so he is. But you can't rely on him."

Setona did not reply. She petted the leopard for a long minute, then helped it to its feet.

"Can't stay here either," she said.

Marsh went into the ransacked shop and came back out with a long chain and a gold harness. As he put it around the leopard's neck, he said, "I hope you don't mind nanoapartments."

"Do I have a choice at this moment?" Setona asked.

"I was talking to the leopard."

# CHAPTER THIRTY-ONE

Nadira could be as objective as she liked—even calm and self-possessed. She staked her reputation on these qualities. But she saw two things that had frightened her today.

The silence inside the Catacombs of Excellent Precision was a balm to her state of mind, but only temporarily. Despite her, her mind charged forward and stumbled over the implications of Trooper Devinez's death and reanimation.

Endless iteration was beautiful in nature and art: fractals, Fibonacci patterns, concentric rings in cross-sections of tree trunks. However, for SeForTecs—who viewed each transfusion as a dutiful iteration—perpetuity was unnecessary, a waste of time and energy.

"We honour life," she had learnt before her first transfusion, "because we honour those who prematurely reached the end of theirs."

Trooper Iryna Devinez was an iteration carried out without her consent. Nadira had considered leaving the examination to another senior technician under her, but the problem was, all technicians were under her. Subject one to the abominable task and the rest would lose respect for her. She had to undertake this burden alone, for the sake of all SeForTecs.

A preliminary examination would normally take her an hour. She took two. She had to ensure there were no longer any signs of life.

Nadira had passed the imitation synthamber cube to the main lab for extraction. She hoped the results would be straightforward enough to offset her sense of imbalance. She sat on a spare bench and replayed the sparring footage several times.

Footsteps running down the corridor. No personnel ran at that clip without a very good reason, but for Dumortier, anything could be a good reason.

He burst into the chamber without greeting her. "Why wasn't I informed?"

Nadira saw his face like a stormfront, all subtlety and refinement displaced by fury. "You could have compromised the situation."

"Don't give me that officious bullshit." He put his hands on his waist. "Both of us are beyond that."

"A Dogtooth was present, and he was killed in front of me."

That took some of the fury from his expression. He stepped closer to Nadira with concern. "There's blood on your face."

Nadira touched a fingertip to her cheek. "Not my blood. Pleo Tanza did it. Killed the Dogtooth."

"How...?"

Nadira wiped the blood off her cheek and pointed at the sparring footage onscreen.

"You saw it?" he asked. "The thoughtform?"

"I saw the actions of it. Pleo Tanza told me she didn't kill Gia. She was telling the truth. Look at the footage again: there are two people in the piste and *two more* presences."

Dumortier played the footage back. He paused at the fatal moment when Gia's neck was yanked back too far. The shadow was behind her head, and when the head dipped, another shadow.

"Slow the frame rate, fifty times."

The image segued from one frame into the next, but Dumortier paused it in time. Caught halfway, Pleo's face emerged from the other shadow, elongated and blurred. The other presence had been trying to pull Gia out of the way of the incoming fan, against the action of Saurebaras's thoughtform, which had been directing the fan at Gia.

"You saw that in Canal Mouth?"

"I told you; I saw what it did and these things *should not be*. And then she made it grab my throat."

Overwhelmed, Dumortier held his hands up. "If you want to get off this case, I understand. I won't hold it against you, and your decision won't show up on your record."

"No," replied Nadria with a deep breath. "And that's final."

Dumortier pursed his lips and nodded. "How does someone evoke a thoughtform?"

"Trauma—induced or shared," Nadira said. "Saurebaras and her reconditioning. With Pleo it's her miner's ancestry, possibly transgenerational. The exact mechanisms involved are still a mystery."

"How do *two* separate people do it, within a short amount of time? Aren't they rare?"

"My guess is, Saurebaras gave Pleo a dose of something unique, possibly self-manufactured."

"I have results regarding the stars thrown at me in DryWare. They were made with a modified version of the biotech used for highlights."

"And who came up with the highlights?"

"Two Polyteknical instructors, Nive and Mangolin. They have previously been cautioned by their institution for extra-curricular activities."

Nadira killed the sparring footage onscreen. "The tech in the stars. Could they apply it to dead bodies?"

"Not unless they had outside assistance. No one in all three systems can."

"Devinez is in the next chamber. You may view her," Nadira added. "I've seen enough."

Dumortier looked at the walls of the chamber as though his eyes could bore through them.

Nadira went out of the chamber. "Preliminary results regarding the cube are in. The cube contains a human embryo. DNA matching Gia Aront."

Dumortier followed her. Suddenly he pounded a fist into the corridor wall.

"There are easier ways to kill your children, damn it. This is too much, even for Tier Dwellers. They fuck each other over for assets and inheritances, but this plotting is on another level."

Nadira asked, "What do we do next?"

Dumortier massaged his hand and blinked at Gia's black dress spread out in its translucent evidence sac, as if it had suddenly snapped into view.

Nadira caught on. "We call in the Aronts for an interview? Present it to them as voluntary."

"Only the father," replied Dumortier. "We'll get more out of him."

Nadira addressed the coloured lights: *Send officers to Aront Tier.*

He went to view Devinez. After a minute he returned, calmer than before.

"You offered to help me with Devinez's case?"

"Yes," Nadira recalled.

"Please help me now."

"How?"

"Use your SeForTec clearance to haul in and grill Sisme Morin, the little shit in charge of Canal Police, now that Devinez's body has turned up. You can do it while I'm with Patriarch Aront, since we don't have the luxury of time. I've long suspected he had something to do with her disappearance, but I can't grill him."

"Because Katyal took you off the Devinez case?"

"No, because I don't want to spill a dirty officer's blood in the Sunlight Corridor."

*Send detainment officer to pick up Sergeant Morin.*

And Nadira dismissed the coloured lights and walked out.

# CHAPTER THIRTY-TWO

Setona and the display leopard clambered up the stairs behind Marsh. A single bulb flickered on the wall in time with the crowning-shield over the nano-apartment block. She had draped the big cat in one of the white sheets used for the shop's display backdrop, but it couldn't conceal its presence in the dimness. It snarled and the teenagers smoking on the landings had retreated into their respective apartments.

A woman clad in a translucent blue raincoat over a bullet-grey sheath dress entered the block. She stepped forward to embrace Setona. He recognised the sintered limbs and fluid gait, and the hustle in her stride.

Members of the old modrani network had arrived. They looked like they worked all over the Systems before joining the network.

"Rhoni!"

She bumped into Marsh, expecting him to step out of

her way, then sized him up. "You're definitely not one of us."

Setona told her, "He's with me."

Rhoni backed off, but only slightly. "A pity your exploits are no longer the highlight of the highlights. What strange and dangerous company you've been keeping lately, Jean-Ling."

The crowning-shield for the entire block suddenly hissed and crackled.

"It's better we go inside." He shouted over the noise and was glad to hear Setona vouch for him, although he pretended to ignore Rhoni's suspicion.

He checked the narrow corridor outside before shutting the apartment door. Reality intruded with the hubbub on the stairs, and restored itself after the strangers had gone in.

"In practical terms," Setona pointed at Marsh and spoke very deliberately, as if she did not want to repeat herself to Rhoni. "Can you turn him into modrani cargo?"

"Permanently?"

"No, despite all we've been through together I'm rather fond of him."

Rhoni looked disappointed and sat on the scoured tiled floor of the living area. "I can do a passable resemblance, but what's the point? He won't be classed as indispensable or expensive like you or the display leopard. Standard rules of carriage will apply to him."

"Paint job, knocked out cold, and shoved in a box?" Setona was a touch dismayed. "He won't make it. Not with Khrysobe delays."

"I don't run the only outfit in town."

"Then don't think I'm giving this job to you exclusively."

Rhoni laughed. "But you are; what choice do you have?"

"Freight entrance or the passenger front?"

"Doesn't make a difference," said Rhoni. "If you can't wait until after the Monument's unveiling."

"So we wait," interjected Marsh, "and then where will we end up?"

"More alive than dead, darling," replied Setona. "It's our best chance."

# CHAPTER THIRTY-THREE

ORCHID GLASS DOORS slid shut. Noises evaporated as Dumortier and Nadira entered the far end of the Sunlight Coridor via separate doors.

It was a picturesque yet unlikely setting for parallel interrogations; few investigators had used the interrogation rooms at the far end of the Sunlight Corridor. The windows showcased the skyline: Lonely Heron Bridge, Leroi Major and Minor Canals, the 'Cinth and the Temple. Below them flowed normalcy: Chatoyants going to work, some retuning from it and joining their families. People who never killed, never stole, and never deceived each other.

The lack of haze from this height turned the views into a tableau. All these damned structures—they held now, and would hold in the future.

The Temple was in the centre at eye level; its deliberate placement exhorted the interrogatee to confront divinity and burn away traces of guilt.

In his room Dumortier made note of the steel interrogation table—it was too wide to reach across and too heavy to flip. He approached the man sitting on the other side of the table like a concerned surgeon, as though he was the latest of the symptoms exhibited by an ailing Chatoyance.

"Haven't you got enough out of me and my wife?" Patriarch Aront demanded.

"We never said we were finished with you," replied Dumortier. "So, let's begin again."

He touched his ear stud to start recording. A reciprocal ascending chime, pre-agreed with Nadira, acknowledged the start of his session and signaled the start of hers in another room, three doors away.

Dumortier placed two items on the table: a rumpled black coat and a cube of synthamber. Aront looked at both objects in front of him and then at Dumortier with disbelief at how out of control things had spun.

"You recognise them, obviously."

Aront sighed to confirm it.

"Shell games, Patriarch? It's all child's play for you—literally. Two children: one dead long before the other."

"I didn't come here for this—"

"I know; you came to get it all off your chest. But you should have gone to the Temple; it's the nuns' job to hear confessions. But it's our job to ask the questions. You of all people should understand that." Dumortier wore the wan smile of an investigator with a duty he was all too glad to discharge.

He crossed over to a wall display and pulled up the

reply from Chatoyance Register Office. "No records of Gia's brother."

"Of course there isn't, he was never born," Aront's reply was so inaudible Dumortier thought his ear stud was faulty. "And neither was Gia."

By way of encouragement, Dumortier killed the wall display.

"Not to say we didn't try our hardest to have children the natural way. I wanted them, but she wanted—no, insisted on—continuity. Our assets hold us captive: homes and businesses are all anchored in the Archer's Ring. It's not easy to move assets around."

"Still better to be rich and scrutinised here than poor and anonymous in Steris?" asked Dumortier.

Aront leaned forward and put his face in his hands. Now done with stalling, Dumortier went on the attack:

"It's one of the oldest schemes: funnel some of that excess wealth to an apparently unrelated child residing off-world. Except the child is actually an embryo. Then a few years later when the child is grown, claim they are sickly and undergoing special medical treatment to explain their continued absence. Then when time is right, claim the child is dead. And ensure the child is dead. In your case it was *two* children. One turned out not to be viable. The other grew into Gia, your daughter."

"I should have stopped her." Patriarch Aront's admission about his wife was meant as much for himself as it was for Dumortier and Nadira. Was a glint of buried humanity peeking through?

Dumortier waited for him to elaborate but it was not

forthcoming.

"Do you remember what I said to you on my Tier?"

Dumortier shrugged.

"'A slow and steady rise is the best.'"

*It's such second nature to him*, noted Dumortier with vague disappointment, to try to derail the momentum of questioning. He did it so unconsciously that it was almost innocent. Aront ought to know better than to try it. Dumortier recalled his assessment after his probationary period: *Can be relied upon to summon the required callousness. Highly recommended for Tier Dweller remit.*

"Filter down, ten percent," Dumortier said. "Don't you find it a little dim in here?"

The sunlight level in the room increased. If it increased any more, orchid glass of a special opacity and secret manufacture would materialise—neither rising nor descending, but coalescing, like a perfect living curtain of black ice, seemingly out of thin air—over the table and between him and Aront. The glass would block Gachala's blinding light only on Dumortier's side of the room.

He noted the position of Gachala in the sky outside. In five minutes, the sun will set and the temple roof would send up its famous flash.

*What're you doing?* Nadira's voice said in his earstud. Her tone told him she knew exactly what he was going to do. In the screen above Patriarch Aront's head, Dumortier saw her place one hand on the window in her room and glance up in direction of the camera. No outward indication of having just spoken and her expression gave nothing away. Her stud was set to audio output, then relayed to his earstud; he lacked such SeForTech capabilities so he could only receive but not reply subvocally via the same channel.

*Get him to narrate as much as possible, even if it means going into any personal history with him. Reinforce rapport, no matter how unbalanced.*

After several seconds, Dumortier replied *yes* in Morse code, tapped out on his ear stud.

*If he's lying, he's only adding to the cognitive load on his brain. It'll break eventually. Stay calm.*

Dumortier glanced at the screen and saw Morin, sitting in the next room with Nadira. He pitied him. She was calm but precise, like slow-acting venom. He wouldn't know he was being skinned alive until it was too late.

So Dumortier tried a different tack. "One of your Dogtooths was killed by Tyro Pleo Tanza in Canal Mouth, in that same hard currency block in which Gia kept a room."

"Swibi and I knew about Gia's room." Aront emitted a mirthless laugh. "We weren't pleased in the beginning, but I commended Gia for her creativity."

"One of your Dogtooths...?" repeated Dumortier.

"Unlucky but replaceable." Aront paused before he got to the point. "But not you, Dumortier, you had much potential but you left us too soon. You could've risen through the Dogtooth ranks."

Nadira's advice about personal history didn't make it easier for Dumortier. "And for what great reward and legacy? One of your canals named after me? I preferred to rise through Khrysobe Spaceport."

"A shame," insisted Aront.

"No greater than Gia."

A spontaneous remark, but it was enough to effect a change in the room like a drop in temperature, combined with Gia's black coat. Dumortier saw remorse seep through his bravura. He began talking as though Gia was eavesdropping on her father's interrogation.

"Gia would have carried on with her life after receiving the tooth flower, as if it was an elaborate joke between mother and daughter. But she was sure of her mother's intentions and tried running away."

"Did you protect her from your wife?" asked Dumortier.

"Of course. But how could I have known? Matriarch Aront had to risk originality. The death had to be accidental yet elaborate, the sort that could happen to someone like Gia."

"And to what end? Taking back and dissolving the various shell companies under her name?"

Aront shook his head. "If her plan followed its ultimate course, she would be presiding over the board of directors of ArontCorp without me and without Gia succeeding me."

Dumortier notified Nadira via earstud Morse code: *Got him.*

*Congratulations. Give me a little more time with Morin.*

"I'm talking to an empty room," said Dumortier.

"What do you mean?"

"Because a dead man is on the other side of this table."

"Which side?" Aront challenged but still flinched in his chair.

Gachala rose to its height. Streaks of brilliant light shone in gaps in the main window filter.

"The temple nuns understand something we don't: light doesn't burn so much as consumes you, becomes part of you." Dumortier called out, "Filter up, one hundred percent." He met Aront's eye. "Or would you rather be a sheltered man instead? You have no choice now."

The perfect curtain of black orchid glass rematerialised over the main window, shielding Aront and Dumortier from Gachala's full blast of judgement.

"Take Aront into custody," Dumortier said to Detainment through his ear stud. "Full protection applies."

# CHAPTER THIRTY-FOUR

SERGEANT MORIN WORE the look of an officer who never expected to find himself on the other side of the extruded interrogation table. The reek of musty uniform and sweat caught Nadira in the nostrils and throat; the climate control could do nothing for the suspect's discomfort. She noted with satisfaction how he couldn't disconnect from his surroundings.

She stood before him and let her silence build for effect. As predicted, his recognition of her had the required effect. Blood slowly drained from Morin's face.

No refined art of interrogation for dirty officers—they didn't deserve any forbearance, elaboration or nuance. It was not Constabulary SOP, but it had been practised enough over the years Nadira was active.

Now she was not so much outraged as disappointed.

"Does Katyal and Sakamoto know what you're doing?"

"Ammonia," muttered Nadira.

Morin asked, "Is there a gas leak up here?"

"No," she said, before reminding him, "but if you pass out I'm going to need it to revive you."

*He's not going to pass out, the little shit doesn't need oxygen to survive,* Dumortier suddenly told her via rapid Morse code. Nadira remembered he was still in the Sunlight Corridor, although Aront had just been taken into custody. *Just pump him. If he denies or obfuscates, pump harder.*

"What's standard behaviour for a dirty officer?" Nadira sounded pedagogic.

"I don't know."

"Exactly. There's no such thing as standard; dirty officers behave the way they see the world, be it gullible, selfish, venal. Dirty SeForTecs get expunged from records and sealed in their vats alive."

"I don't envy your colleagues."

"You betrayed your entire force. No need to ask questions; they'll be pure formality in this case. Quicker to throw you off the roof."

"You won't dare."

"We're most certainly cleared to."

Nadira's statement took the remaining colour and animation out of his face. Morin slumped back like an abandoned doll.

"Your kind," said Nadira, "I've seen quite a few. Not exactly dangerous, but a conduit—via action or inaction—for dubious and corrupt action. Canal police all do what you say. Except for one."

"The rookie."

"How did she end up like that?"

Morin turned to face the view of Chatoyance. "Nothing to do with me."

"Reroute your officers to Blue Taro and Boxthorn to pick up one suspect. Why?"

"I'm telling you we were understaffed."

"I've checked Desk Sargeant's log for that day. You're aware of understaffing, yet volunteer your own personnel."

"What's wrong with showing some initiative?"

"Nothing, but you were overstepping your boundary."

"Desk Sarge requested them."

Nadira shook her head. "Desk Sarge only informs and requests. They don't make decisions. Even a cadet during their first week at academy knows that."

Morin drummed the section of table in front of him. "The two instructors from Polyteknical, they told me they needed bodies for their experiments."

"What experiments?"

"I don't know, but something fucked up. Preferably recent, but they had to be whole."

"Nive and Mangolin, the two Polyteknical instructors, were paying you and some of your officers hush money to look the other way when they collected the dead from the canals. Devinez tried to speak up against this, and you revealed yourself trying to behave not as you've done before."

"So, I took that money," replied Morin. "But about Devinez ending up dead, I don't know what you mean."

"You apparently 'showed initiative.'" Nadria narrowed her eyes at him. "But no, you wanted Devinez there at

Blue Taro and Boxthorn. You wanted Nive and Mangolin to catch a glimpse of her, their next victim."

Morin rose from the table. "You've been too long on the Tier Dweller remit with Dumortier. It's contagious: makes you see plots everywhere. I didn't mean for her to end up that way."

Nadira let his last statement ring out in the room. "Thank you, sergeant."

She performed a saccade, and a colured light tapped out *Got him* in Morse code to the man waiting and watching in the other room.

# CHAPTER THIRTY-FIVE

DUMORTIER AND DEPUTY Hitei broke free from the throng of mendicants as the Monument To The Thousand Falcons loomed over their heads. Blurring his vision, a shimmering golden mist of nanoscale machines coalesced to track all movements. Mias was operating at full capacity today.

Red paper nightingales were to be released from a giant net. The crowd joined in with their contributions; some folded them out of leftover coffee filters, pamphlets and sugar paper. Children were told to write their wishes on their own birds to make them come true.

"Most will fall into the aquifers beyond the checkpoints," said Hitei, "to be collected and recycled as paper pulp. They'll end up as next year's tribute."

*The wind will always bring dust,*
*After a sandstorm the sun shines brighter.*

*No longer on the ships to nowhere,*
*We cross the abyss towards home.*

A Corund member read out a stanza from a popular poem *Dust and Argol*. As soon she finished, the monument was unveiled. The orange fabric fell away, revealing four looming monoliths covered with laser-engravings. This display and the huge net of paper nightingales suggested underlying tension between regimentation and resistance. The unblinking eyes of Mias knew where you were coming from, but not where you were going.

The susurration of rain had finally stopped and announcements were made; the nightingales were to be released.

Dumortier kept track of communications, nervously anticipating the silence before an explosion:

"—Keep crowd behind barricades, they're spilling onto the Avenue."

"—Advise on canal approach with Newts."

"—Maintain Shirpen speed and distribution of officers."

NADIRA WAS GLAD for the monument's beauty, for its own sake, for the sake of what it commemorated and for the sake of where it stood. *The Thousand Echoes* and the Forty together. Why should a commemoration be denied to them? Nothing should have to spoil the glory of this day.

*Queen is red and in the crowd,* Dumortier had broadcast. If all Pleo did was stay in the crowd Nadira could enjoy this day as a civilian. It was as if all activity and communications had slowed down. Constabulary and Spinels stayed glued to their devices; no incident had happened yet.

Up on a wide purpose-built stage, the same Corund official cut a thick ribbon around the net. The crowd applauded as the paper birds floated away.

All of them, that is, but for a cluster which remained stubbornly on the ground. Smiling out of incomprehension, the official tried to rake them up with his bare hands. Something invisible slapped him to the stage floor.

"The main stage! Move!"

Dumortier tried to go around the edges of the crowd, who were panicking. Could Pleo project her thoughtform from a distance? The official tried to get up, but was struck again.

*Damn it, where are you, Pleo Tanza?*

"Request for firearms use," Nadira said over the comms.

"State your request."

"Glass heart rifle," said Nadira, enunciating each word as to leave no doubt. "With flexi-mounting."

"Denied."

Dumortier made it to the stage and grabbed the official. He passed him to a pair of officers who whisked him to safety.

"I have previous use of glass heart," insisted Nadira.

"Noted but still denied—"

"Dumortier 0986," he interrupted. "I second the request for glass heart."

"Noted again. Still denied. You're free to observe for the sniper unit." SeForTec clearance had its limits, but snipers were useless unless they could see their target.

Dumortier checked the stage: still clear. He yelled, "Where are you?"

In response, the cluster of paper nightingales suddenly flew up into his face.

"She's climbing onto the Aront Barge," Dumortier heard Nadira say over his personal comms.

Then who was controlling the action onstage? He swatted paper birds out of his face and saw Saurebaras standing in the wings. She winked at him and turned to leave.

PLEO STOOD ON the deck of the Aront barge, a confection of gold and spun materials for cruising along their new canal. She dripped water onto the fine carpet as she made a beeline for the Aronts sitting near the prow. She directed her thoughtform and it swatted Dogtooths aside.

"I'm here for you. Karma is too slow!"

Matriarch Aront retreated before Pleo, looking panicked.

"This is for Cerussa and Gia."

She moved to strike the Matriarch down.

An explosion rocked the barge before she could reach her.

\*     \*     \*

DUMORTIER HEARD IT before he saw it: a flash of light and flames licking the once-intact structure of the barge.

*Does it end here?*

He must have spoken to Nadira unaware, because she replied over the comms, "I hope so."

# EPILOGUE

The hooded figures waited at the end of one of the Harp reservoirs for the automated light submersible. When it surfaced, it bore a body wearing a knee-length black shift, its limp fingers revealing no trace of the forceps contained within.

Nive murmured praise to the crystalline deities. "They can repair her and we still need her."

"There's potential," Madrigal said, "but I don't think we can harness her."

"Our masters see otherwise."

"Think she can walk, after treatment?"

Nive looked up at Gachala's emerald disk. "Yes. She might even soar."

# ACKNOWLEDGEMENTS

No writer works and writes in complete isolation and so follows a list of those to most gratefully thank:

To my parents for putting up with their overgrown child with her head stuck in too many books and imagined worlds.

To my brother for leaving piles of his old science fiction paperbacks and comics lying around the house at a formative age and setting me off on various journeys.

To David Thomas Moore: thank you for taking a chance with this novel, editing, for your boundless patience and encouraging emails—drinks will be on me.

To Kate Coe: thank you for your time, editing, and insights while going through this novel. Your discerning eye helped so much—drinks will be on me as well.

To my beta readers of this novel over the years. You all know who you are and thank you all.

# ABOUT THE AUTHOR

**EeLeen Lee** was born in London, UK, but has roots in Malaysia. After graduating from Royal Holloway College, she worked for several years as a lecturer and a copywriter until she took the leap into writing. Her fiction since has appeared in various magazines and anthologies in the UK, Australia, Singapore and Malaysia, such as *Asian Monsters* from Fox Spirit Books, and *Amok: An Anthology of Asia-Pacific Speculative Fiction*. When she is not writing she can be found editing fiction and non-fiction, being an armchair gemmologist, and tweeting at odd hours at @EeleenLee.

# FIND US ONLINE!

## www.rebellionpublishing.com

/rebellionpub         /rebellionpublishing         /rebellionpub

## SIGN UP TO OUR NEWSLETTER!

rebellionpublishing.com/sign-up

## YOUR REVIEWS MATTER!

Enjoy this book? Got something to say?

Leave a review on Amazon, GoodReads or with your
favourite bookseller and let the world know!

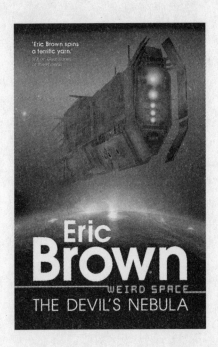

'Eric Brown spins
a terrific yarn.'

Eric
**Brown**
WEIRD SPACE
THE DEVIL'S NEBULA

Ed Carew and his small ragtag crew are smugglers and ne'er-do-
wells, thumbing their noses at the Expansion, the vast human
hegemony extending across thousands of worlds... until the day
they are caught, and offered a choice between working for the
Expansion and an ignominious death. They must trespass across
the domain of humanity's neighbours, the Vetch – the inscrutable
alien race with whom humanity has warred, at terrible cost of life,
and only recently arrived at an uneasy peace – and into uncharted
space beyond, among the strange worlds of the Devil's Nebula,
looking for long-lost settlers.

A new evil threatens not only the Expansion itself, but the Vetch as
well. In the long run, the survival of both races may depend on their
ability to lay aside their differences and co-operate.

DEREK KÜNSKEN

"An audacious con job,
scintillating future technology,
and meditations on the nature of
fractured humanity."
Yoon Ha Lee

THE QUANTUM
MAGICIAN
BOOK ONE OF THE QUANTUM EVOLUTION

## THE ULTIMATE HEIST

Belisarius is a Homo quantus, engineered with impossible insight.
But his gift is also a curse—an uncontrollable, even suicidal drive to
know, to understand. Genetically flawed, he leaves his people to find
a different life, and ends up becoming the galaxy's greatest con man
and thief.

But the jobs are getting too easy and his extraordinary brain is
chafing at the neglect. When a client offers him untold wealth to
move a squadron of secret warships across an enemy wormhole,
Belisarius jumps at it. Now he must embrace his true nature to pull
off the job, alongside a crew of extraordinary men and women.

If he succeeds, he could trigger an interstellar war... or the next step
in human evolution.

WWW.SOLARISBOOKS.COM